Laughter After

Laughter After

Ashton A Bohannon

Contents

Preamble

Laughter After is a story about healing, discovery, and spiritual warfare. Amanda, a wife experiencing domestic violence, shares her journey to healing and total victory through her relationship with God. This story perfectly depicts the forces of good and evil in the lives of ordinary people, and it emphasizes the truth that devils are behind all cases of domestic violence. Domestic violence is spiritual and it is the demonic manifesting itself openly.

People who have been negatively affected by domestic violence need a strategic plan on how to deal with it. Many churches are totally unprepared to handle the devils behind domestic violence. As a result, many victims of violence go to their church for help, but they are turned away to services outside of the church, if they are acknowledged at all. In fact, some people working in the church may perpetuate the violence or fail to intervene on behalf of the vulnerable soul in front of them.

God doesn't intend for His people to be under the domination and control of devils. He doesn't want anyone who loves Him to suffer and be subjected to abuse and violence, chiefly from the home front. Until the Church understands and confronts these forces from the realm of the spirit world, the forces will continue to dominate and at times even take the lives of those God commands us to protect. Whether you are a victim, a perpetrator, or a bystander, this book will change your perspective forever on domestic violence. It will help you know how to identify evil and how to drive it out from a Biblical perspective while simultaneously bringing hope and healing to the victims of the crime.

{ 1 }

Premonition

She saw what was coming like one sees a storm approaching on a weather radar. As she looked out into the future, she knew that this man she loved was not going to be a part of her life for much longer. The passion and the love they once shared were coming to an end and quickly. Often the world does not give us time to process the changes in our lives. One day we are at the pool in summer, and the next we are wearing warm winter jackets because a new season has come.

Amanda wasn't sure why God let her see what was going to happen. It had to be because He loved her, but why? She knew she had never been loved before— by anyone. The passion and the commitment she had to a man were never reciprocated. Her own father had disowned her and left her to discover the world alone as a young girl. As he pretended to save other women he lusted after and others, many of whom were undeserving through his job in law enforcement, he simultaneously forgot about her in her innocence.

Today in the modern world people love to insinuate that women and girls do not need protection. But Amanda knew that this was a lie because she did need protection and she always had. *Vulnerable.* The word and the state of vulnerability could not properly describe the way she had always felt. She was left susceptible to attacks from both people and spirits for as long as she could remember. The things of this world and the things beyond were always after her. They didn't wait for her to mature and become of age. The battle began while she was yet a child.

As she pondered and remembered her life, as a woman who had suffered so much loss and heartache, she didn't fully grasp and understand why the Creator of the universe would care to tell her anything, help her with anything, or save her from the impending storm. The man she had joined herself to, out of her own ignorance and folly, was going to be destroyed, but she knew she would not follow him into his eternal state of judgment and sorrow. Her God had another plan for her.

Amanda was not better than him. She did not commit fewer crimes or live a life that was superior to his. In fact, they had drank together, used drugs, and slept together long before they were ever married. Even before that she had never lived like a saint. She was a former hoe, a prostitute, a woman who slept with many men, lusted after them, and lived completely separated from God. And that is why none of this made sense to her brain. Salvation? Security? Redemption and help? Why? Why would a good man like Jesus choose her and help her, and why would this other man, who was not that different from her, die long before his time?

The answer can only come from something supernatural and beyond this world. Amanda had made a decision, a decision when she was still young, right after the onset of their romantic relationship, a decision that would separate her from him. After so much hurting and pain, and after years of living life as a harlot, Amanda knew that if there was not more to God, then she didn't want to continue living. Sex, drugs, and an immoral lifestyle weren't fun, and unfortunately, she had found that out the hard way.

When Amanda was young, she saw some of the adults in her life watching pornographic movies, drinking alcohol, and partying all around her. She was such a young girl, so impressionable, so innocent, and she wanted to be happy, like those she saw dancing, screaming, and laughing at the party. It seemed like they had something she didn't. It seemed like they didn't care about any of the pain present in the world.

Had this pain never hurt them? Had they lived lives void of struggle or heartache? Or were they able to overcome the pain and push through, and the alcohol and the sex helped them to do it? From a young, underdeveloped mind, Amanda assumed it must be the drugs and the alcohol, the sex, and the wild friends that helped them to become superhuman and happy. Plus, she had never fit in with those who had good homes, normal lives, and acceptable standards anyway, because deep down they didn't like her. Honestly, they knew what she was capable of, long before she knew it herself.

Amanda didn't blame her mom at first. She always thought her mom was a victim, a woman who had been abandoned, neglected, and abused by the men in her life too. For so many years Amanda felt sorry for her mom, and she had a deep longing to fix her life. To rescue her and help her, like the men around her never seemed to do. Her idealization of her mom was justified after all. Because she was a good person, she just needed someone to see it, right?

Let's not talk too much about the past, Amanda thought. *I hate the past. I don't want to see it, feel it, or acknowledge it.* Many people feel like Amanda. They hate their past. They hate their parents, and they hate the things that happened to them that made them who they were before they had a chance to choose for themselves. Childhood can be so traumatic. It can cause so many scars and wounds, and it doesn't seem right because children don't choose to be born into a family of dysfunction. They just discover themselves there.

On the day that Amanda decided she didn't want to be a part of this family of dysfunction anymore, and she wanted to separate herself from it, she was twenty-one years old. Enough was enough. *I am not going to be like these people. I am not going to continue living like this,* she thought. A few nights before, she had dreamed about her uncle, an uncle who had hosted the wild parties at his house. She saw him riding a boat, saying goodbye, and leaving her as she begged him to stay.

What did this dream mean? she thought when she woke up the following morning. But later that day she encountered the meaning: Her uncle was dead. He had died, and she saw it ahead of time in her dream. *There must be a God,* she thought. *There is no way I saw him die right before he died. How did I know? I am not God! And why would God reveal this to me? Why am I seeing someone die before they do?*

The death of her uncle landed her in a church for the first time in many years. His funeral was held there, and a pastor talked about eternity, God, and His plan for our lives. Amanda didn't listen much to what the pastor was actually saying. She was in her own head, thinking, pondering, and suffering, wondering why life hurt so much. *Is there really a God? Is this man preaching telling me the truth? My uncle didn't seem like a godly man. He was kind of course, but he didn't live like Jesus.*

It was during this memorial funeral service that Amanda prayed: "God, if you are real, you have to tell me, and you have to show me. Are you this God? The God of Christianity? Prove it to me if you are real. Speak to me now." As the prayer finished Amanda received a text message from a guy she had been dating. They had been in an argument, and he had broken up with her that week, but she had been praying to God to have him respond. She had been asking God not to leave her alone. She asked God to have this man speak to her if He was real.

Looking back on it now, how silly that a man who didn't even love her could be used to demonstrate God's reality in the world and in her life. By sending that text message, he didn't know he was going to be giving her hope in God's reality because only God knew what she had been praying and how she would respond. Amanda gasped, "Whoa! God is real! He answered me. He hears me." So later that afternoon Amanda went to a local Christian bookstore. She bought several books and a Bible, and she began to read the Bible for real for the first time in her life.

That night, with her Bible in her hand, Amanda started praying and asking God for answers to her questions, and to her amazement and astonishment, He was answering her direct questions with scriptures. *How is this possible? How can God speak to me directly through this book?* she thought. But one thing was for sure: He was! He was speaking to her and giving her direct responses to the things she was asking for. He was communicating . . . with her.

Now I am going to be transparent and honest with you. Amanda's life did not transform overnight from one conversation with God. There were many dysfunctions in her life, her mind, and her heart. She was messed up. She didn't understand right from wrong, and she was in desperate need of rehabilitation. Amanda was used to using her body and sexuality to gain the attention of men. She was used to using drugs to cope with her pain, and she was used to partying and finding her peace through dancing, clubbing, and hanging out with other people who were messed up.

All of Amanda's friends were still living how they had always lived. They hadn't had an experience with God just because she had. They were still the same, and they were now looking at her as if she were crazy and a prude because she had started wanting to change and do things differently. *Am I crazy?* she wondered. *I don't see anything different about my life outside. I look the same, I live in the same apartment, and I have the same associations and friends.*

What makes me think God would talk to me anyway? Who do I think I am? Amanda thought. Day after day and night after night she battled in her mind. She waivered back and forth, feeling like God was real but not understanding what that meant for her in her life. She wanted to be different. She wanted to live a different life, but how was that even possible? *Look at me,* she thought, looking into the bathroom mirror. *I am still just a hoe.*

Amanda had more than one boyfriend at the time. She had her primary one, the one who had texted her, but he was a soldier living in Afghanistan at the time. But because he was gone she needed male companionship, so she found other guys to text, hang out with, and chat with too. During one of the late nights, a private message came through Facebook. A message from a longtime friend, from her days in high school. He said, "Hey long time no talk. Do you want to hang out sometime?"

Ohhhh. I remember this guy! Amanda thought as she looked through his profile pictures. He was so sweet and nice. He was kinda nerdy. He had never tried to assault her or push up on her like a lot of the other guys. He would give her rides and hugs. Amanda's memories of this dude were fond. She remembered him as being caring and thoughtful and kind. *What perfect timing!* she thought. *I do need a good friend right now! I am trying to change my life.*

"Heyyy!" Amanda responded. "I remember you! Maybe we can hang out sometime." Bing. Bing. Bing. The communication had begun, and before she knew it they were making plans to hang out and reconnect. Amanda still remembers the first time she saw Nathanial again. He showed up in the city outside of her apartment building, wearing a black peacoat and smiling from ear to ear. He was so excited to see her, and the first hug from him reminded her of something. It reminded her of her childhood, a time when she felt just a little more safe and secure than she felt today.

The two became friends. They found rest in each other because both of them were running from the past into the future and their lives were in transition. Things were changing for both of them, and the companionship was nice, new, but also familiar in a strange way. His ex-girlfriend hated Amanda. She started messaging her on Facebook, insinuating that she was going to tell Amanda's boyfriend in Afghanistan about her relationship with Nathanial.

My relationship with Nathanial? Ha! Amanda thought. She replied, "I have not had a relationship with this man. Trust me, I have had many relationships with dudes, and my friendship with Nathanial is just that. A friendship. We have never done anything! We just hang out, talk, and spend time together as friends." But before she knew it, her boyfriend was messaging her and asking her about her friendship with Nathanial. He asked, "Why is this girl telling me you're cheating on me?" "I am not, babe!" she responded to him. "We are just friends."

Amanda was used to boyfriends who were fit. Guys who everyone wanted. She was a gym freak and she was hot. She and all the dudes she had been messing with were dolls. They were not like Nathanial at all. He was very out of shape. He was also poor, and she was used to dating dudes who had good jobs, like cops and military officers. She could not imagine being with a dude like Nathaniel. In fact, that is what felt so safe about him. He was different, and he was not going to push her to do things or cause her to be something she didn't want to be.

Amanda's boyfriend didn't believe her though. He became jealous and inquisitive about the friendship and the time she was spending with Nathanial. Things got out of hand quickly, and it was almost as if the universe had pushed these two together. One part of the sandwich was her boyfriend, who was envious of the relationship, and the other was his ex-girlfriend, who felt the same way. Amanda and Nathanial must have wondered why others felt they were an item, and they must have begun to think about the potential of them being one.

It was the end of the year 2014 and New Year's Eve. Amanda decided she was going to stay home. Her boyfriend was already on edge, suspicious of her lifestyle, and about to break up with her. She didn't want to upset God either. She really did want to change her life, and she was trying in her own effort to make sure she did the right things. "I am going to start a new year, and I am going to just stay in," she said.

Nathanial didn't agree. He wanted to go out and party. All of his friends had gotten tickets to go to Washington, DC's Echostage's

EDM performance, and he really wanted Amanda there with him to bring in the new year. New Year's was his favorite holiday, and it would not be complete unless Amanda was there. You see, Nathanial had a secret that Amanda knew nothing about. Nathanial was in love with her, and he had always been since he was sixteen. He knew she was the woman for him, but he had not told her that.

The desire to have Amanda there was intense. The more time he had spent hanging out with her lately, the more he was drawn to her like a magnet. He was obsessed with the thought of them being together—a thing he had waited on for years. He was closer than he had ever been to having her as his own girl and was on the verge of taking her to be his woman. He was determined to not give up now! "You have to come out with us," he pleaded.

"No. I am just going to stay home this year. I don't want to go out. I am trying to change my life. I want to have a better year this year," Amanda said. "Come on!" Nathanial said. "It will be fun. I need you to come with me! I promise I will take care of you." Amanda protested, "Dude, I am gonna stay home. I don't want to go. You will be fine. Just go without me." But Nathanial wouldn't give in. He stood at her apartment door for over thirty minutes insisting that she come with him, and finally she let him in and agreed.

Amanda took a shower and got ready. They then went downstairs and hopped into the back of his friend's car. Amanda didn't know where they were going, where they were staying, or who these people she was riding with were, but she knew Nathanial. They were his friends, so she felt she would be okay. He had promised her that he would take care of her. He'd said he was going to be sure she was safe if she agreed to come. He wanted her there. He cared about her as his long-lost friend, right?

On the way to Washington, DC, the group stopped to have a meal at a restaurant. Once they got to the city they checked into a hotel and began preparing to go out that night. The hotel was close enough to the club that they were able to walk there. Once they got to the club and made their way inside, Nathanial and his friends walked Amanda upstairs to a private lounge they had booked for their group. She didn't know any of these people, but she sat there quietly, trying to blend in.

Amanda started drinking, and everyone there appeared to be having a good time. The night was young, and the music had just begun. After a few hours, Amanda was wasted. She was even cut off by the bartender, something that had never happened to her before. At this point, she had no clue where Nathanial was. She found herself completely alone in a club, in the nation's capital, intoxicated and vulnerable— again.

Amanda went outside to have a cigarette. A cigarette was what she needed. It would calm her down, sober her up, and give her some relief since she couldn't get any more alcohol. "Oh there you are!" she said to Nathanial, who was also outside smoking. "Where have you been?" she asked. "I am having a good time! Are you?" he inquired. *Not really*, she thought to herself, but she was just glad to have found him again, and so her mouth blurted out a "yes."

Amanda later remembered hearing Nathanial talking about taking a random pill from a dude he didn't know on the patio. But after that, she didn't remember anything. She would eventually find herself bent over a counter in the hotel room. And who was behind her? Nathanial? *Why are my clothes off? Why am I bent over? How did I get to this room?* she wondered. *No! Nathanial, we are friends! You said you were going to keep me safe. Why are you doing this to me?* she thought.

Amanda was able to tell him she wanted to stop and put her clothes on before he was able to sleep with her, but apparently there was a huge fight. His friends said the next morning that the night before was terrible and that they'd gotten into a really bad argument and it was ugly. Amanda wanted nothing more than to go home. She grabbed her phone and her bag, and she went downstairs and sat in the hotel lobby where people were eating breakfast. She reached out to her boyfriend and told him she was sorry about everything. She hated where she was and that she was going to change her life for real.

What a way to start the new year, Amanda thought. *I hate this dude and I hate his friends. I want to go home, and I want to get away from them.* She decided to post on her Facebook page about wanting to change her life. She knew that by posting it she would be validated by others who also wanted to change their lives for the new year. She knew her boyfriend would see it, too, and maybe he would finally believe her. He had warned her about Nathanial. He was suspicious of the relationship, but she didn't see it. She didn't know that Nathanial would try anything like this with her because she had trusted him.

Amanda had been raped before, and she just never saw Nathanial as a rapist. He didn't look like a rapist. He didn't seem like a dude who was overly sexual. He didn't care about his appearance. He wasn't hot. He was nothing like the other people she knew, who were overly sexualized and lustful. He was just a regular guy, and he had never given her creep vibes. In fact, he had always been so subtle and sweet, pretending to really care. This was the opposite of what she had experienced before.

Ughhh. I just wanna go home, she thought. Without a car she couldn't go anywhere, and she was very far away from her apartment. *I will just be nice enough to get home and then I will never talk to any of these people again,* she told herself. Just then, Nathanial got off the elevator and went into the lobby. "Hey I am really sorry about last night," he said. "I was really messed up and I didn't know what I was doing. Someone gave me a pill. I was not acting like myself. Will you forgive me? Can I have a hug?" he asked.

"Get away from me, Nathanial," Amanda barked. "I just want to go home. Leave me alone and let me go home." But Nathanial was cunning, and he continued begging Amanda to forgive him. He swore he didn't mean to. He swore he was sorry. He cried and told her he loved her. He was only acting out of character because he had been drunk and high. "Can you please just forgive me?" he pleaded. "This isn't like me!" he promised.

Well, it did seem like this was very out of character for him. He had never done anything like this before. Maybe he was really just drunk and had made a bad decision. Everyone makes bad choices sometimes, right? "Okay dude. I will forgive you," she said, "but I still want some space, and I want to go home." Nathanial told her, "Well, we aren't going home yet. We are in DC! We are going to explore the city some and hang out here for the day."

Ughhh, Amanda thought to herself. *He never told me we were going to be staying in DC for another day, but what choice do I have? I don't have a way to get home, so I guess I will just be cool and then we will get home soon.* During the car ride through the city Amanda was locked in on her phone. She was reading the Bible app on her phone. She was praying and searching the Scriptures, talking to God like never before. He was her only hope to get through this. He was the only thing she cared about.

There was a day when she thought Nathanial was safe and the person she could count on, but that day was now over, and she now had no one on this side of Heaven. This was likely the last time Amanda put her trust in a man, because men sucked, and they were mean. But God was talking to her. He was helping her, and He really did want her to be safe and cared for, unlike anyone else she could think of.

To make matters worse, her boyfriend from Afghanistan . . . he broke up with her that same day because he wanted to change his life too. He also didn't think she was good for him. He felt that way because Amanda didn't act as if she cared about him at all. She was out partying again. She was hanging out with another guy, and she was being a crappy girlfriend.

Amanda was devastated. She couldn't believe she had lost her boyfriend for someone she now loathed, a guy who pretended to be a friend when he wasn't. Nathaniel wasn't her friend, and she knew it somewhere deep in her heart and soul, but it would take her a while to admit the truth about him and their relationship. It would take many more betrayals before she finally saw him for what he really was inside his heart.

Fast forward many years to the year 2025. It was New Year's once again, and there was a positive expectation for the things to come. Amanda looked around her living room and saw Nathanial and their now three children. The two had been married for ten years, and they had built a life together, a life she thought was a dream and a love story, at least for a little while.

As the New Year was upon them, Amanda prepared herself for a fast with her church. She had advanced in her faith and her relationship with the Lord, and she had been baptized right after New Year's 2014. She really had changed her life and become someone new, and over the last ten years the Lord had worked in her life, removing drugs, alcohol, partying, and sexual immorality. God had taken the desire for these things away from her entirely, and He had worked with her to be a strong wife and mother.

But Nathanial was still struggling. He was a drunk, drinking alcohol almost every day. In addition, he was still dabbling with drugs and choosing to smoke marijuana, which was now legal in the country. He claimed to have his addictions under control and frequently said, "I don't have a problem. I am a good husband and dad. And I am a successful business owner." He proclaimed proudly, "Our life is fine. I am fine." But when Amanda tried to confront him about his bad choices, he would retort, "You think you are a goody two-shoes! You think you are more than me, but you're not."

Well, that is not really true, Amanda would think to herself. *I don't think I am better than anyone. I just want to do the right thing. I want God to be happy with me. I want to be a good wife and a good mom, and I am trusting God to help me become who He wants me to become.* Recently the Lord had been speaking to Amanda about oral sex. He told her that it was causing a problem in her marriage because Nathanial only increasingly wanted to participate in it and rarely wanted her.

She felt neglected with her sexuality, and for years she would tell Nathanial that she didn't want to do oral anymore. She wanted to have intercourse with him. She wanted to have him love her and make love to her. She also desired more children. She loved being a mom and she didn't think she was done having children. But Nathanial hated this idea. He didn't want more children. He didn't even really like the ones he had. He regularly made comments idealizing what his life would be like if he didn't have a wife and children.

These comments cut Amanda to the core. She couldn't believe he would feel that way or that he would dare to vocalize it, sometimes even where the children could hear it. She hated the life she had created for her children. She wanted to get out so badly, as she had wanted to get out of DC that day long ago, but she couldn't get out now. She was married and had children. She was also dependent on his income because she had chosen to stay home and raise their babies for their betterment. So, Amanda would pray and ask God for help. She would ask the Lord to please help her and her children.

Many years went by where Amanda would share with God the heartache she was experiencing as a wife and a mother. Nathanial was hateful. He regularly cussed at her and called her crazy. He regularly threatened to kill her and bury her body in their backyard. "It was a joke of course," he would say, as he smiled at her, making these vicious comments. "You are so sensitive and weak. I am only joking. What is wrong with you? Can't you take a joke?"

Amanda knew that these things were more than jokes, but what was she supposed to do? She didn't know, so she prayed to Jesus, the One who had always been there for her and listened to her when she was in trouble. It was during one of her conversations with Jesus during a fast in the early moments of 2026 that she knew the truth about Nathanial and his fate. Jesus peeled back the truth. He revealed to her what she needed to know, even though it hurt. Jesus told her the truth about her husband, her abuser.

"Nathanial is a drunk," Jesus said. "Furthermore, he has hurt you for many years in more ways than you know or have known. There is going to be a big betrayal: a big catastrophe in his life. I am going to take Nathanial's life from him, and he is going to be out of your life. You are going to be a widow, and your children are going to be fatherless. But don't worry about anything, because I am going to give you a plan. I am going to prepare you to take care of yourself and your children, and I am going to stay with you and ensure that you and your children are safe now and forever."

Amanda wondered if this was true. She wanted to make sure she heard correctly what Jesus was saying. She was on the first three-day fast she had ever taken, and, like Gideon in the Bible, she needed God to tell her for sure if this was true. She didn't want to make a mistake. She didn't want to say something, believe something, or plan for something to happen to Nathanial if she was mistaken. "Lord, is this you? Are you telling me what I think you are?" she prayed. "Yes, Amanda," Jesus said. "I know it is hard to process. I know it hurts."

A few days before this, Nathanial had said something that he had never said before, and God said he was going to receive the death penalty for it. When Amanda told Nathanial she didn't want to have oral sex anymore he kept pushing. He didn't want to accept it. He told her they were going to do it, or else they were going to have to go to counseling for it. Then he told her that he would work with her. He was going to have more sex with her and reduce the amount of oral he required. But Amanda, for the first time in their marriage, had set a boundary, and she was not moving.

God told her that oral sex was a barrier in the marriage. He showed her that it was keeping her from intimacy with her husband, and it was keeping her from conceiving more children, something He wanted her to do too. So Amanda refused to participate in oral sex, but this enraged her husband. They spent much time fighting and ultimately not having sex anymore because of the refusal to do oral sex.

This solidified what Amanda knew. The oral sex was a barrier in the marriage, because Nathanial would straight-up refuse to be intimate with her if she didn't perform it. But she wasn't willing to go back on what she knew was right. She was going to stand firm and try to bring them together in intimacy and love by refusing to participate in something that was tearing them apart.

Right after the New Year, on New Year's Day, Amanda said no again, and this time he went ballistic. "I have been doing what you want. I have been considerate and doing what you want to do," he shouted. "Now it is time for you to do what I want you to do." Amanda responded by calmly saying, "I have been doing what you want me to do for years, and it has caused a problem in our lovemaking. I am not going to keep doing that. I don't feel comfortable with it. I want to have sex with you. I want us to actually make love." He shouted back, "You just want me to get you pregnant, and I don't want to do that. And if you don't give me what I want I am going to get it from somewhere else!"

Amanda was struck speechless. She knew the words he spoke were straight from his heart and that he desired to be with someone other than her because she didn't want to have oral sex with him. For the first time she knew that he didn't love her, because if he loved her nothing would keep him from being intimate with her.

Amanda got hot all over her chest and body. She felt anger and she was hurt, but this was what he wanted. This was what he had chosen, and she had nothing to do with it. There was nothing she could do to change his mind. There was nothing she could do to make him take back what he had just said.

Jesus said that if a man looks lustfully after a woman, they have committed the crime. The Scriptures also say that adultery is a sin punishable by death, a sin deserving of stoning. In a few days Amanda would discover how mad Nathanial's comment had made the Lord. God was finally done with the sexual violence, emotional violence, and physical violence that he inflicted upon his wife. God was not going to continue to allow this man to abuse someone so valuable and precious. He was not going to turn a blind eye to the cruelty and the suffering of a woman who continued to plead with Him for her safety and the safety of her children.

After a few days of communing with God, Amanda would discover the truth about her husband's fate. God would reveal to her the execution timeline as well as the plans that needed to be made to ensure her safety and security. She had a realization of the crimes committed against her and saw that her husband was in danger and would soon be destroyed and killed for his sins. As for the premonition of the future, even though it was hard, she was thankful for her Lord and Savior. God saw her and protected her from a man who was commanded to do just that but refused to.

Amanda knew when God pronounced death on a person that person was a dead man. She looked over at her husband, who at the time was very much still alive, and she knew he wouldn't be for much longer. Amanda saw that he was already gone. A dead man, because the Judge had ruled against him for his sins and aggression. Amanda prayed, asking, "God, is there hope for him? Can he be forgiven?"

"Yes, of course," God said, "but he won't be because he refuses to surrender and repent for what he has done. I would forgive him, just like I have forgiven you for your sins of sexual immorality and unhealthy romantic relationships. I would give him a clean slate, a new chance, and the ability to live and thrive if he was willing to lay aside his pride and hatred of me and my word." He continued, "He won't change because he doesn't want to. So, I have hardened his heart, and all of these things I have said about him will shortly come to pass, and you will see it. Now prepare yourself so you won't be affected and left without a way out."

A plan—a way out, Amanda thought. *Wow. That is a new one. I have never had a man prepare me ahead of time for what was coming. The men I have known always left me stuck without a plan in a vulnerable place. Jesus wants me to be prepared. He wants me to be in control. He doesn't want me weak and unable to prevent what is happening or what is going to happen to me. What a great man.* She prayed, "Thank you, Jesus. You are unlike anyone else I have ever known. You are a righteous redeemer. I love you more than anything, and I will do what you say, even when it isn't easy, because I know you love me and care about my future."

And that is when she realized that God had always tried to tell her about what was going to happen. He had always given her visions, dreams, and premonitions about who people were and what they were going to do. She didn't know then how to interpret His messages because she didn't trust Him enough or know His voice. But today was a new day. From this day forward, she would heed His every word. She would obey and listen to His proclamations of the things to come, and she would never look back, because why would she? Her future was bright, and God could be trusted.

The LORD is my shepherd, I lack nothing. He makes me lie down in green pastures, he leads me beside quiet waters, he refreshes my soul. He guides me along the right paths for his name's sake. Even though I walk through the darkest valley, I will fear no evil, for you are with me; your rod and your staff, they comfort me. You prepare a table before me in the presence of my enemies. You anoint my head with oil; my cup overflows (Ps. 23:1–5).

{ 2 }

Angelic Intervention

How did Amanda end up married to Nathanial? How did they end up together with three children, years after he first sexually and physically attacked her? Why didn't she leave? Why didn't she stay away from him when he proved himself to be aggressive and mean toward her?

It is easy to judge others when you've never been in their shoes. From afar people can say what they would do and what they wouldn't. If you have never been in an abusive situation or an abusive intimate relationship, you are blessed not have gone through what those who are or have been have experienced.

It really isn't uncommon for women to remain in abusive homes or relationships. There is a sense of loyalty that comes from trauma bonding. In the psychological phenomenon called Stockholm syndrome, people begin to sympathize with their abusers and attackers and often bond with them. The brain, when in emergency situations, oftentimes tries to resolve the conflict and the danger through compassion and understanding, withdrawal and submission.

Consider a person who has been taken hostage and held for a long time. If the captor hasn't killed them and gives them food and water, allows them to take showers and do necessities, then the captured person may think this person is compassionate when indeed they are not. Of course, logically speaking, we know that no one deserves to be held in captivity at all, but when one has become captive and is in a state of survival, they may cope with the danger and the abuse through normalizing and sympathizing with their attacker.

Conditions like these can be amplified when a woman or a child has been sexually abused or attacked by someone. Scripture tells us that a woman named Dinah was raped and captured by people outside of her camp. After the rape she was willing to marry the man who raped her because she knew that marriage, even to a terrible man, would be better than a lack of safety or protection in a world full of violence and male aggression and headship.

Genesis 34:2 explains, *"When Shechem son of Hamor the Hivite, the ruler of that area, saw her, he took her and raped her. His heart was drawn to Dinah the daughter of Jacob; he loved the young woman and spoke tenderly to her. And Shechem said to his father Hamor, "Get me this girl as a wife."*

This abusive man claimed to love Dinah. He said he wanted to marry her and that he cared for her. Abusers will at times proclaim to love the woman they are abusing. They will tell lies, give engagement rings, and convince others of their affection toward the woman they have already harmed and shamed. And in the case of Amanda, she experienced all of this, but she was too young and naive to know what she was experiencing until it was far too late.

Young girls need the protection of their fathers and brothers. Women were created by God to be honored, protected, and provided for. When a father fails in his calling to protect and provide for a young girl, then younger men will feel that they need to take up the charge and protect them. Oftentimes, however, due to their own immaturity they make mistakes in administering justice. Dinah's brothers wanted to protect her and honor her. They wanted to handle the abuse, but because of their immaturity, they handled it without wisdom.

When Jacob heard that his daughter Dinah had been defiled, his sons were in the fields with his livestock; so he did nothing until they came home. Then Shechem's father Hamor went out to speak with Jacob. Meanwhile, Jacob's sons had come in from the fields as soon as they heard what had happened.

They were shocked and furious, because Shechem had done an outrageous thing in Israel by sleeping with Jacob's daughter—a thing that should not be done (Gen. 34:5–7).

Why did Jacob wait for his sons? Why did he not intervene and handle the situation like a man and a father should have? Jacob was wise in many endeavors, primarily in his business dealings, but in this case, he did not do what he should have done. Amanda's dad was the same way. He worked as a police officer, claiming to help victims of crimes. He paraded himself in the community as a man of valor and wisdom and strength, but because he failed to administer protection and provision in his own house, Amanda was left without protection from the man she needed it from the most.

Women are the weaker vessel. They do need the protection of men. Men will not be held blameless when they neglect the women and girls in their lives. God expects men to step up and provide protection, especially from sexual assault and other forms of violence. When men refuse to take their job seriously, women will be hurt and then hurt again because a woman's or child's psychology will enslave them into a system of trauma bonding and abuse, a tactic Satan knows all too well.

When Satan is permitted to perform an act of violence on a woman, he gains a level of domination in the emotional realm. He is given access he shouldn't have, and unless a woman is taken in and cared for by someone else, Satan often will keep the woman in a pattern of bondage and submission to his will and schemes. As Amanda lived her life without the protection of her father, other men came in and abused her. With each abusive act, she became more desperate for protection from a man, but this proved incredibly dangerous for her.

When a woman feels unsafe, she runs to a man, but what happens when there are no good men for her to run to? What happens when the men she is running to for safety, protection, and aid are a part of her problem? Tamar, another woman in scripture who was raped by a man who should have protected her, ran to her brother Absalom after her attack. Yet some girls do not have brothers. They don't have anyone to come to their rescue, and Satan knows it.

These women are easier to trap. These vulnerable, precious girls need help, and Satan will package their help in the form of a man. This plan works because God's plan is for men to come and protect women, but not all men are created equal. Some men are good and some are evil. Nathanial was evil. He pretended to be Amanda's answer to prayer. He pretended to be her protector and helper, at least for a little while.

After that terrible night in DC, Nathanial started going to church with Amanda. During the first church service he attended with her, he cried and said he felt God talk to him. He attested that he was going to change his life. He said, "I am going to be different, and we are going to do this together." Amanda was thrilled. She knew God's power to change a life. She knew that change was possible for anyone! It didn't take long for her to begin imagining a life of safety and love and godliness with Nathanial. They could be unlike anything she had experienced before. They could be a Christian couple changed and transformed by God's power.

Unbeknownst to Amanda Nathanial was putting on a show. He never planned to be a Christian or to change his life. He just saw her desire for God and her love for the church, and he exploited it to capture her in a relationship. For Nathanial, church and God were not a genuine call or experience. It was a ticket to Amanda's heart and trust, a ticket he was willing to purchase if it meant he could sleep with her and call her his own.

Before long the two were officially dating, and Amanda had high hopes for their future because they were both committed to God . . . or so she thought! As far as she was concerned this man was genuine, and why wouldn't he be? She couldn't imagine a man lying about his conversion to Christianity or his love for God. A man surely wouldn't do that. So, after a few months of dating and being a couple, this man began to push her to sleep with him, something that seemed harmless to her at the time because he had waited for her and that was different too!

To a woman accustomed to one-night stands and quick hookup culture, a man who had waited a few weeks and gone to church with her was very different from the rest. And Amanda had completely forgotten about the experience in DC by now, because of course that was the Christian thing to do after all. He was changed. He was different, and she shouldn't hold his past against him anymore. She wouldn't want someone to hold her past against her after her conversion to Christ, so why would she do that to someone else?

The first time Nathanial was successful in sleeping with Amanda, he ejaculated inside of her without her permission. Then, he began to tell her what a great mother she would be and how he wanted to have children with her. He said he loved her so much and that they were going to have a great future. Amanda was shocked. She didn't want him to impose himself on her this way so quickly, but a part of her did long for children, marriage, and a home, so she felt very conflicted and uncomfortable. And every time she slept with him, she felt convicted, a conviction she had never felt before—and she knew it was God.

Before Amanda's baptism and conversion to Christ, hooking up with men didn't feel wrong. She didn't see anything disgusting about the behavior, but after her conversion she knew this was wrong. She felt God telling her to stop. She shared this shame and guilt with Nathanial, and he said he understood because he knew she was serious. She would stop the relationship if he didn't do something quickly, so he went out and bought an engagement ring and proposed to her, saying, "I want you forever."

Amanda had never been proposed to before—a moment she had waited for her entire life. The proposal was on her 22nd birthday, and Nathanial planned a special lunch and trip to the beach for them alongside the proposal. Amanda was excited. She felt like this relationship was genuine and that he respected her needs and wishes. He was playing the perfect part and doing the things she wanted him to do. She had no clue how sinister all his motives and plans really were. Everything Nathanial was doing was for his own benefit. All he did was done so that he could fulfill his lust and have total sexual conquest of her.

A few weeks after the engagement the couple went out to dinner in downtown Richmond Virginia. They were drinking margaritas at the local Mexican restaurant, Little Mexico. Things quickly turned ugly, and Nathanial got infuriated over money. Amanda had more money than he had at the time because her grandmother had given her some of her grandfather's inheritance. Of course Nathanial hated that Amanda had financial support and ability, and he constantly told her it was a problem in the relationship. She thought she was better than him! She used her money as a wedge between them, he would say.

Amanda had no idea what Nathanial was talking about. Her money had nothing to do with him. She was not asking him to do anything for her. She could pay her own way. Why was this man so sensitive about money? None of it made any sense to her. She didn't get why he had such a hangup with money, but whenever he was challenged he would say, "You have had everything given to you, and I have had to work hard for everything I have had. I have never had anyone help me. It must be nice."

Nathanial wanted Amanda to feel sorry for him. He wanted her to think he was a victim of his parents' and family's rejection and neglect. This trick worked so well because Amanda really was neglected and rejected by the men who were supposed to protect her. She had a special place in her heart for people who had never been properly protected and cared for by their fathers. Like Nathanial, Amanda wasn't close to her dad, and she had a deep father wound that Nathanial exploited so they could "trauma bond and connect."

But back to the fight that night at Little Mexico in Richmond. When it was time for the bill, the two got into a big disagreement. Nathanial left Amanda inside the restaurant to pay while he fumed in anger outside smoking a cigarette. When Amanda went outside, Nathanial was blasting violent music by a band whos music is all about murder and death. He was fueling his hatred and aggression through music created to do just that.

As the two walked toward the car they yelled back and forth in disagreement. Then seemingly out of nowhere something happened . . . something that Amanda was not prepared for or expecting. Nathanial attacked her. He grabbed her, ripped her clothes, and began throwing her like she was a doll. He grabbed her hand and ripped off the engagement ring. He took her car keys and put them in his pocket, and then he pulled her shoes off and took her phone from her.

Just then, Amanda heard a man yelling at them and looked up. He was screaming at Nathanial and telling him to get off that girl and leave her alone! "What the hell are you doing?" he yelled. Nathanial snapped out of it and realized that he had been spotted. He took the car keys, got into the car, and sped off, leaving Amanda downtown with no shoes, a ripped outfit, and a broken heart.

Amanda was hysterical. She had never had a man be this physically aggressive with her before. She was scared. She also had no way to get back into her apartment because the keys were on her car key ring. What was she going to do? She walked through the city trying to make her way toward her apartment. She was weeping, bawling, and crying out to God like never before. She said, "God! God, if you are real and you are here, please, please help me. I need help."

Just then, Amanda heard a voice say, "Hey, are you okay?" She looked up, tears covering her face, and said, "Not really." The voice was the voice of a stranger. She didn't know these people, but before her sat two people, a girl and a boy. "Can we ask you a random question?" they inquired. "Uh, yeah. Sure," Amanda sniffled back. "Do you believe in God?" they asked her. *What in the world?* Amanda thought. *This has never happened before.* Two people asking her about God while she was in the middle of a prayer begging God for help? In fact, she did not expect anyone, especially anyone in downtown Richmond on a Friday night, to talk to her about Jesus.

Amanda knew these people were an answer to the prayer she had prayed a few moments earlier. She knew that this encounter was not an accident or coincidence. These people had been sent by God to help her, as she had asked. They were not average Richmond people. They were different, and they seemed so out of place in a wicked city full of sexual immorality, partying, and ungodliness. But here they were, nonetheless. Two people sitting on a wall in front of an apartment building asking her about God.

Amanda stopped and began talking to these two strangers. She told them about what had just happened to her. They were so bothered by the news, and they were very concerned for her safety. They asked her where she was going and if she was going to be okay when she got there. They took her into the apartment they lived in, got her some clothes, and let her call her sister from their phone. After spending some time with Amanda, they then gave her a ride back to her apartment, but before they dropped her off, they said one important thing to her: "Do you really think that God would want you to be with this kind of man? God loves you. Leave this man alone. Don't forgive him, and don't go back to him."

Yeah, you are right, Amanda thought. She knew that these strangers were right, but what was she supposed to do? He was her fiancé after all, and she loved him. He wanted to change and honor God. They must not know him. He could still change and be a good man. He was just drunk and made a bad decision. *He wouldn't have done this otherwise,* she argued within her mind. When Amanda got back to her apartment her car was parked out back. She knew Nathanial was inside waiting for her.

The strangers asked Amanda if she was sure that she wanted to go inside. *I just want to go home,* she thought. *Maybe if I can take a shower and get some sleep all of this will just go away.* "I will be okay," she assured them. "Thank you for all of your help. I really do appreciate it so much!" she said to the strangers as she got out of their car. Amanda went inside and found Nathanial sitting at her kitchen table. He said, "I just wanted to make sure you got back home safely, but I really am done with you. I am leaving." And he got up and walked out the door.

Amanda's heart was broken. Her engagement was over. Her hopes and dreams of marriage, love, and unity with a godly man were finished. But then, after a few long, hard days, Amanda started getting texts from Nathanial again. "I am really sorry for what happened, baby. I love you so much. I do want to marry you. I do want to be together," he asserted. "I didn't mean what happened. I was drunk. Please forgive me," he begged. After a little coaxing, Amanda agreed to talk to him again and meet up. Before she knew it they were engaged again, and her ring was returned to her hand. Her future was restored, and she could just forget about that terrible nightmare that was a one-time accident.

Looking back on it today, Amanda knows the two people were angels. These angels were sent into the city for her, so she could be given a ride home, a phone to call her sister, and a place to calm down. God sent the angels to warn her and to direct her about what she was supposed to do. They wanted her to know she was loved and that God had a better plan for her. But why didn't she see it? Why didn't she heed their warnings? She didn't know, but she was sure sorry. She was sorry she hadn't listened to the voice of the angels, because Nathanial wasn't the man God had for her. He was a monster and deceiver, an agent of Satan meant to destroy her life and her future.

Exodus 23:20–23 teaches, *"See, I am sending an angel ahead of you to guard you along the way and to bring you to the place I have prepared. Pay attention to him and listen to what he says. Do not rebel against him; he will not forgive your rebellion, since my Name is in him. If you listen carefully to what he says and do all that I say, I will be an enemy to your enemies and will oppose those who oppose you. My angel will go ahead of you and bring you into the land of the Amorites, Hittites, Perizzites, Canaanites, Hivites and Jebusites, and I will wipe them out."*

The next time God would send her an angel, she would heed his voice. Way into her future, after finding herself in a similar situation again, this time with more to protect: the lives of her children. And Amanda would listen. She would obey the voice of the angel and speak against this evil man who was sitting in her home. She knew God would do what He promised to do. She knew that He would take out her enemy. She knew the Lord was with her because He loved her and had more for her life. And it was only a matter of time before justice was served, and her freedom and happiness would spring forth.

"Thank you, Jesus, for the angels," Amanda prayed. "I am so thankful you have sent me help." I am so thankful for your love and your protection. I am so sorry I didn't listen before. I am so sorry I have brought this heartache onto myself and into the lives of my kids. Please help me and help my children. Please have mercy on us and let us be a part of your family. I love you, Jesus. I love you, God. Thank you."

{ 3 }

Healing Power

Some rollercoasters are designed to go backward. When you go to an amusement park it is common to find rides that propel in a backward motion so the riders can have fun. Amanda always loved rollercoasters and theme parks, but going backward wasn't always easy, especially when you weren't riding a ride. God was taking Amanda on a journey through her past. He was taking her backward so she could heal and find joy again. But Amanda had to fasten her seatbelt because this ride hurt a lot. She wanted to get off, but she knew she couldn't if she wanted to heal and find her joy again.

How could Amanda see the truth about Nathanial and their entire relationship and not mourn, weep, and be in agony? She had loved this man. He was her husband and the father of her children. He was the man she had spent the last eleven years with as a partner and a friend. Everything she had done for him and with him was genuine. She really did love him and care for him, yet she had no clue that he was so deceptive and operating with guile. *I really fell in love with a monster*, she thought to herself. *How could I have been so naive?*

The Lord had given her warnings. He had told her many times to get away from this man. Right before the two were married, Amanda was sitting in her car and prayed to ask God if she was supposed to marry Nathanial. He told her no as the scripture in her Bible jumped off the page: "Do not be unequally yoked with unbelievers." Amanda slammed her Bible shut. She was already on the way to marry him, so how in the world would she get out of the car and change her mind now? *What would he say? What would he do?* she wondered.

As she looked up from her Bible, she saw the license plate of the car in front of her "Mr. and Mrs.," it read. *Oh, this must be a sign from God,* she thought. But Amanda was so mistaken. This was not a sign from God. It was a sign from her enemy, Satan, who can manipulate things in the natural world to seem supernatural to deceive and trap the ignorant.

Upon seeing the sign, Amanda ignored the Bible verse. She said to herself, "It will be okay. I am doing the right thing anyway. God doesn't want me to be in a sexually immoral relationship, and if I am going to continue sleeping with this man, then I need to marry him. That will protect me from being in trouble with God. I need to get married to be pure. I need to do the right thing even when I am scared and hesitant."

People often say that hindsight is 20/20, or that you can see things better in reverse. Some things can only be understood that way. Some things remain hidden, unless you are willing to go back and discover the truth behind them. Second Thessalonians 2:9–10 tells us, "*The coming of the lawless one will be in accordance with how Satan works. He will use all sorts of displays of power through signs and wonders that serve the lie, and all the ways that wickedness deceives those who are perishing. They perish because they refused to love the truth and be saved.*"

The man of sin, the Antichrist, will be able to perform miracles and signs. He will be able to manipulate human reason and the human brain because he is operating with spiritual power. Demon power is real. Demons do have power and ability. We need God in our lives to know when we are interacting with a devil and when we are hearing from angels or from Him. Not all supernatural signs and wonders are good. Some of them are very very bad, and if you don't know how to discern and tell the difference, it can be vital for your life.

Vital moments in life are the important moments. When you get married, the marriage certificate is filed with the vital records department. Birth, death, and marriage are some vital moments in our human experience. Amanda knew these moments with Jesus were the vital informing of her future, and she knew that these moments witnessing to Nathanial were vital as well. She repented for not taking the marriage as a vital moment in the past, and she trusted Jesus with the vital moments that would come in the future.

One day Nathanial would look back on his life and realize who Amanda was in the spirit. He would remember vividly the vital words she spoke to him in early January 2026. Nathanial didn't know it now, but one day in reverse, he would remember her warning him and pleading with him to change from his demonic associations and to repent. Amanda looked at Nathanial and warned him with passion and conviction. She told him what was coming for him if he didn't change and repent from his sins and hatred of God. But he laughed at her and mocked God all the more.

"Yeah, you have angels that protect you. And go ahead! I am not afraid. Do what you have to do, God," he sneered. "Do it now!" He taunted, "What are you waiting for, God? Kill me now." Nathanial didn't see it, nor did he get what Amanda was saying. His life was in danger. God had placed a death sentence over his head, and he was now on death row in the court of Heaven. He didn't take it seriously, however, and he didn't want to change or admit his sin even when faced with the reality of his future.

"Nathanial, please!" Amanda cried. "Do you not want to see your daughter walk down the aisle on her wedding day? Do you not want to celebrate fifty years of marriage with me?" "I will do those things!" he asserted proudly. "I am doing just fine. I am doing better than ever." But Amanda warned him. "No, Nathanial. You don't hear what I am saying. Please listen to me. Please don't turn your back on God's warning. God has informed me that your life is indeed in danger if you don't repent. Your actions and words have offended God. He is going to take your life soon if you don't repent."

"You are so insane and crazy, Amanda!" he shouted at her. "I am so effin' tired of being a part of this continual church. I want to get some fresh air. I want to breathe and get out of church. You know the feeling of being stuck in a church service and not being able to get out, and then once you get out and breathe you are finally good? That is how I feel being around you! You are so annoying. I hate having to constantly hear about Jesus."

The reality of the verdict against his life and the refusal to repent were heavy on Amanda. She hurt for him. She felt grief. For the last few days, ever since Jesus spoke to her about Nathanial's fate, she was in mourning. She wondered, *Why doesn't this man value his life? Why do I seem to care more about his future than he does? I wish he would just change. I wish he would repent and become what God wants him to become. His life doesn't have to be this way. He still has a chance to repent, but he doesn't care. He doesn't want Jesus's help.*

Amanda knew that Jesus would forgive anything. She knew that He was capable of restoring, healing, and forgiving all offenses. If Nathanial would just hear Jesus's words and simply repent genuinely for his ungodly choices and life, then Jesus would welcome him and help him. He would forgive him and be a part of his life permitting him to live. His story didn't have to end this way. Even as mean and hateful, deceptive and harmful as Nathanial had been, God could and would forgive him if he would only turn from his wicked ways and ask for forgiveness.

"If my people, who are called by my name, will humble themselves and pray and seek my face and turn from their wicked ways, then I will hear from heaven, and I will forgive their sin and will heal their land. Now my eyes will be open and my ears attentive to the prayers offered in this place. I have chosen and consecrated this temple so that my Name may be there forever. My eyes and my heart will always be there. As for you, if you walk before me faithfully as David your father did, and do all I command, and observe

my decrees and laws, I will establish your royal throne, as I covenanted with David your father when I said, 'You shall never fail to have a successor to rule over Israel'" (2 Chron. 7:14–18).

When God spoke these words, He was establishing His healing covenant and professing His love for His people. God wants people to honor Him and to keep His decrees. He is willing to forgive all former transgressions and wrongdoings, but in order to be eligible for the forgiveness, blessing, and help, people have to want to change and repent. They have to show God that they were sorry and willing to do what He wanted them to do.

God is gracious, loving, and kind. He wants to restore people and to forgive them, but sometimes God will not see His plans and purposes for a life come to pass. There are times when people refuse to heed the warnings of God or His plans for their lives. If they continue to walk in disobedience and refuse to turn and change and go another direction, then they will not be saved, healed, or taken from their problematic situations.

Walking with the Lord may at times feel like it is backward, especially when you are used to walking in human reason. God is a spirit. His ways are not like our ways as people. The way forward with Jesus may feel like a backward rollercoaster. It may feel like we are going the wrong way, when in reality, the way forward is through the thing we think is backward. God established the heavens and the earth to work in a certain way, and this way is not the same as our presumed way.

Isaiah 55:9–11 says, *"As the heavens are higher than the earth, so are my ways higher than your ways and my thoughts than your thoughts. As the rain and the snow come down from heaven, and do not return to it without watering the earth and making it bud and flourish, so that it yields seed for the sower and bread for the eater, so is my word that goes out from my mouth: It will not return to me empty, but will accomplish what I desire and achieve the purpose for which I sent it."*

Sometimes people think they are going forward in the direction they are supposed to go. These people, because they live by their own human understanding and reasoning, think that they are headed onward and advancing outside of the commands and words of the Lord. Life seems fun, and the ride is exhilarating. *I am having a great time, and I don't need to change,* they may think. All the while, the Lord's voice is saying, "Get off the ride or turn the ride around, so you can live and enjoy the life I have given you."

Just as believers can hear the words of the Devil or see the signs sent from enemy forces, unbelievers can hear the words of God and see the signs of the direction of Heaven. God will speak to unbelievers. God spoke to Pharaoh through Moses. He spoke to Pontius Pilate through his wife in a dream. Other unbelievers who received words from the Lord were Jezebel and Ahab through the prophet Elijah, and Balaam, a wicked prophet who believed he was working for God.

Balaam even prophesied and did some of the Lord's work, but in the end, he was destroyed by God because he was corrupt and full of deception and lies within his heart. *"Balaam answered, 'Did I not tell you I must do whatever the LORD says?'"* (Num. 23:26). Baalam appeared to do the right thing outwardly, but inside his heart sided with evil. This proves to us that God does speak to people who are going to be destroyed.

The elders of Moab and Midian left, taking with them the fee for divination. When they came to Balaam, they told him what Balak had said. "Spend the night here," Balaam said to them, "and I will report back to you with the answer the Lord gives me." So the Moabite officials stayed with him. God came to Balaam and asked, "Who are these men with you?" Balaam said to God, "Balak son of Zippor, king of Moab, sent me this message: 'A people that has come out of Egypt covers the face of the land. Now come and put a curse on them for me. Perhaps then I will be able to fight them and drive them away.'"

But God said to Balaam, "Do not go with them. You must not put a curse on those people, because they are blessed." The next morning Balaam got up and said to Balak's officials, "Go back to your own country, for the LORD has refused to let me go with you." So the Moabite officials returned to Balak and said, "Balaam refused to come with us." Then Balak sent other officials, more numerous and more distinguished than the first. They came to Balaam and said:

"This is what Balak son of Zippor says: Do not let anything keep you from coming to me, because I will reward you handsomely and do whatever you say. Come and put a curse on these people for me." But Balaam answered them, "Even if Balak gave me all the silver and gold in his palace, I could not do anything great or small to go beyond the command of the LORD my God. Now spend the night here so that I can find out what else the LORD will tell me" (Num. 22:7–19).

God had already commanded Balaam to not go with the evil men. He told him the first time to stay away from the men and to have nothing to do with them. Balaam thought he could change God's mind and join himself to an evil agenda because he wanted the money and power associated with the men who were summoning him. This man even performed religious ceremonies and burned things on the alter, claiming to be working for the Lord. However, the Scriptures assure us that he was not accepted or approved of by God.

Revelation 2:14 explains, "Nevertheless, I have a few things against you: There are some among you who hold to the teaching of Balaam, who taught Balak to entice the Israelites to sin so that they ate food sacrificed to idols and committed sexual immorality." When Jesus was speaking to the Church through this prophecy, He was warning them to be on guard for sexual immorality and intermingling with the world. He warned the Church to be separate from the world, as He had commanded Balaam, not permitting evil to come into your house.

Sometimes the Devil will come to Christians offering them relationships, money, or other things that are appealing to human desires or the flesh. But when Christians join themselves to people, places, and things that are unholy and defiled, then they are in danger of losing their standing in the house of God because God does not want to be joined with corruption and evil. The Lord will remove the corruption and the impure from His people, but they must be willing to first stand against evil and obey His commands to hate evil and flee from it in their hearts and their actions.

Balaam was doing the right things outwardly. He seemed to be obeying the voice of God, at least at first. But the Lord knew that Balaam's heart was still positioned toward evil. Even though it looked like Balaam wanted to obey God, within his heart he still desired to be accepted by the world. If a woman wants to be set free, she must hate evil and love God more than anything else offered to her. This includes marriages that are against God and His plan.

Again Jesus called the crowd to him and said, "Listen to me, everyone, and understand this. Nothing outside a person can defile them by going into them. Rather, it is what comes out of a person that defiles them."

After he had left the crowd and entered the house, his disciples asked him about this parable. "Are you so dull?" he asked. "Don't you see that nothing that enters a person from the outside can defile them? For it doesn't go into their heart but into their stomach, and then out of the body." (In saying this, Jesus declared all foods clean.)

He went on: "What comes out of a person is what defiles them. For it is from within, out of a person's heart, that evil thoughts come—sexual immorality, theft, murder, adultery, greed, malice, deceit, lewdness, envy, slander, arrogance and folly. All these evils come from inside and defile a person" (Mark 7:14–23).

God knows and sees the heart of a person. He knows when someone is appearing to go forward but they are really going backward. Conversely, he knows when someone appears to be going backward, but because their heart is positioned toward him and his truth, they are really moving forward. Our minds often confuse the spirit's will and our own will if we are not intentional in pressing into the things of God. There are things in life that will perplex our minds but ring true to our spirits, and only a man or a woman who loves God and seeks His will can find the truth.

Amanda had always loved God. She wanted to do the right thing, and she tried to obey God throughout the duration of her relationship with her husband. She seemed to be operating foolishly to continue to forgive and love a man who was so hateful and mean to her. It seemed like she should have left him and made a public spectacle of him, bringing him shame and humiliation for the things that he was doing and had always done to her. But Amanda knew something that only a select few people ever discover.

God was moving her forward by what seemed to be going backward. As she put her trust in Him and His righteousness, and as she wanted to obey Him and His word more than she wanted anything else, God was going to remove her husband from her life because he was corrupting this mission. In her obedience to God, she had to lose her husband because he was not headed in the same direction as her. He was heading right toward destruction.

God was watching everything. He wasn't going to allow His daughter, who had unwavering faith in Him and His word, to be destroyed. He was not going to allow this man to take her captive anymore into her future because her future wasn't bleak—it was very bright. Proverbs 4:18 explains, *"The path of the righteous is like the morning sun, shining ever brighter till the full light of day."*

If Nathanial stayed in her life, then God's word couldn't come forth in her life because He was leading their family in another direction (backward). God loved her and her children far too much to allow this to happen to them. God wanted them to have what He promised them to have. He was a man of His word, and He was going to ensure that the enemies to her destiny were removed. *"But the way of the wicked is like deep darkness; they do not know what makes them stumble"* (Prov. 4:19).

All these years Nathanial thought he was headed forward with his deception and trickery. He assumed that because he sometimes heard the voice of God and got signs that he was on the right track and headed for greatness. The Devil is a deceiver, and he will go to great measures to keep people walking in the way of darkness. And God will allow it because people allow it and want it to be a part of their lives.

When a heart turns away from the truth, it has no choice but to wind up in a web of lies. Lies multiply, they continue to accumulate, and at some point people find themselves surrounded by them and entangled by them. Nathanial would soon find out that while he felt in control, and he felt superior in his ability to deceive and trick Amanda, the truth was that she was going to remain and continue on forever, living a life of luxury and happiness with Jesus. He was going to find himself in chains for what he had done, and he would never get out.

All the while he felt he was powerful and in control of her, keeping her under his dominion and watch. For years, he laughed at her ignorance and her pain. He assumed she was weak and stupid, incapable and easily persuaded. But in the end, that is his story, not hers. He is the one who was taken captive and kept under the dominion of a serpent. He was the one who was ignorant and suffering while believing he was fine. In the end he will know he was the weak one, the stupid one, the incapable one of seeing the truth.

Nathanial will know that he was easily persuaded by his enemy, the Devil, but now there is no chance to go backward and change the narrative and story. There is no chance to rewind, because in eternity there are no more second chances. Once God has set a course, a decree, or a plan into action you are on that rollercoaster forever, and you can't get off the ride. You can't change your mind once the restraints are put on and you are moving forward, backward, or whichever way the ride goes.

Therefore this is what the LORD Almighty says concerning the prophets: "I will make them eat bitter food and drink poisoned water, because from the prophets of Jerusalem ungodliness has spread throughout the land."

This is what the LORD Almighty says: "Do not listen to what the prophets are prophesying to you; they fill you with false hopes. They speak visions from their own minds, not from the mouth of the LORD. They keep saying to those who despise me, 'The LORD says: You will have peace.' And to all who follow the stubbornness of their hearts they say, 'No harm will come to you.' But which of them has stood in the council of the LORD to see or to hear his word? Who has listened and heard his word? See, the storm of the LORD will burst out in wrath, a whirlwind swirling down on the heads of the wicked. The anger of the LORD will not turn back until he fully accomplishes the purposes of his heart. In days to come you will understand it clearly. I did not send these prophets, yet they have run with their message; I did not speak to them, yet they have prophesied. But if they had stood in my council, they would have proclaimed my words to my people and would have turned them from their evil ways and from their evil deeds.

"Am I only a God nearby," declares the LORD, "and not a God far away? Who can hide in secret places so that I cannot see them?" declares the LORD. "Do not I fill heaven and earth?" declares the LORD.

"I have heard what the prophets say who prophesy lies in my name. They say, 'I had a dream! I had a dream!' How long will this continue in the hearts of these lying prophets, who prophesy the delusions of their own minds? They think the dreams they tell one another will make my people forget my name, just as their ancestors forgot my name through Baal worship. Let the prophet who has a dream recount the dream, but let the one who has my word speak it faithfully. For what has straw to do with grain?" declares the LORD. "Is not my word like fire," declares the LORD, "and like a hammer that breaks a rock in pieces?

"Therefore," declares the LORD, "I am against the prophets who steal from one another words supposedly from me. Yes," declares the LORD, "I am against the prophets who wag their own tongues and yet declare, 'The LORD declares.' Indeed, I am against those who prophesy false dreams," declares the LORD. "They tell them and lead my people astray with their reckless lies, yet I did not send or appoint them. They do not benefit these people in the least," declares the LORD.

"When these people, or a prophet or a priest, ask you, 'What is the message from the LORD?' say to them, 'What message? I will forsake you, declares the LORD.' If a prophet or a priest or anyone else claims, 'This is a message from the LORD,' I will punish them and their household. This is what each of you keeps saying to your friends and other Israelites: 'What is the LORD's answer?' or 'What has the LORD spoken?' But you must not mention 'a message from the LORD' again, because each one's word becomes their own message. So you distort the words of the living God, the LORD Almighty, our God.

This is what you keep saying to a prophet: 'What is the LORD's answer to you?' or 'What has the LORD spoken?' Although you claim, 'This is a message from the LORD,' this is what the LORD says: You used the words, 'This is a message from the LORD,' even though I told you that you must not claim, 'This is a message from the LORD.' Therefore, I will surely forget you and cast you out of my presence along with the city I gave to you and your ancestors. I will bring on you everlasting disgrace—everlasting shame that will not be forgotten" (Jer. 23:15–40).

True prophets speak the truth from God regardless of who doesn't like the message. A prophet who is sold out for the Lord is a prophet who tells the truth of God's word. They warn people when destruction is coming for their lives. They tell people that if they don't repent, the Lord will soon bring judgment upon them. Amanda was a prophet who was willing to warn the man she had once loved and joined herself to about his death, but he didn't hear her. He didn't care. He assumed she was only crazy, weak, and foolish in her speaking.

At one time in her Christian life Amanda was new at interpreting the spiritual signs and the situations around her. She thought the Mr. and Mrs. sign on the car in front of them was good news. She ignored the word of God when He told her not to marry Nathanial. Amanda thought, *Of course the Lord knows we are going to be wedded, and this will be good. That makes sense, right?* But now she knows the Devil sends people, signs, and messages. The Devil will speak and act in ways that seem supernatural and convincing. When God says no, you must listen, because it is only in obedience to God's commands that you will find the path of life.

Jeremiah 24:6–7 teaches, "My eyes will watch over them for their good, and I will bring them back to this land. I will build them up and not tear them down; I will plant them and not uproot them. I will give them a heart to know me, that I am the LORD. They will be my people, and I will be their God, for they will return to me with all their heart."

Resurrection of Joy
Unspeakable

Amanda woke up from a strange dream. In her dream she was running around a theme park trying to have fun. There was a huge hill, a mountain region, and she was grabbing hold of the fence, thinking, *I cannot get up this hill. This is so hard! Ugh, I want to ride the ride, but why in the world is this line so crazy? Why do I have to climb and work so hard to get to the top of this hill to get on this ride? And it is dark. Everything around me is dark. Why am I here?*

As Amanda got to the top of the hill, she began making her way through the winding stanchions separating the groups of people waiting for the ride. She came across two boys who worked for the park. They were mean, and they were yelling at people, making fun of those trying to have a good time. The boys started yelling at her, too, and when they did, she began recording them on her phone. This infuriated one of the boys, and as she confronted him, he came up to her and spat in her face.

"Whoa yuck!" Amanda shouted in her dream. What was wrong with this dude? She was just there trying to have fun, and he was the one who was attacking her. Why was he spitting at her for simply recording his actions? Didn't he know that he was the problem, not her? As she walked away from the boys, she tried to call the police. She kept dialing 911, but every time she dialed she couldn't get anyone to pick up the phone.

"Hmm. This is really weird," Amanda said to herself. Didn't this place have police? It was late, but most places had police officers who were available when someone called. Why couldn't she get through? It was probably best to just forget what happened and keep trying to have a good time. At least she got away from the boys and wouldn't see them again. She reasoned, "Let me just leave them alone, stay away from them, and then it should be okay."

When Amanda finally got onto the ride, she saw herself swinging back and forth high above the ground, but she wasn't having fun. She wasn't laughing, yet the other people around her were laughing hysterically. *What is wrong with me?* Amanda thought. *Why am I not having fun? Why am I not laughing? Why am I not happy? I should be happy. I have nothing to complain about. I need to be more grateful.*

As she was swinging, she noticed a name written on the ground beneath her feet. *Huh? What is that? She wondered. Why is there a name on the ground? Is that a grave? What a strange place to be buried. Maybe this is an old burial ground, and it was here before the park, so they just didn't move it.* One thing that stood out to her, though, was the name on the grave. She squinted her eyes to look closer. "It says Xai. Who is Xai?" she wondered, and then she woke up from her dream.

The first thing Amanda did when she woke up was Google the name Xai. She learned from walking with the Lord that it was important to write down her dreams as soon as she woke up, because if she didn't, she was likely to forget the specifics of the dream. If she didn't have the specifics, she wouldn't be able to get the Lord's interpretation. "Amanda gasped when she read the meaning of the name Xai. "Xai means joy, happiness, and victory!" she exclaimed. "I must write this down so God can explain to me the purpose of my dream."

As Amanda penned the dream on a piece of paper, she began to understand what God was trying to teach her. God wanted her to know that she had been unable to get help for her abuse and her trauma for a long time. She had been working hard to get through the darkness and the pain, trying her best to have fun, all the while questioning her own sanity and ability to persevere. She thought it was her fault that she couldn't have fun and find joy anymore. She thought she was doing something wrong and that she needed to be better, stronger, happier, and more grateful.

But none of this was her fault. There was a mean boy on her path, and this man was adamant that her suffering remain unnoticed and that his sins remain unreported and unobserved. He didn't want to be discovered for who he really was. He didn't want people to know what he was doing to her and her children, who were trying to live a normal life and have fun. Whenever she confronted this man he would spit in her face, and it would be worse for her, so Amanda got quiet. She became reserved and afraid to speak out because she didn't think anyone could help her anyway.

The criminal justice system in the United States requires a person to have a substantial amount of evidence and proof. While this can be a good thing, when someone isn't guilty of a crime, or if they are criminals and they seek to remain undetected for their crimes, this isn't a good thing for those who are victimized and abused and remain hidden and unprotected from the law enforcement officers and judges who could potentially help them.

Before Amanda began to date Nathanial, she was raped by a friend. This guy drugged her, took her cellphone, and drove her into the countryside, where there was no one around. He raped her there, and when she went to the police for help, they determined the man was indeed guilty of the crime. Amanda had a friend who testified that the man answered her phone at 2 a.m., saying, "She is too messed up to pick up right now."

The man also admitted that he had slept with her. The police determined that there was enough evidence to arrest him and give Amanda a restraining order against him. However, when it came time to go to court, the prosecutor decided to drop the case, attesting that there wasn't enough evidence to convict him of the crime. The police and others involved told Amanda to stay away from the man, and they told him to stay away from her. They expected her to just go on with her life as if it had never happened.

Amanda's whole life was uprooted by this event. She lost her job because the rapist was a member of the gym where she worked. She couldn't work out at her gym anymore, either, which was unfortunate, as the gym was her whole life and the way she coped with the struggles of life. In addition, she lost a lot of her friends because they knew this guy. She was unable to talk about the crime or mention it because the police informed her that it wasn't wise to do so.

How could Amanda's life go back to normal? How could she just be expected to pretend this never happened? Amanda decided right then and there that the police could not help her. She turned her back and her heart on trusting the police once and for all. Even though she had been raised as the daughter of a police officer, she no longer thought they could help her. After all, this guy who assaulted her was himself a corrections officer working at the prison. And the night of the attack, she had texted a police officer friend after being drugged in the club, saying, "Help me," and he did nothing to aid her.

The sexual assault by her supposed friend had only happened six months before Nathanial started coming around. She had not even had time to heal from the rape before she was exposed to more male violence in that DC hotel room. All of it was raw, so she didn't trust the cops. There was no point in calling them that time either, because they hadn't helped her. They had only made it worse. Didn't they know how hard it was to show up at court and see your rapist, only to be told nothing was going to be done to him?

This same mindset and attitude carried into Amanda's relationship with Nathanial. The first time he attacked her on the street, she didn't call the cops. Why would she? She didn't have any more evidence than she had with her rapist. They weren't going to do anything anyway. It would only make things worse. Plus, the second time he attacked her at her mother's house, grabbing her and throwing her on the bed with all his force, he told her he was going to kill her whole family if she said anything.

Amanda didn't want anything worse to happen. She didn't want anyone around her to be harmed, so she just dealt with it and hoped it would go away and get better. She hoped she would be able to survive and keep the peace. That would make all of this go away. If she were just strong enough and she acted good enough, he wouldn't get mad, right? She imagined that if she could just appease him and be kind, then he would stop hurting her, and no one else around her would get hurt.

A few months later, after the second attack, the couple got into a disagreement in their new apartment they had just leased together. Nathanial climbed on top of her in their bed and choked her, almost killing her. He only removed his hands a few seconds before she would have died. He kept telling her how much of a whore she was and how much he hated her. His words hurt, but so did his actions. She couldn't believe this man, who claimed to love her, had done this. Why would he be doing this?

Amanda fled the apartment. She went and stayed at Nathanial's parents' house that night because she didn't want her parents to know what had happened. But when she went to school the next day, some of her friends urged her to go to the police and the domestic violence center. They said, "This isn't right. You need to do something. At least go talk to the advocates at the center. They won't tell the police who did this, but they will be able to help you." She reluctantly agreed to talk to the advocates, and they then determined she needed to go to the hospital for evaluation because she had bruises all over her neck.

Amanda also called their pastor on the school's office phone. Like before, during a vicious attack, Nathanial took her phone and kept her from having one. The only difference this time was that the phone was in his name because he had urged her to get a new number, cut off old associations, and start new on a new line that he would pay for, because it was better for their relationship. At this point in their relationship, they were involved in a church, and their pastor knew who they were. The pastor told Amanda that he was sorry that this had happened to her and that it wasn't right, but he left it at that. She wouldn't hear from him again until she reached out to him later in the future.

As Amanda sat in the hospital room, the Richmond police officers came in. They said to her, "Don't be stupid. Tell us who he is, or he will kill you. Trust us, we know these kinds of dudes. If they strangle you then they will kill you next time. You must tell us who he is." But she was jaded by the cops, and they weren't being nice to her anyway. They were just as harsh and rude when she needed help, so she told them no thank you. She instead continued to talk to the advocates and the nurses who were helping her through her medical treatment.

Amanda hoped all of this would stop. She wanted it all to just go away. She eventually gave in and called her sister and her parents because she needed someone to help her. She didn't have anywhere to go. She couldn't go home to him. The domestic violence advocates gave her a phone to use, and then she went to stay with her sister for a few weeks. She didn't want Nathanial to know where she was or how to get to her, and since he'd never been to her sister's house, that was the safest place.

After a few weeks of separation Amanda longed to go home. She loved her sister and her sister's family, but she knew it wasn't right to live on their couch. She also didn't want to go home to her parents. She was an adult and she had lived on her own for a while now, so she couldn't go back home. And, of course, Nathanial had found God again. He was remorseful, posting things on Facebook and Instagram about full sobriety, the Lord, and His new tattoo, which read: overcomer.

Nathanial talked to his mom and convinced her to gain the trust of his girlfriend. He told her to figure out how he could get in touch with her, and so his mom agreed to be his accomplice. She reached out to Amanda, posing as a confidant and friend. She pretended to be understanding, caring, and compassionate about the crime, but what she really wanted to know was if Amanda was thinking about pressing charges against her son.

Later in the relationship Amanda discovered the truth about Nathanial's mother, but in the beginning she thought the caring woman was a friend who really loved her and wanted her to be safe. So, during this encounter with his mom, Amanda was honest and vulnerable, open and intimate, with someone she should never have trusted with personal information or her heart. It didn't take long for Nathanial's mom to start pushing Amanda to return to her son. She said he had really changed and that he loved her so much.

Amanda finally gave in and began talking to Nathanial again, and before they knew it, they were back together as if nothing had happened. Nathanial pleaded, "Listen. We must get married. Let's just get married tonight, that way we can honor God and do the right thing. The engagement is taking too long, and once we are married it will all be okay. Show me you love me and just marry me tonight, okay?"

In haste, Amanda showered and headed to the courthouse with Nathanial. *Maybe once we are married all of this will go away,* she thought. They found someone to marry them that night, downtown in the city near the place they had held their first date. And for a little while, everything seemed to be better. Nathanial went with Amanda to church, to counseling, and to meetings for his sobriety. He made friends with people in the recovery groups at church, and he downloaded the Bible app and completed Bible plans with his new wife.

All of this went on for a few months, but out of nowhere Nathanial decided he had enough of sobriety. "Why do we need to get sober?" he would ask. "We can do this ourselves. We don't need to be sober, and we don't need support groups. Those are for weak people. Don't you see that, Amanda? Religion is also a crutch. It is for people who have no personal willpower. I don't need God. I can just be a good person."

Then, he didn't want Amanda to go to church anymore either. He accused her of wanting someone else who was better than him- a Christian man. One night, he threw her down on the ground, picked her back up again by her shirt, dropped her on the ground again, and repeated the cycle. He continued to throw her down until finally he decided to grab her by her hood and pull her across the carpet. Amanda's whole back was scraped and covered with carpet burns. It hurt badly.

Nathanial told her she was a liar and that she was a whore. He said she was unfaithful to him and he knew it! "Admit you are a whore!" he would scream. "You are and always have been! I should have never married you. I hate you!" He then fled the apartment and stayed out for the remainder of the night. When Amanda woke up the next morning to go to work, she discovered that her car window was shattered. Nathanial denied having anything to do with it, promising he had not done it. Of course many years later when things had quieted down, he finally admitted he was the culprit.

Nathanial always accused Amanda of pretending to be saved, good, or pure. He reminded her daily of her past sins during her life before she surrendered to Christ. In the beginning Amanda would hear his accusations and have nothing to say to defend herself. She had been a whore before she found Jesus. She had slept around, and she had done drugs, but when she gave her life to Jesus, she tried to be different. She hated her sin and she wanted to stop sinning.

Looking back on it, Nathanial would often set traps for her by trying to get her to drink with him, use drugs with him, or do perverted sexual things. He wanted her to participate in evil with him, but then he would condemn her for doing those same things in her past. Amanda didn't see it for what it was at the time though. She just thought he wanted to "bond with her" and that these behaviors were his only way of doing it. After all, that is what he did with all his friends.

God was always present in Amanda's life, helping her and protecting her, even throughout this chaos. He continuously sent her messages of faith, power, and transformation. He constantly reminded her that He loved her and wanted to be a part of her life. God also sent people to encourage her, and one of those people knocked on Amanda's door after the night she was thrown on the floor and dragged on the carpet.

When Nathanial was gone, their neighbor from the apartment directly beside them knocked on the door in his police uniform. He said, "I wanted you to know if you ever need anything I am next door." No doubt, this man had heard the fight, and he knew that Nathanial had attacked her. The apartment walls were not that thick, and she had been thrown all over the apartment. "Oh, thank you," she said as she shut the door.

Years later when Amanda and Nathanial bought their home, another police officer bought the house directly beside them. This man was also placed beside them, Amanda believes, because God wanted her to know He was always watching her, her husband, and her children. Nathanial hated police officers. He regularly would go on rants about how terrible they were and how they deserved to die. He didn't care that Amanda's dad was a cop. He persisted in his violence toward the police, a hatred that was proof of his refusal to change or be different.

People don't hate the police unless they have a reason to. Only when you are doing something wrong do you hate the police. Amanda didn't trust them, but she also didn't hate them. *I bet he says what he says about the police because he doesn't want me to talk to them or trust them. He doesn't want me to go to them for help, and he wants to condition me to distrust them,* she thought. Amanda realized a few months before his death, *I finally get it now. I finally see why he spoke so harshly of the police and the church! It was to keep me from going to them.*

God kept revealing the truth to Amanda little by little, piece by piece. He was unveiling and showing Amanda exactly what Nathanial had been up to all of these years. *All the things that he did were calculated. They were intentional*, she thought. "Wow, God," she prayed. "I really trusted this man who trapped me and kept me trapped on purpose." When you've been brainwashed and deceived for so long, it is perplexing to interpret and see the truth.

Day after day when the Lord revealed the truth to Amanda, she stood amazed. "How did I not see this, God?" she prayed. "Why did I ever love this man? All the while he has been lying to me, playing me, and manipulating me. All the while he has been trying to keep me as his slave and his victim. Man, this hurts, but it is good to know. Thank you, God, for showing me the truth, even when it hurts."

The truth is that these things did happen. They were real. She was a victim of many crimes. She was hurt, abused, and mistreated. She was taken as a captive, sexually abused, physically abused, and emotionally abused. She was currently married to a man who didn't love her and had never loved her. All of these things were true, and they did happen. She couldn't pretend as if they didn't, like she was told to with the other rape a few months before this relationship.

The authorities were going to help her. Maybe not the ones on the earth, but the ones who are in Heaven. Those authorities have all the evidence. They have all the details of the crimes perpetrated against her and against her children. The angels in Heaven, Jesus, and the Father all knew what had been done to her with certainty. They knew who was and who wasn't lying, and they could prove it. God was going to handle this for Amanda. He was bringing forth judgment and punishment quickly, and all the people around her would see.

And it was in the realization of the truth, the facing of the truth, that Amanda would finally find peace and joy again. As Amanda confronted and accepted the truth she would be set free and find her laughter once again. The joy and the happiness that had long been hidden and buried beneath the ground were going to be resurrected because the God that she served was a resurrecting God. The power that she held was the power that raised Christ from the dead, and she wasn't willing to lay down this power and this relationship for anyone or anything. She wanted to be revived. She wanted to be restored and healed, full of positive expectations of the future, because she knew that she was worth it.

Praise be to the God and Father of our Lord Jesus Christ, who has blessed us in the heavenly realms with every spiritual blessing in Christ. For he chose us in him before the creation of the world to be holy and blameless in his sight. In love he predestined us for adoption to sonship through Jesus Christ, in accordance with his pleasure and will—to the praise of his glorious grace, which he has freely given us in the One he loves. In him we have redemption through his blood, the forgiveness of sins, in accordance with the riches of God's grace that he lavished on us. With all wisdom and understanding, he made known to us the mystery of his will according to his good pleasure, which he purposed in Christ, to be put into effect when the times reach their fulfillment—to bring unity to all things in heaven and on earth under Christ.

In him we were also chosen, having been predestined according to the plan of him who works out everything in conformity with the purpose of his will, in order that we, who were the first to put our hope in Christ, might be for the praise of his glory. And you also were included in Christ when you heard the message of truth, the gospel of your salvation. When you believed, you were marked in him with a seal, the promised Holy Spirit, who is a deposit guaranteeing our inheritance until the redemption of those who are God's possession—to the praise of his glory.

For this reason, ever since I heard about your faith in the Lord Jesus and your love for all God's people, I have not stopped giving thanks for you, remembering you in my prayers. I keep asking that the God of our Lord Jesus Christ, the glorious Father, may give you the Spirit of wisdom and revelation, so that you may know him better. I pray that the eyes of your heart may be enlightened in order that you may know the hope to which he has called you, the riches of his glorious inheritance in his holy people, and his incomparably great power for us who believe. That power is the same as the mighty strength he exerted when he raised Christ from the dead and seated him at his right hand in the heavenly realms, far above all rule and authority, power and dominion, and every name that is invoked, not only in the present age but also in the one to come. And God placed all things under his feet and appointed him to be head over everything for the church, which is his body, the fullness of him who fills everything in every way (Eph. 1:3–23).

{ 5 }

Time to Fight—No More Flight

Psychologists have studied human responses to trauma with an evolutionary worldview. They view their subjects with the assumption that people have predetermined trauma responses that are hardwired and cannot be changed. These psychologists will say that when certain individuals are confronted with a battle, they will inevitably flee from the problem because they don't have another choice. Likewise, those who fight are predestined or determined to fight, because they, too, are hardwired to do so.

Determinism is a demonic doctrine of philosophy that views certain outcomes as inevitable and existing independently of human interventions or the will to change the situation. Psychologists who follow deterministic theories are wrong, because determinism is in direct opposition to the Lord's proclamations of human agency and ability to overcome a challenge when they are partnered with Him. *I can do all this through him who gives me strength* (Phil. 4:13).

If someone thinks that they are evolutionary or animalistic, and that they cannot control their behavior or their choices, then they will act in ways that are animalistic. If you teach people that they are animals, they will act like animals. Evolutionary teachings are directly responsible for continuing cycles of human abuse and mistreatment. These teachings tell people they are going to do vile and disgusting things because they teach people that these things are unavoidable, natural, and a part of evolution.

After all, if you believe in evolution you believe in the survival of the fittest, a demonic doctrine ascribing worth and value to some life while simultaneously advocating for the destruction and damnation of others. God is not an evolutionist. He doesn't believe that some people are more adept at surviving, thriving, and persevering, and He doesn't believe that humans are incapable of acting in honest, just, and moral ways. Jesus taught people to operate in wisdom and self-control. He taught people to value life through His restorative actions.

Jesus proved to us that people from a variety of backgrounds could be redeemed and set free from their sins and their bondage. He showed us that God isn't a respecter of persons. Jesus came as a sacrifice for the whole world. He came to set all people free from the torments and captivities of Satan.

Romans 2:11–16 teaches, *"For God does not show favoritism. All who sin apart from the law will also perish apart from the law, and all who sin under the law will be judged by the law. For it is not those who hear the law who are righteous in God's sight, but it is those who obey the law who will be declared righteous. (Indeed, when Gentiles, who do not have the law, do by nature things required by the law, they are a law for themselves, even though they do not have the law. They show that the requirements of the law are written on their hearts, their consciences also bearing witness, and their thoughts sometimes accusing them and at other times even defending them.) This will take place on the day when God judges people's secrets through Jesus Christ, as my gospel declares."*

Many of the Pharisees felt that some people were not eligible or worthy for salvation based on their works. They held this same demonic doctrine while proclaiming themselves to be religious and holy people. The Lord has never liked doctrines that ascribe worth and value to people based on outward appearances or through religious acts alone. God hates theories like the theory of evolution, because they teach people that some people are more valuable than others, and that we as humanity have no ability to control ourselves.

Jesus taught us that we are to control ourselves and subject ourselves to the word of God. He never gave people the right to sin or to act animalistically. Animals have no conscience or regard for what they are doing, but this is not the case for humans. Humans have a conscience. They can discern right from wrong, and this ability makes them liable and responsible for what they do to others while they are alive. Humans have a choice. They can determine their lives.

Joshua 24:14–15 says, *"Now fear the Lord and serve him with all faithfulness. Throw away the gods your ancestors worshiped beyond the Euphrates River and in Egypt, and serve the LORD. But if serving the LORD seems undesirable to you, then choose for yourselves this day whom you will serve, whether the gods your ancestors served beyond the Euphrates, or the gods of the Amorites, in whose land you are living. But as for me and my household, we will serve the Lord."*

People who do not want to be held accountable for what they are doing love doctrines and theories that teach them they are not going to be held responsible for their choices. This news sounds great to a carnal or a wicked man or woman, because they don't want to change or do what is right in the eyes of God. When someone gives them a license to sin and tells them, "God understands your sin. God will permit this, or He knew you were going to sin, and you can do the wrong thing, and it will be fine," the Lord is furious because people are being lied to in the name of religion.

Jeremiah 48:10 explains, *"A curse on anyone who is lax in doing the LORD's work! A curse on anyone who keeps their sword from bloodshed!"* God's people in particular are going to be held accountable for the management and handling of the truth they have been given. People who know the Lord and know His word will give an account for the work they have done for God, with or without His agreement. If the Lord holds even His own people accountable, how much more will the wicked give an account?

We are in a spiritual battle every day when we wake up. This battle has been raging long before we were alive, and it will continue to rage after we are gone if the Lord doesn't return for His Church in our lifetimes. God expects all people to take responsibility for their lives and their choices. We are not doing anyone any good when we refuse to hold them responsible for their behavior toward others or themselves.

Only a righteous man is willing to use the word of God appropriately as a sword. A righteous man will bring forth judgment and correction on others who need to be sharpened or taken out through the sword he holds in his hand. A righteous man or woman knows what God's word says, and they refuse to hold back the truth, regardless of the consequences or the cost, because they know that it is only God's word that can heal, deliver, or restore a life. Only God's word can implement God's perfect will.

Amanda had once attended some Christian recovery meetings with her husband. She had once sat in a circle with other women who were crying about their codependency and their abuse. These meetings were held in the church, and they seemed to be true, helpful, and aiding in the hope and healing of those in attendance. At one time, Amanda was thankful for the meetings because after Nathanial had choked her, he had gone to a church and sat in a meeting, and he seemed to be closer to God for it, at least for a little while.

But here's the thing: These meetings were deceptive. They were doctrines of devils dressed up as doctrines of grace. In these meetings, the participants would chant the Serenity Prayer, saying, "God, grant me the serenity to accept the things I cannot change." *Wait a second. I thought the Lord told us we can change our circumstances and outcomes through obedience and behavior? Why would there be things we can't change about our lives?* Amanda wondered one day after discovering the programs weren't helping her husband.

You see, whenever Nathanial would go to these meetings, he would leave feeling like he couldn't change things about himself that God said he could change. He would leave feeling empowered in his sin because he felt as if sin had power over him. Christian counseling or Christian groups can quickly become problematic if they don't confront the sin in a life and drive it out. These groups can quickly become unbiblical if the participants don't hold each other accountable and tell each other that they can do all things through Christ.

When a bunch of people with problems hang out and talk about their sins, and then they glorify or magnify their sins, the sins will only increase in their lives. There is no good in meeting and assembling to sulk and cry about the former things. In fact, this is directly opposed to God's command to forget the former things and become new. Many counseling groups, even Christian ones, magnify the problem and minimize the power. They enable the perpetrator and rebuke the victim because they don't want to take responsibility for their failure to serve God fully.

When we accept Jesus as our Savior things don't immediately level themselves out in all domains. It takes time to learn, grow, and develop in Christ. But Christians, upon accepting Christ, become new creations. The former things are dead and the new has come, and if the former us is really dead, then it isn't us anymore and it doesn't have a right to stay in our life. James 4:7 says, *"Submit yourselves, then, to God. Resist the devil, and he will flee from you."*

Resisting is a fighting word, a word that means to stand against. When we resist the Devil we stand against him and we confront him. As we submit to God, we are told to simultaneously resist or fight against all evil in our lives. This will help us to overcome, persevere, and continue to do the good things that God has commanded us to do because we are committed to him and we are willing to resist all other behaviors, thoughts, and lifestyles in opposition to Him. James 4:8 teaches, *"Come near to God and he will come near to you. Wash your hands, you sinners, and purify your hearts, you double-minded."*

When you wash your hands you are removing the filth. You are stopping the works of evil and instead choosing to do the works of God. God doesn't give people the right to continue in their sin once they have been saved. He doesn't tell us that we are still codependent, alcoholic, or abusive, and that this is our portion in life. He doesn't tell us that we will always struggle with sin and be slaves to sin. He tells us the opposite.

The LORD will make you the head, not the tail. If you pay attention to the commands of the LORD your God that I give you this day and carefully follow them, you will always be at the top, never at the bottom (Deut. 28:13).

Amanda was convinced that the Christian recovery meetings and the Christian counseling she and her husband participated in were a part of his failure to repent, especially in the beginning when his heart was more willing. The Church had many opportunities to speak into his life and minister to him through the demonstrations of the Holy Spirit's power. He was a captive audience because he attended church services with his wife at first, so he could woo her into submission and domination.

It is very possible that a passionate and on-fire believer could have impacted his mind and his heart in the early days, causing him to genuinely repent and change from his wicked ways. But week after week, month after month, after being subjected to weak, milk-based, watered-down gospel messages, full of grace and understanding for sin, this man grew more and more distant from God and disrespectful toward God. He didn't see a reason to change or to serve God. The Church appeared weak and incapable of healing, even its own, so why would he believe it could heal him?

When Christians fail to gain victory in their lives and fail to walk in the power of the Holy Spirit, it has an impact on those around them. Every time pastors choose to teach on something they deem valuable, without asking the Lord what He would have them preach, they endanger and do a disservice to the people in the pews. Religious traditions and a form of godliness will not get people into Heaven. Religious tradition won't heal the brokenhearted and restore the sinner to Christ, because there is no power in religion outside of God.

Amanda had a friend named Elizabeth. Amanda and Elizabeth had met at church at a children's program, where their children were in the same nursery classroom. Her friend was in an abusive relationship like she was, and the two would go to the gym together when their children were young. During some of their workouts, they would talk about God and His plan for their lives. They would talk about motherhood and marriage, and they were honest and open with each other about their husbands' abuse.

This was the first time that Amanda opened up about her abuse to anyone outside of her house in a long time. For many years she tried to hide it because she didn't want it to ruin her family's reputation, especially in the church. A part of being a Christian is being a good wife, a good mom, and having all of your priorities in line. A part of being a good Christian is appearing religious and godly, right? So, Amanda stayed quiet until that day when she felt safe to share the truth with her close friend.

Elizabeth opened up to her as well, and she shared that, like Amanda, she was being abused by her husband. Her husband had also choked her in the early stages of their relationship. She shared that he continued to be emotionally abusive toward her. It was good to have a friend who understood her. Amanda hated what was being done to Elizabeth, but she liked having someone else to be honest with and to connect with. It had been a long time since Amanda could be honest about her marriage, and it felt good to let it out.

Some time went by and Amanda had a dream about her friend. She saw her friend's daughter being chased by a bear, and she saw her friend preoccupied. She wondered what this dream meant. She wrote down the dream, then she texted her friend to check in on her. What she discovered next was shocking. Elizabeth was leaving her husband and filing for divorce. The couple had been having a lot of issues, and she wanted to get out to protect her daughter.

Amanda didn't know what to say. She loved her friend and wanted her to be okay, but she just felt like something was wrong.

She didn't want her friend to be in danger, and she didn't want her friend's daughter to be either. Amanda told her friend the truth. She didn't think it was a good decision to leave her husband based on the information she had at the time. The dream that Amanda had the night before, and the way that she felt in her spirit about what her friend was saying, told Amanda that something about this situation just wasn't right.

Even though Amanda knew that her friend didn't deserve what was being done to her, and she knew that her friend loved God, she felt like her friend was trying to run away from the situation instead of facing it. Sometimes when we are confronted with hard things we are tempted to run away, and this response is what psychologists call the flight response to trauma. And Amanda knew that God didn't call His people to run away in the face of danger. He called them to confront and stand to fight, especially when they were not the ones acting against God's commands.

Throughout Scripture God delivered his people from oppressors and enemy forces. When an enemy would rise up to hurt one of God's children, if the child stood in faith, then the Lord would stand with them and take up their case. Stories like Daniel in the lion's den and David and Goliath exemplify these truths because when they could have given in, run, and hidden, they didn't because they knew they were endowed with God's power.

David's brothers acted very differently from David when faced with a challenge or an enemy. David, through his union and relationship with God, knew that the unbelieving giant, who was worshipping false gods and doing evil to God's people, wouldn't be a match for him if he confronted him in faith. David knew two things: First, that the person against him was against God, and second, that God was with him. Knowing these two things changed everything.

God's people do not have to run and hide from enemies or threats. In fact, when Elijah ran from his enemy Jezebel, he found himself suicidal and worse off than when he was confronting his enemies and their false prophets. God reassured Elijah in his weakened, saddened place and commanded him to go forward in faith and to believe that he had a mighty army willing and ready to fight for His plans and purposes in His children's futures.

When Elijah heard it, he pulled his cloak over his face and went out and stood at the mouth of the cave. Then a voice said to him, "What are you doing here, Elijah?" He replied, "I have been very jealous for the LORD God Almighty. The Israelites have forsaken your covenant, torn down your altars, and put your prophets to death with the sword. I am the only one left, and now they are trying to kill me too" (1 Kings 19:13–14).

When you feel that there is a threat to your life it is normal to experience the sensation of fear. Elijah felt that his life was in danger, and this caused him to run away from the situation. Yet, when he ran, he didn't find peace and joy. In fact, he found the opposite because he had run from the people he was supposed to confront. He cowered away from the truth instead of standing proudly and boldly in it.

When God's people were escaping Egypt, some of the Israelites were afraid of the giants, and some believed they could overtake the giants if God was with them. The question is, which group do you belong to? Are you going to run in fear or are you going to stand and fight?

When we fight against evil forces, like the forces operating behind abusive men, we must ensure we are fighting with God's power and not our own. When we try to face giants in our own strength we can be defeated like the Sons of Sceva, who attempted to do an exorcism with religious words and traditions. There was a vastly different outcome for Paul than there was for these men, because devils cannot be driven out of a life unless the Spirit of God is manifested and present in the life of a man or woman of God.

God did extraordinary miracles through Paul, so that even handkerchiefs and aprons that had touched him were taken to the sick, and their illnesses were cured and the evil spirits left them. Some Jews who went around driving out evil spirits tried to invoke the name of the Lord Jesus over those who were demon-possessed. They would say, "In the name of the Jesus whom Paul preaches, I command you to come out." Seven sons of Sceva, a Jewish chief priest, were doing this. One day the evil spirit answered them, "Jesus I know, and Paul I know about, but who are you?" Then the man who had the evil spirit jumped on them and overpowered them all. He gave them such a beating that they ran out of the house naked and bleeding (Acts 19:11–16).

Joshua and Caleb took the promised land because God's Spirit was with them. Paul did many miracles and cast out devils because God's Spirit was working in His life. David took down Goliath because the Spirit of God rested upon him. And Daniel wasn't devoured by the lions because he refused to bow down to evil, fully submitted himself to God, and the Spirit of the Lord was very present in His life. The common denominator in all of these amazing stories isn't the power of the man, but the power of God within the man or woman who surrendered their own desires and plans and gave full service to God's plan, regardless of the circumstances they found themselves in.

If a woman is not absolutely assured that she is in God's good graces and that He is on her side, then she shouldn't try to go against the devil in her husband. A woman also shouldn't go against the devils in her life in the name of Christ alone without a relationship with Him. Women should only go against devils if they are absolutely sure that the Spirit of the Lord rests on their life and that He goes with them and surrounds them as their helper and shield. It would be foolish to go into a battle without armor, and it is foolish for a woman without God to stand against devils and assume they will not be harmed.

It isn't recommended for anyone to challenge evil forces unless they are standing strong with the holy ones. A failure to understand these concepts can result in fatalities, and that isn't God's plan. Our preparation and our personal responsibility in these matters are vital. It is life and death, and if a woman is at war, or if she plans to confront and engage in battle, then she better be sure that she isn't alone. She better be confident in the God who is with her, because one misstep could prove hazardous.

The Devil doesn't have power and authority over the Christian. The Christian has power and authority over him, but if a Christian doesn't understand their authority, and they don't obey the Lord's commands to submit to God's word and resist the Devil, then the Devil could win in a battle he was never intended to win. If there is sin in a house or camp, or if there is compromise with the enemy in life, even when the sin is hidden from others in the church or the friends and family members of the person, then it could cause the battle to be lost to enemy forces.

Only when we abide in the covenant and we keep the covenant can we be victorious in our battles. Judges 2:12–14 says, *"They forsook the LORD, the God of their ancestors, who had brought them out of Egypt. They followed and worshiped various gods of the peoples around them. They aroused the LORD's anger because they forsook him and served Baal and the Ashtoreths. In his anger against Israel the LORD gave them into the hands of raiders who plundered them. He sold them into the hands of their enemies all around, whom they were no longer able to resist."*

When a man or woman is preparing to stand against their enemies, they must prepare. They must begin by searching their own heart and ensuring they are in perfect alignment with God and His word. This principle was one David understood well. He said, *"Search me, God, and know my heart; test me and know my anxious thoughts. See if there is any offensive way in me, and lead me in the way everlasting* (Ps. 139:23–24).

Christians must operate in wisdom and self-control. They must not make impulsive, emotional decisions or fear-based ones. They need to know that they have a pure heart, and they must know if they are anxious and giving way to fear, or what David called anxiety, because if you are going to submit yourselves to the spirit of fear you cannot win the battle. Fear is an enemy to our faith. Fear must be resisted if you are going to win. Fear is a spirit. It is a devil. 2 Timothy 1:7 says, *"For the Spirit God gave us does not make us timid, but gives us power, love and self-discipline."*

Amanda knew she was going to win this battle against the forces of Hell. She knew that her husband had been hired by Satan to try to take her out and destroy her life. As hard as that was to admit, and although she was saddened by the truth, she knew that it was indeed the truth because the Lord told her it was. God called her to this battle. He had trained her hands for war, and this battle she was fighting wasn't going to be won with natural weapons and natural armor. It couldn't be won with religious tradition or man-made rituals. If she was going to win she would need God's power.

Amanda needed the supernatural provision and protection of Jesus. She needed to be right before God if she was going to stand a chance of survival. But the good news is, she was sure she had it, so she knew she would win. Amanda knew she had power and authority over all demons and demonic power. She knew she was fully prepared and equipped with the Holy Spirit because she knew Jesus Christ her Savior and she knew Him well. He was her everything, and if she had to she would lay down her life for Him. She knew He would never allow that to happen, because He was an honorable and noble man, a man who would lay down His life for her, not the other way around.

After all, Amanda was Jesus's soon-to-be bride. *"One of the seven angels who had the seven bowls full of the seven last plagues came and said to me, 'Come, I will show you the bride, the wife of the Lamb'"* (Rev. 21:9). Amanda was valuable to Him, and because of their relationship, Jesus had gifted her an endowment or symbol of the promise, like an engagement ring. And with this promise, this sign, the whole world would know they were together. Everyone would see who Amanda belonged to, and they would know she wasn't fighting alone. *"But you will receive power when the Holy Spirit comes on you; and you will be my witnesses in Jerusalem, and in all Judea and Samaria, and to the ends of the earth"* (Acts 1:8).

{ 6 }

You Shall Overtake Them

Once Jesus began to prophecy to Amanda and tell her about the soon-to-be fate of her husband, a devil of fear came to her one night on the way home from a church event. An hour or two prior, she had been speaking faith, believing God for deliverance, and standing on the promises of God for her future and the future of her children. Amanda was sharing with two other people in her life, her mom and her grandma, about the power of God and the ability to overcome all the attacks of the Devil. But on the way home riding in the car with her children, the enemy began telling her his lies.

These lies were loud. They roared through her ears, and she saw images in her mind that matched the lies she was hearing. As she heard the voice of her enemy, her mind was plagued with images that had their roots in the demonic realm. The Devil said, "He is going to kill you. You are not safe. Once you lie down to go to sleep, he could smother you with a pillow. He could take a knife from your kitchen and stab you in the neck. You can't overcome him. What would you do? There is no hope for you against him. You and your children aren't safe. Don't go home."

As Amanda heard the words, she could visualize them, but she refused to accept them. As the pictures and the words popped up, she would cast them down like a person shuts down an unwanted tab on their computer. This wasn't her first rodeo with a devil of fear. She had experienced fearmongering devils more than once in her life, and she knew exactly what this devil wanted her to do. He wanted her to retreat, to run, and to cower back in fear. This demon wanted her to believe she didn't have the victory. It wanted her to believe she couldn't have what God promised her she could have.

"I resist you, Satan," she said. "What God says will surely come to pass. I plead the blood of Jesus over my life and the lives of my children. No weapon formed against us shall prosper. No weapon formed against us will prevail. I am the head and not the tail. I am above and not beneath. I am going to live, and so will my children. If Nathanial even dares to attempt to attack me tonight, this will be his last night on the earth. The Lord will not allow me to die in shame. He will not allow me to lose this battle."

When Amanda got home, she found that everything was seemingly normal. Her husband was making dinner for her, something that rarely happened, and he was making her something special that only she would eat. He was welcoming as she came through the door, and Amanda knew immediately that the devil had gone because she had resisted him. There was no validity to the threats and no conquering that was going to occur. But this devil wanted her to believe the lie because it is only in believing a lie that you can be overtaken.

The hardest part about the revelations that God had given Amanda up to this point was trying to go on with life like business was usual. She had warned Nathanial about his fate, but she was still wrestling with the idea inside of herself, because naturally it seemed like things would go back to normal, their fights would resolve, and everything would be okay. However, she knew deep within her spirit that this wasn't the case. Things would never be the same again, and even if it seemed to be okay right now, his fate was sealed. He was finished because God said that he was.

How can I go on and eat dinner with my family like everything is normal? How can I pretend that this man isn't a liar, an abuser, and a manipulator? How can I unsee that the things he has done and the words he has spoken were vile and intentionally meant to degrade and destroy? How can I ever be in love again knowing the truth about him and his heart, she wondered. And maybe the point wasn't that God wanted her to unsee or to fake fine. Maybe the point was to show her that she was genuine and loving, kind and honest. She was having a hard time with the news about her husband. It hurt her because she didn't want it to be true.

Amanda wanted Nathanial to turn to Christ. She wanted them to walk together into the future, build a home, have more children, and worship and praise God together. She wanted him to see her ministry explode. She wanted him to see what Jesus was going to do in her life. She knew God could make him into something phenomenal and exceptional. She knew that Jesus could change it all for him if he would only repent. And this all hurt so much because Amanda knew the possibilities, but she also knew those possibilities were dead. The man she was married to didn't want to accept Jesus. He didn't want to change.

People are given choices to become or not to become. God doesn't go around looking for people to kill, harm, or destroy. The Lord wants all people to come to know Him and to walk with Him, but the sad reality is that many never will because the love and the desire aren't reciprocated. God isn't a rapist or an abuser. He isn't a man who will make someone love Him, stay with Him, or do what He says. God allows us to choose what we want to do. He wants us to consent.

When a person is truly in love there is no fear and forced compliance through fear. Fear is from our enemy, Satan. Fear is a demonic spirit. If Amanda and Nathanial were in love, she wouldn't have felt the immense spirit of fear in the room. She wouldn't have gone to bed asking the Lord to keep His angels encamped around her and her home. Real love wouldn't cause a woman to flinch back in fear from their spouse. True love wouldn't produce such a strong reaction and relationship with a devil.

When someone can induce fear into another person's environment or into their heart, they are able to do so because they carry that spirit with them. Spirits are transferable. People can receive an impartation of another person's spirit, both good and evil. A Christian carrying God's power can lay their hands on someone and impart the Holy Spirit. And a demonically possessed person carrying a spirit of fear, when given an opportunity, will do the same.

For someone to receive the baptism of the Holy Spirit or a spiritual transfer, they must come to the altar and have a minister impart upon them the gift from Heaven. Acts 8:17 tells us, *"Then Peter and John placed their hands on them, and they received the Holy Spirit."* What a person carries can be given to another person, but only when the person is willing to receive what is being offered to them. That is why God commands us to resist the Devil, because when the Devil tries to impart a spirit that is unclean into our minds, lives, or situation, we have the power to resist it and reject it, saying no thank you, which causes it to flee.

Christians have more spiritual power and authority than a devil does. Devils have power, but their power is inferior to ours. In the book of Acts, we read about a sorcerer who had spiritual power. He was carrying a demon spirit, and he used the demonic power to influence others in his environment. He assumed that the Holy Spirit was like other spirits he had encountered. He assumed it was just another spirit that he could have as a part of his life that would perform miracles, signs, and wonders.

When Simon saw that the Spirit was given at the laying on of the apostles' hands, he offered them money and said, "Give me also this ability so that everyone on whom I lay my hands may receive the Holy Spirit." Peter answered: "May your money perish with you, because you thought you could buy the gift of God with money! You have no part or share in this ministry, because your heart is not right before God. Repent of this wickedness and pray to the Lord in the hope that he may forgive you for having such a thought in your heart. For I see that you are full of bitterness and captive to sin (Acts 8: 18–23).

Simon knew that there was spiritual power, but he was not able to properly determine or differentiate between the powers of light and the powers of darkness. Peter, however, because he carried God's Spirit, knew the difference between the spirits being carried in Simon. He saw what Simon was captive to. He saw what the spirits and the sins in his life were specifically and in depth. God gives His people the ability to discern between spirits. He gives us wisdom and vision into the spiritual world.

Being able to see who your enemy is and what they carry is an essential part of war. When you know who your enemy is, what they carry with them, and if you are going to receive the victory during a battle, then you have all the information you need to engage in battle. When David was going to pursue the enemy forces who had raided their troops' homes, he knew who had perpetrated the attack, and he knew what they had with them. Then God gave him insight into where they were and where they were going, and he told David to pursue them and take back everything they had stolen.

David asked him, "Who do you belong to? Where do you come from?" He said, "I am an Egyptian, the slave of an Amalekite. My master abandoned me when I became ill three days ago. We raided the Negev of the Kerethites, some territory belonging to Judah and the Negev of Caleb. And we burned Ziklag."

David asked him, "Can you lead me down to this raiding party?" He answered, "Swear to me before God that you will not kill me or hand me over to my master, and I will take you down to them." He led David down, and there they were, scattered over the countryside, eating, drinking and reveling because of the great amount of plunder they had taken from the land of the Philistines and from Judah. David fought them from dusk until the evening of the next day, and none of them got away, except four hundred young men who rode off on camels and fled.

David recovered everything the Amalekites had taken, including his two wives. Nothing was missing: young or old, boy or girl, plunder or anything else they had taken. David brought everything back. He took all the flocks and herds, and his men drove them ahead of the other livestock, saying, "This is David's plunder" (1 Sam. 30:13–20).

God gave David specifics about his enemy. He told him what he was looking at, and He gave him a play-by-play instruction manual of what to do, where to go, and how to get the job done. God wants us to be prepared. He wants us to have vision and to see clearly what we are up against. When we are walking with Him, there will be no doubt about our victory and our supernatural assistance from God. David knew that God was with Him. He knew that the information he was getting was supernatural and from Heaven.

1 Samuel 30:8 tell us, *"David inquired of the LORD, 'Shall I pursue this raiding party? Will I overtake them?' 'Pursue them,' he answered. 'You will certainly overtake them and succeed in the rescue.'"* David knew in advance that he had the victory. He didn't wait to see the results to know the outcome. He was living under the old covenant, before the death and resurrection of Christ. How much more should we operate today in spiritual power and insight into knowing our enemy and their weaponry and knowing what we are to do and what we are going to receive when we engage in the war?

Hebrews 8:6 says, *"But in fact the ministry Jesus has received is as superior to theirs as the covenant of which he is mediator is superior to the old one, since the new covenant is established on better promises."* Amanda knew that as she walked with Jesus, under the new covenant, He was fulfilling every single promise in the Bible. He was telling her who her enemy was and what he carried, and He told her what she needed to do and how the battle was going to end. Jesus made sure Amanda knew there was a reward for her conquering of the giant.

The enemy wanted her to think she was done and that her life was over. He wanted her to think she wouldn't be able to preach and teach God's word of healing and deliverance to the next generation. The enemy wanted her to believe she had a reason to run and hide and flee from her oppressor, and he wanted her to give up before she got back everything God wanted her to have and then some. The truth was that Amanda wasn't going to be "as good as she was be-fore." She was going to be better, stronger, and happier than ever. She was going to have an abundant life because that was what Christ wanted her to have.

There will be rejoicing and dancing soon. I won't be subjected to the spirit of fear from within my home anymore, Amanda thought. *My kids won't have to encounter this devil every day while they are simply trying to eat their breakfast and do their schoolwork. We will be free. We will be liberated and happy. We will be at peace. Thank you, Jesus.* Amanda knew some-thing many don't: Fear is a spirit. It isn't an emotion. It's a devil that wants to kill you and steal everything you have, but it can't succeed when you resist. It can't win, but it wants you to think it can.

There is no fear in love. But perfect love drives out fear, because fear has to do with punishment. The one who fears is not made perfect in love (1 John 4:18). The pure love of Jesus was going to cast out the fear. It was go-ing to remove the fear and the carrier of the fear from her because it wasn't loving to allow it to remain.

Jesus promised to remove our heavy burdens. He promised to chal-lenge the forces that want to destroy us and to give us victory in every circumstance. The question is, do you believe it? *"I have given you au-thority to trample on snakes and scorpions and to overcome all the power of the enemy; nothing will harm you"* (Luke 10:19).

You can believe Jesus, or you can believe another spirit, like the spirit of fear. You can let the spirit of fear tell you what is true, or you can let Jesus tell you. The choice is yours, but your choice does matter. If you fight or if you flee, those decisions will impact your destiny. God's people are depending on you. If David hadn't fought this battle with the enemy, no one would have recovered their possessions. And if He hadn't fought the first battle with Goliath, God's people would have continued to be conquered by their enemies.

Amanda's children were about to have their lives forever changed because she chose to fight. And the thousands of women and children who were in abusive relationships and needed to know what God would do for them wouldn't have the chance to know if she didn't pick up her spiritual weapons and teach them to fight. Amanda wanted to fight. She wanted to defeat God's enemies and help God's people. She was on His side, no matter what. His battles were her battles, and her battles were His.

David said to the Philistine, "You come against me with sword and spear and javelin, but I come against you in the name of the LORD Almighty, the God of the armies of Israel, whom you have defied. This day the LORD will deliver you into my hands, and I'll strike you down and cut off your head. This very day I will give the carcasses of the Philistine army to the birds and the wild animals, and the whole world will know that there is a God in Israel. All those gathered here will know that it is not by sword or spear that the LORD saves; for the battle is the LORD's, and he will give all of you into our hands" (1 Sam. 17:45–47).

Amanda knew she had won the victory, even if the giant was still in front of her today. She knew she was not going to be defeated, so she ignored the Devil's taunts and pathetic cries. She silenced the words and the images of her enemy, and she called the shots. She told the Devil what was going to happen, and she knew that because she wouldn't quit, he would have to. Amanda was not moved by what she saw that day because she was moved by what she knew the next day would be.

Luke 10:20 tells us, *"However, do not rejoice that the spirits submit to you, but rejoice that your names are written in heaven."* Amanda's future was Heaven. Her children also had their futures there, and nothing was going to stand against their relationship with God and their place in Heaven. Nothing was permitted to remain that was contrary to the goal of knowing Christ and walking in His perfect glory until they enter eternity. God does have a plan for His people. He does care about their lives and their futures, and if anyone on the outside tries to resist Him, they will find out that they have made a grave mistake.

One thing was for certain. Amanda's husband could kill her if she didn't have Jesus. He was able and willing to harm her, as he made sure she knew on multiple occasions. He would tell her, "Do you want me to take you in the backyard and bury you? I could shoot you right in the head. POW. Don't you think I could kill you and get away with it? Haha!" There wasn't a week that went by without her being threatened in one way or another. There wasn't a month that passed that she didn't hear those words of violence.

"Well, he is only kidding," some would say. But Amanda knew that his words were far more than improper jokes. They were weapons of war formed against her by her enemy. Words that were meant to destroy her faith and weaken her ability to speak up and to fight. These words were intentional and vile. They were positioned and pointed right at her heart and her soul, intending to stop her from becoming who God wanted her to become, and God had finally had enough. Her silence was going to come to an end soon. The intimidation and the threats would soon be over, and she would sleep in perfect peace because she knew who was going to help her to win the battle. She knew who never left her side and witnessed every single word and deed.

"No weapon forged against you will prevail, and you will refute every tongue that accuses you. This is the heritage of the servants of the LORD, and this is their vindication from me," declares the LORD" (Isa. 54:17).

Every time the enemy thought he was stealing her peace, her happiness, her confidence, and her fervency for the Lord and getting away with it, he wasn't. The Devil thought he could use fear to take her out. He thought he could laugh and celebrate the presumed defeat of a Christian life, but God is the One who will have the last laugh. He is the One who will have the last say, and Amanda would surely recover all. She would sing, dance, and laugh without fear of the future. Proverbs 31:25 tells us, *"She is clothed with strength and dignity; she can laugh at the days to come."*

{ 7 }

Mourning

Mourning is formally defined as a time of grief and sadness, suffering and agony. When people are in mourning, they feel rejected and hopeless, and they are full of negative expectations of tomorrow. People can mourn many things, but the main season of mourning generally occurs after a death or loss. Mourning is a spiritual thing. It is a representation of our perceptions and our realities about what has happened around us.

One of the scariest things in Amanda's life for a long time was imagining losing her husband, her best friend, and her companion in life. She heard people talk about losing their spouses or situations of divorce, and she thought, *Nothing can be worse than that. What a tragedy.* But today, as she was confronted with the reality of Nathanial's impending death, she mourned. She also prepared, not for a life of defeat, sadness, and misery, but for a life that is plentiful and good.

People can have varied responses to the death of their loved ones. Naomi, a woman in scripture who lost her husband and her sons through death, felt like her life was over. She even changed her name to represent sadness and misery. She didn't want people to call her by her former name, as Naomi means pleasant one or delight. Instead, she wanted people to call her Mara, which was a name that meant bitterness. When our lives change, we have a choice: Are we going to trust God or are we going to hold onto the past and be bitter?

Naomi's daughter-in-law Ruth also lost her husband. She experienced a loss, but she didn't view her loss as a setback or an eternal fate of gloom and misery. Instead, she believed she could go forward. She didn't care what it looked like because she trusted God with her future. Ruth 1:16 tells us, *"But Ruth replied, 'Don't urge me to leave you or to turn back from you. Where you go I will go, and where you stay I will stay. Your people will be my people and your God my God.'"*

Moving on and going forward is always God's plan for His people's lives. He does not want us to remain stuck in a place of sadness, grief, and suffering. He promises us that we will live full lives and continue to grow, advance, and prosper. Ignorance can cause people to stay stuck or to improperly process what is happening to them. As we mentioned earlier, if people do not know what they are supposed to be doing, where they are headed, or what has happened in their lives, then they are more likely to fall prey to Satan and his schemes of destruction and gloom.

David and his men initially mourned the loss of the camp when they discovered that things had been taken from them. But when David encouraged himself in the Lord, he could continue pressing forward, and he discovered that he hadn't lost anything of value. At times, Satan makes people think they've experienced a loss when they have not. *"So David and his men wept aloud until they had no strength left to weep. David's two wives had been captured—Ahinoam of Jezreel and Abigail, the widow of Nabal of Carmel. David was greatly distressed because the men were talking of stoning him; each one was bitter in spirit because of his sons and daughters. But David found strength in the LORD his God"* (1 Sam. 30:4–6).

Amanda's grandfather died a few years before her husband, and this loss was hard because he was a Christian and a good man. However, because he was a believer, the loss was easier to process because Amanda knew he was with Jesus. The hardest part about his death was the fact that he was murdered by his wife. She used hospice to kill him because he was older than her and she didn't want to continue aiding in his care. Wrongful death is mourned by God, as death before its time is also seen and experienced by Him.

When you lose someone or something of great value and importance, mourning is often more intense, especially in circumstances where a life has been stolen prematurely when it shouldn't have been. David was mourning his valuables. He was mourning the loss of something profoundly important. His wife and children were not appointed to die. They were not supposed to be harmed and conquered by their enemies.

When Basheba's husband was murdered, she mourned his death, and so did God. God's will was not for this man to die. He didn't like that the man was wrongfully killed. 2 Samuel 11:26–27 explains, *"When Uriah's wife heard that her husband was dead, she mourned for him. After the time of mourning was over, David had her brought to his house, and she became his wife and bore him a son. But the thing David had done displeased the LORD."*

If someone has been wrongfully killed, as in the cases of murder, then the Lord is displeased with the murder, and he mourns alongside the victims of the death. This, however, is quite different from the death of an immoral or corrupt man or woman. While there may be mourning over the loss of life, because life is valuable and sacred to God, there is also a degree of rejoicing and victory. The evil being perpetrated on the earth because of the choices of that individual has not been permitted to prevail.

Police officers do not like arresting and putting people in prison, and no judge likes to sentence a person to death row. Yet there are times when people have committed such violence or malice toward others in their lives or in their communities that these tough decisions must be made to ensure true justice is served on behalf of the victims. God is not a murderer. He is a judge who ensures justice for those who have been mistreated or hurt.

Romans 13:4 explains, *"For the one in authority is God's servant for your good. But if you do wrong, be afraid, for rulers do not bear the sword for no reason. They are God's servants, agents of wrath to bring punishment on the wrongdoer."* Exodus 21:12 teaches, *"Anyone who strikes a person with a fatal blow is to be put to death."* And Numbers 35:30 says, *"Anyone who kills a person is to be put to death as a murderer only on the testimony of witnesses. But no one is to be put to death on the testimony of only one witness."*

Some people think that the people who work for the government or the police are the only ones who bring forth judgment in a life. But the Scriptures tell us that God places divine authority into the hands of His people. He tells us that there are times when He will give an order to His people, and like how a police officer obeys a judge, the orders are then carried out. If a judge tells the police officers to take a man to prison, he is going, and it doesn't matter what the police officers think about the judge's ruling.

God's plans and purposes are not for us to alter, change, or fix. When you trust Jesus with your life you realize that if He has ordered something or tells you to do something, then you are wise to obey. His instructions are for your good. When you are doing the right thing, you have no reason to be afraid of negative repercussions. Only people who do evil should be afraid of the governing authorities.

God has many ways of collecting evidence and finding witnesses to attest to the crimes that have been committed in a life. Angels are one, people are another, and God himself can stand as a witness to crimes done on the earth. *"The eyes of the Lord are everywhere, keeping watch on the wicked and the good"* (Prov. 15:3). Nathanial believed he was not being seen. He thought he was being covert, discreet, and inconspicuous. He believed everyone thought he was good and that his legacy would be one of positivity and purity, even when he didn't deserve this title.

The things that God sees, records, and knows about a man or a woman permit Him to mourn their death or to see it as a necessity in the big scheme of life. At times, evil people will not stop perpetrating crimes against others, even when they are warned and given consequences. There are some offenders who are so vile and heinous that they will persist in their lawbreaking efforts, despite multiple attempts at rehabilitation. And in these unfortunate circumstances, God will intervene and sentence them in a way that may seem harsh to us, but if we really trust God, we will know that He works all things together for our good because He loves us.

The Egyptians were warned and given consequences for the way that they were treating God's people. God warned them that there would be tangible consequences for their misconduct. Yet these people didn't heed the warnings and stop their pursuit, so the Lord killed them in the Red Sea. But how many times did God say to them beforehand: "Let my people go!" How many times did the Lord warn them and tell them: "Stop what you are doing. Or else!"

Some people refuse to quit, even when they have been warned by the Lord and by His servants. They do not fear God or the consequences of their behavior. Matt. 10:28 explains to us who and what we should fear. People shouldn't fear the opinions of others, the court system, or their pastor or friends. They should fear God because He is the One who is always watching, always recording, and always judging right from wrong. *"Do not be afraid of those who kill the body but cannot kill the soul. Rather, be afraid of the One who can destroy both soul and body in hell."*

What is God supposed to do when someone continues to violate His commands and is heading toward an attack on His children? Do you think it would be fair or just to allow evil people to continue in their evil? Or would a good God, a loving God, stop the abuse and the trauma? Would He stand up for His people and give them a chance for life? God values His people. *"Are not two sparrows sold for a penny? Yet not one of them will fall to the ground outside your Father's care. And even the very hairs of your head are all numbered. So don't be afraid; you are worth more than many sparrows"* (Matt. 10:29–31).

Wow, Amanda thought. *This all makes so much sense now. I am finally understanding everything so clearly. God doesn't want to see people die. He hates it when death is a part of life because death was brought to the world by Satan. But because God is good and loving, He must punish people who are hurting others! Like a good person would stop someone from being robbed, a good God will stop someone from being continuously abused and harmed.*

Through this entire experience, Amanda realized just how much God loved her. He was willing to take extreme measures, even measures of life and death, to protect her future and her children's futures. God loved her so much that He was willing to implement justice on her behalf because her abuser wouldn't heed the warnings God had been giving him for years. The truth was, God had warned him. He had warned him many times, and she knew it. She was a witness to the things God had said to him because sometimes it was from her own mouth!

Nathanial refused, like Pharaoh, Amanda realized. He was warned. He was given many chances, but he didn't care. He continued to taunt God. He continued to ignore the covenant God had made with His people. She wondered how many deaths she'd seen around her were actually divine judgment. She began to ponder. One thing was for sure: God knew what was going to happen, and He is the One who judges if something was murder or a sentence from Him.

We should mourn for people when they are alive! Amanda thought. *It is only when they are alive and being given a chance to repent that we should mourn. Once they have sealed their eternal fate, we shouldn't mourn anymore.* We shouldn't continue to go back and talk about how the Egyptians died in the sea from a sad and dejected perspective. They made their choice, and God's people rejoiced, not mourned, on that day because they knew their God had delivered them from their oppressors and enemies.

"Jesus said to him, 'Let the dead bury their own dead, but you go and proclaim the kingdom of God" (Luke 9:60). There are people who work on the opposing side. These people are not fighting the same battle you are fighting. They are not on the same mission you are on. When

these deaths occur, you don't have to celebrate and throw a party, but you also don't need to mourn, weep, and cry over the loss like their army will. If a person is evil, the Devil and his associates may weep, but why should you?

Likewise, when a Christian person, a good person, is murdered or harmed, like in the martyrdom of the apostles, then we shouldn't expect Hell to mourn their death because they are the ones behind it. If a Christian dies, Hell rejoices, and we don't because we are burying "our dead." All of us must choose a side. We must determine if we are on the side of darkness or the side of light. The side we are on determines how we mourn the death of those who are either for us or against us. Not all deaths are to be mourned equally. Not all deaths are worthy of tears.

{ 8 }

Heavenly Demonstrations

"One two three say cheese! Oh my God! You guys are just too cute. I love it!" the photographer exclaimed as she shot the last family photoshoot they would ever have. "You are just so lucky. Look at y'all. Aww," she said. "Okay, well, I will be sending these photos over to you in a few days or up to a week, okay? It usually takes me a few days to get the edits done. I will send you the photos to your inbox, Amanda," she explained as they packed up to depart the photo shoot.

"Okay, thanks so much!" Amanda replied. The photo session was a birthday gift to her because photos were always so important to her. She always loved pictures and photography. Now that she was a wife and a mother she wanted to make sure she remembered the life she was building. She wanted to make sure she never forgot all the memories her family was making as they grew and developed together.

Amanda had no clue that this experience was going to be their last family photos as a family with a mom and a dad with their children. She didn't have any idea of the giant wave heading toward the beach of their life. At the time it just seemed like another photo shoot, another memory. One of many in their family photo book. And from the outside, everything looked perfect. Everything looked like a dream.

Amanda and Nathanial had lived in their first home together for years. They had just experienced the birth of their third child in that house, their first home. Nathanial was a contractor and worked on people's houses for a living. When an opportunity presented itself for him to purchase a house at a deal and to renovate it for them to move into, he went for it. Amanda never liked the house. She didn't want to move. She felt like God had told her to stay where she was, but Nathanial didn't want to hear that. He loved this house and they were GOING to move into it.

The first time they walked through the house Amanda sensed an evil presence. Something didn't feel right, particularly in the laundry room and basement. When she walked downstairs into the basement, she immediately began to speak in tongues because she was keenly aware of the presence of something sinister and dark. Something evil. But what in the world was there? Everything looked pretty cool, and the house had potential to be made better. After all, this was a good deal, so maybe Nathanial was right. Maybe they should consider moving.

At first Nathanial said that the house was going to be a business deal, and that is how he got Amanda to agree to going forward with the offer and the purchase. But right before the closing and the sale happened, Nathanial said, "This house should be ours. Let's put our names on it." Amanda didn't know what to say. She wanted her husband to be happy, and he loved this house. He was so excited for it, and she hadn't seen him happy very much. "Okay," she sheepishly agreed. "If you think that you can make it nice for us, I guess we should."

For the next few months Nathanial and his brother worked on the house. They did all the renovations. It looked so beautiful on the outside. Everything seemed so picture-perfect. This house was a dream! It was gorgeous, and it was so much closer to everything in town as well. *We are getting a fresh start. A new beginning,* Amanda thought. Maybe a new beginning is what they needed. Maybe this move would change everything they were struggling with in their marriage.

The night the house went into their names, before the renovations had begun, Amanda saw a devil in her dream. It called her on an old-time phone. Brinnnng! Brinnnng! the phone rang. "Hello," Amanda said as she picked up the phone. "Welcome!" the devil said. "I am the butler of this house. Let me show you around." Amanda was so confused. *Who is this? Why am I here? And what is the point of this encounter?* she wondered.

"Look at these pitiful church members. They are singing in the choir and singing praises to God, but they can't help you, can they? They have no power to stop us," the devil taunted. He took her into another room, then quoted Deuteronomy 32:30 to her: *"How could one man chase a thousand, or two put ten thousand to flight, unless their Rock had sold them, unless the LORD had given them up?"* This devil wanted her to think God was against her and the church was against her. He wanted her to think she had no help in the battle.

Upon recounting her life months later Amanda could see the appropriate scripture to speak back to this demon: *"Unless the LORD builds the house, the builders labor in vain. Unless the LORD watches over the city, the guards stand watch in vain"* (Ps. 127:1). This demon thought he had possession over a house. He thought he was in control. That he could intimidate and stop Amanda from prospering by messing with their finances. But in the end, all work done outside of God is worthless anyway. There are some things not worth building because God isn't in it.

All the money, all the time, all the work that was done in that house amounted to very little. Their family moved into the house, then quickly moved back out, returning to their home they should have never left in the first place. The devil took her husband on a wasted journey, a wasted experience, because he wanted to and felt like it would be good for him. This devil felt empowered in what he did and what he said. He felt like he was going to have the last say. It only took a few days living in the house that Nathanial said, "I can't be here. I can't live here."

They had to remain in the house for a few weeks before moving because their other house had been ripped apart in order to be renovated. In the few weeks that they lived in the new home, Nathanial had become increasingly suicidal. He said he legitimately wanted to kill himself.

In addition, Amanda felt very depressed because she didn't really like the house and had never wanted to be there. Everything felt out of place, but she didn't really know why. The home was in great outward condition. "This house has newer appliances than our other house. Everything is immaculate. I don't know what is wrong with me. Why am I sad?" she asked Nathanial. "Something is really wrong. Something is not right here. There is something evil here," she insisted. Nathanial agreed. He was having dreams about snakes and had even found two snakes, one of them in the house, down in the basement.

Their son was acting out of character too. He told Amanda that he didn't really like her, and he had never said something like that before. She knew that this was spiritual. Even though she couldn't see anything in the house, there was something there. One Sunday when she was watching a sermon on their TV, the TV stopped working without rhyme or reason. The internet and TV connection for the house was strange in general. They had a hard time getting any type of internet service to work.

"I am trying to make sure the kids get their schoolwork done on the iPad. They need to be able to watch their homeschool videos," Amanda explained when the internet connection was down. "Yeah, I don't know what is up with the internet here," Nathanial replied. There seemed to be some kind of interception. The demon did call her on a phone, and the Wi-Fi works through things we can't see. "I don't get it, but something is so weird!" she said to him.

"Nathanial, I think something evil is in this house. We need to get out," Amanda insisted. Nathanial nodded and said, "I know. I am working on it, but this just sucks. I have put so much money and effort into this house. I can't believe we aren't going to live here." Things only got worse when they finally listed the house to learn that they weren't going to be able to get what they planned to get out of the house. The couple was set to lose $50,000.

Buzzz. Amanda looked down at her phone to find a message from a girl she talked to sometimes at church. "Oh wow! You guys are selling your house? That must be so hard. It is so beautiful!" it said. Amanda tried to explain that she was glad to be leaving the house. She wanted to convey that she really wasn't sad and that she simply wanted to get back to her old home. The girl seemed to understand. She replied, "I hope everything works out for y'all."

Everyone on the outside thinks our life is perfect. Everyone thinks I wanted this house, Amanda thought. *If people only knew the truth about our finances and how terrible this experience has been. If people could only see what was actually going on in our lives and what pressure we are under.* "Man this is funny. People really don't have a clue what is going on in someone's life, do they?" she said to Nathanial. "Everyone thinks we are doing so well with this house. People think we are silly for going back to our other home." Nathanial nodded. "Yeah, people really don't know what is going on."

In the Bible, we learn about a prophet named Ezekiel. Ezekiel was a demonstrative prophet, and God frequently had him act out skits or dramas to teach a spiritual lesson. One day, after acting out many skits, God told Ezekiel that he was going to lose his wife. *"The word of the Lord came to me: 'Son of man, with one blow I am about to take away from you the delight of your eyes. Yet do not lament or weep or shed any tears. Groan quietly; do not mourn for the dead"* (Ezek. 24:15–17).

This news came as a surprise to Ezekiel, but because he had a close relationship with God, he was able to trust God with his life. He could demonstrate a lesson to the people in the way that the Lord commanded him to. Ezekiel had to act normal when things weren't normal. He had to show no grief at a time when he felt grief. In Ezekiel's life things weren't as they seemed.

Oftentimes, spiritual things are not manifested in the physical realm. People can look beautiful, put together, and perfect on the outside, but inside they are broken, miserable, awful people. In reverse, people can look like they are struggling or like they are having a hard time, but they are alive and thriving on the inside. Amanda had been changed when she accepted Jesus as her Savior at twenty-one. She was different from the way she was prior to her salvation, but on the outside, at least at first, she didn't look like she had changed at all.

Nathanial never appreciated the change in Amanda. He never saw her for who she became the day she accepted Jesus. He didn't see what God was doing to renovate her house. When he looked at Amanda, he hated her even more than the day he met her because he thought she was a fake. He assumed she was just a dumb whore who only pretended to be better but inside wasn't any different. As he would sometimes say, "You can put lipstick on a pig, but it is still a pig."

But the truth was, Amanda had changed when she gave her life to Jesus that day at the altar. She was not a whore anymore. She wasn't unworthy, unvaluable, and ugly on the inside. Even though she looked the same at first, she wasn't the same at all. When someone gives their life to Christ they become a new creature, and sometimes it may not look like anything changed on the outside. You may not see the change for a little while after Jesus builds up the house, but be assured the house has changed ownership. A new person has moved in, and the person who was there before isn't allowed to claim that house anymore.

2 Corinthians 5:17 tells us, *"Therefore, if anyone is in Christ, the new creation has come: The old has gone, the new is here!"* When Jesus begins building something in a life, the house will become more and more beautiful. The former state of the house isn't important anymore because when people see the house in the future they will think to themselves, "Oh my, this is beautiful." The people who never saw

the former house won't even believe the former state. They never saw the destruction and filth that once were a part of the house before the renovation began.

People who have never been born again don't understand the new birth. They assume everyone is simply playing religion like they are and that Christianity is something you put on, something you act out, and something you pretend to do before others. But nothing could be further from the truth! A Christian is indeed different. A Christian is not someone who puts on, pretends, and acts holy. A Christian is someone who has changed and committed their lives to Christ, and with this conversion they will do, act, and perform whatever He tells them to perform, even when the world thinks it looks bizarre and crazy.

So I spoke to the people in the morning, and in the evening my wife died. The next morning I did as I had been commanded. Then the people asked me, "Won't you tell us what these things have to do with us? Why are you acting like this?"

So I said to them, "The word of the LORD came to me: Say to the people of Israel, 'This is what the Sovereign LORD says: I am about to desecrate my sanctuary—the stronghold in which you take pride, the delight of your eyes, the object of your affection. The sons and daughters you left behind will fall by the sword. And you will do as I have done. You will not cover your mustache and beard or eat the customary food of mourners. You will keep your turbans on your heads and your sandals on your feet. You will not mourn or weep but will waste away because of your sins and groan among yourselves. Ezekiel will be a sign to you; you will do just as he has done. When this happens, you will know that I am the Sovereign LORD.'

'And you, son of man, on the day I take away their stronghold, their joy and glory, the delight of their eyes, their heart's desire, and their sons and daughters as well— on that day a fugitive will come to tell you the news. At that time your mouth will be opened; you will speak with him and will no longer be silent. So you will be a sign to them, and they will know that I am the LORD'" (Ezek. 24:18–27).

God wanted Ezekiel to demonstrate his love for godliness, not religion. He wanted Ezekiel to speak out, demonstrate, and show the world that the Lord doesn't want religious ceremonies, beautiful temples, and a form of godliness without the power. God desires for His people to love Him with all of their hearts. He wants people to serve Him, obey Him, and do the things He has commanded them to do.

A relationship with Jesus isn't an act. Our love for God isn't a show or a performance. A relationship with God is a genuine relationship, one where He leads and we follow. The people who know God know what we are doing, even when it seems bizarre, peculiar, and strange to the watching world, even those who are inside the Church.

Amanda pondered on these things. How many people today have a form of godliness but deny the power of God? How many church members sit in the church today, ignorant, blind, and dull to the cries of the prophets who are warning them of the impending doom that will come upon those who don't have a close personal relationship with God? A true prophet tells the truth. A prophet gives information from God, and if you don't like it, then take it up with God, not the prophets.

Many people want a feel-good gospel. They want a gospel that doesn't confront or address the problems in people's lives. But if the gospel is going to set people free, then they must first know the truth even when it hurts! When Ezekiel lost his wife it hurt, but he knew God had a bigger plan. He trusted God's plans. He followed God because God was his everything, and he loved God even more than his wife.

"So, because you are lukewarm—neither hot nor cold—I am about to spit you out of my mouth. You say, 'I am rich; I have acquired wealth and do not need a thing.' But you do not realize that you are wretched, pitiful, poor, blind and naked. I counsel you to buy from me gold refined in the fire, so you can become rich; and white clothes to wear, so you can cover your shameful

nakedness; and salve to put on your eyes, so you can see. Those whom I love I rebuke and discipline. So be earnest and repent" (Rev. 3:16–19).

{ **9** }

The Funeral

Today was the day of her husband's funeral. People in the community had gotten word of her husband's death, and today she had to face them as a widow. Amanda was a young woman, only in her thirties, and so many people were shocked by the news of her husband's passing. People tried to reach out to her and send her flowers, food, and alms to cover the funeral expenses.

Don't these people know that I don't need their pity? This is hardly the time to offer me help. The time to help would have been before my husband died, not after, she thought. *There is nothing that can be done now. He is gone. He is no longer able to decide about his eternity. The decision has been made, and he didn't make a good one.*

I wish I could just fast-forward through this. What am I going to tell the children? When will the time be right to explain to them what has happened in our lives? Surely, I can't tell them everything right now. They are still so young, so innocent. One day I will tell them everything. One day it will all be clear to them. I know they will be better off without their dad. As hard as it sounds, he was a harsh and mean man. He didn't love God, and he didn't want us to either, she spoke quietly within her heart.

Many times when Amanda heard the Lord's voice tell her to do something, she would do it. Her husband, when he was alive, would scream, cuss, and yell at her, demanding that she stop doing what God said to do. One week, she was set to speak at the church his grandparents attended, and he continued to barrage her, saying things like, "This is such a mistake. It's so weird. Why are you doing that?" On more than one occasion, in things like tithing or her ministry work, her husband would mock her, make fun of her, and tell her that God wasn't real.

Nathanial was adamant that everything Amanda was doing for the Lord was a waste of time. He would ask her, "What has God done for you? How much money have you made? Why do you keep wasting your time? God isn't real! It is all in your imagination!" He would scream, "All the things you are doing are so stupid. You are so naive, so foolish. You are wasting your money. You are wasting your time. I am not going to support any of this. If you want to do what God is telling you to do, you better not touch any of MY MONEY."

Amanda knew that God was working in her life. He knew that she was not tithing or putting her money toward building something for Him for nothing. She knew that God had called her to teach and preach, too, and every time she worked for the Lord, He would give her exactly what to say and what to do. He would tell her specifics about everything, including her tithes and offerings. Amanda was assured she wasn't doing all the things she was doing for nothing, but how could she convince him of that?

"All these d******* preachers want is your money. If I find out that you are giving any more of our money to the church, it is going to be bad for you. Do you understand me?" Nathanial would shout. "I'd better not find out you've given any more of our money to these crooks. If you want to be an idiot, you can do it on your own, but don't touch my money! All your pastor wants is your money. He is just stealing! Pastors are the worst people in the world. They are literally a plague to humanity, and religion needs to be wiped off the face of the earth."

"Nathanial, you shouldn't talk about God's men and women like this," Amanda warned him. It is a foolish thing to speak badly about the Church, especially pastors who are doing the work of the Lord. God doesn't like it when people speak badly about preachers. He doesn't like it when people talk badly about His children."

Nathanial would shout back, "I don't give a f**k about these people. They aren't s**t! And why don't you go suck their d***? What has the Church ever done for you? One day you will see, Amanda. One day you will understand!" He would then say smugly with a smile, "Right now, you're just too stupid to see the truth, but don't worry, you will get there." Amanda would respond, " No I won't. I am not going to change my mind. I know that God is real. I know that there are good pastors. I know that God has even called me to preach and teach! And one day people will give to my ministry too. Are you saying people shouldn't give to people who are working for Jesus?"

"Hell to the NO!" he would say. "The Church should be taxed. The Church should be done away with. It is terrible! And you shouldn't do anything you are doing. It is dumb!" This was a frequent argument from him, but Amanda knew he was wrong. She knew that God was recording every sermon, every spiritual encounter where she prayed for others. She knew that every time she gave something to someone in faith and love for them, God was going to repay her for it. So she just ignored Nathanial, week after week, month after month, and she continued doing what Jesus had said to do.

Amanda and Nathanial disagreed often about money because Nathanial didn't want to support the Church or advance the gospel in any way, shape, or form. He didn't want to put money toward her ministry. He didn't want to give to the Church. If Amanda ever felt the Holy Spirit speak to her and tell her to give something or to do something for the kingdom that involved finances, she would immediately feel nervous because she knew that she was going to have to explain the situation to Nathanial and hope that he wouldn't completely flip out on her.

Many times, her family members around her would support her ministry by giving her the money to do the things God had told her to do. Amanda didn't work outside of the home. God had commanded her to stay home and raise her children, homeschooling them and remaining at home during their foundational years of life.

Even though Amanda was highly educated, she didn't have a formal job because working outside of the house wasn't what God asked her to do.

She would help her husband with his work. She always renovated houses, got supplies, advertised, and did financial work for the business. She participated in his business while working for the family, doing all the laundry, the cooking, the child-rearing, and the schooling. Nathanial made sure she knew he wasn't going to clean, cook, or help with the children. In fact, if he ever got asked to change a diaper, to help cook food, or clean up his plate, he would respond with cursing and contempt. "Do I got to do everything now?" he would complain.

"Just forget it, Nathanial." Amanda would awkwardly say. "I can handle it." For years, Amanda helped Nathanial grow his business, but she never asked him to do anything. She just worked as if she was working for the Lord, and she was thankful that God had made a way for her to stay home with her children because she loved being a mom more than anything else in her life. Her children genuinely loved her, something she had always wanted.

But sometimes things got really overwhelming at home, especially after the birth of their third child. Having three children, home-schooling, potty training, cooking, cleaning, helping his business, and doing all the other things that needed to be done in order to effectively run a home was hard work. Amanda never got time off. She never had days off. She worked from sunup to sundown, many days with no break. And if she wanted any time to herself, she would have to wake up way before her family, so she could have a few minutes to take a shower or do a workout.

Amanda loved her children and she loved working. She didn't despise being at home or raising them. She loved everything about her life, but sometimes, because she was human, she would get tired. But whenever Amanda mentioned her need for a break to Nathanial, he would begin to make fun of her. "You don't even work! What do you do all day? The more I am around you, the more I can see you don't do anything. Why are you complaining? If everything is so hard, just send the kids to school," he would shout. "I didn't sign up to home-school them. I would just send their asses to school!"

Nathanial knew that sending the children to school wasn't an option for Amanda. He knew that by playing that card he could cause her to bottle up all of her tiredness and her struggles because she would persevere, keep doing everything, and leave him alone. He used the "just send them to school thing" to get her to shut up and stop asking for any help. Amanda told Nathanial a few months before he died, "Didn't you know that even if the kids went to school, you'd have to sign papers, check off work, and return things to school? You would still have to make sure they do homework."

Gruffly he said, "Yeah, but that would be easier than what you are doing." Nathanial was always looking for the easy way out. He wanted to be lazy and do as little as possible while still receiving all the benefits of hard work. Through his entire career and in his inter-personal relationships, Nathanial barely breezed by. He did the bare minimum and then called it good and expected everyone around him to praise him for his minute accomplishments. He was also highly critical of everyone else.

"Your dad was such a bad dad. He did a s*** job," he would say. "Your mom was an idiot. She wasn't very smart. She thinks she is fooling everyone, but she isn't fooling me. That is why she had such an easy job, and even then she could barely do that." It wasn't just Amanda and her parents that would receive criticism though. It was all of his clients, all of his family members, and even his brother, who worked for him. In Nathanial's eyes, everyone was an idiot and an underachiever compared to him. After all, he was the best and every-one else sucked.

For a little while Amanda heard his words and started to be crit-ical of her parents. Her parents weren't perfect by any means, but they did at least try to work hard and be kind to others. Peering back into the past, Amanda saw that the enemy used Nathanial to breed and amplify her pain toward her parents. He wanted her to see all the ugly in them because then she would be all alone without any help, unless of course she obeyed every one of Nathanial's commands.

This was the perfect plot of the enemy. He believed he could cut her off from everyone else who loved her by fueling her heartache from her childhood. If Satan could turn Amanda's heart against the only other people who knew her and loved her and were willing to help her with her children or her ministry, then he could keep her under his domination, doing what he said and only what he said. A few months before Nathanial's death, the Lord revealed to Amanda the truth about her parents. She had been intentionally cut off from them. She had been separated from them by her husband because he hated that she had their help and love.

Abusers want to keep their victims under total domination and control. Financial control is just one of the ways that abusers can keep victims doing what they say and tolerating their abuse. That is why Nathanial always worked to get rid of a separate phone, a separate relationship, or even her car. He destroyed her car's window in that early argument, leaving her without a phone or a car downtown. If Amanda had nothing and no one to turn to or ask for help, then she would be forced to listen to him, regardless of the request or the situation.

God didn't want this for Amanda. He didn't want her to be alone. He didn't want her to suffer, struggle, or beg for money or for acceptance from an evil man. God wanted Amanda to be free. He wanted her to be financially strong, relying on him as her source. When God removed Ezekiel's wife from him, one of the things He told him was not to take the cakes and other gifts from the people that were offered to him. *"And you will do as I [Ezekiel] have done. You will not cover your mustache and beard or eat the customary food of mourners [brought to you by others]"* (Ezek. 24:22).

God wanted the people to know that Ezekiel was dependent upon Him for provision and nourishment. Matthew 4:4 teaches, *"It is written: 'Man shall not live on bread alone, but on every word that comes from the mouth of God.'"* God will oftentimes provide for His children through other people. But Christians must remember that people are not their source—God is.

God will take care of His people in a plethora of ways. He demonstrated this to us when the ravens brought Elijah food in the desert, and when Jesus caught a fish with a gold coin in its mouth. Another example comes from the story of Melchizedek, where a mysterious man, maybe an angel, supplied God's people. God is not limited in how He will provide for His people. He can do all kinds of things, using animals, people, angels, or other methods.

"I know You will provide for me," Amanda would pray. "It may not make sense. I don't have a job, and I don't want to keep bothering my parents either. I want to be able to help my parents. I don't want them to keep helping me." God heard her prayers of honor toward her parents. Even though she didn't have the money now to repay her parents, she would one day, and she would honor them through her life and her testimony, where many would know what they did for her.

The truth was that her parents were not perfect people, and she didn't come from a perfect home. Amanda always wanted a family, a family where a mother and a father were together and in love. She always blamed her parents for her pain. She didn't understand why her home was not solidified and put together. They were still good people who loved her though. They may not have made all the right decisions. They didn't stay married. But they didn't want to hurt Amanda. They didn't hate her as the head of her new family did.

Amanda made a big mistake marrying Nathanial. She thought she was going to form a new family, create something better and new. She thought she could run away from her parents and have a life that didn't resemble suffering or pain, but this led her right into the arms of her abuser, a man who used her past against her. A man who was used by Satan to pinpoint her weak points and exploit them for his own advantage and gain.

For our struggle is not against flesh and blood, but against the rulers, against the authorities, against the powers of this dark world and against the spiritual forces of evil in the heavenly realms (Eph. 6:12).

Amanda's parents had their own issues. Her dad, the police officer, wanted to do right, but he was trying to do it by himself, through his own effort, and through being strong as a man. Her mother, the one who had taken her around to the parties, knew the truth, but she was not willing to admit it, because for a long time, as Amanda did, she found comfort in hiding the problem and hiding the struggle. But when people do either one of these extremes, the problem doesn't go away, because the devil behind the problem isn't dealt with.

People cannot overcome and conquer demonic problems in their own effort and strength. Some things have to be taken care of in the realm of the spirit to be dealt with. When a demon-possessed boy was brought to Jesus, his father needed help with his faith and his son's deliverance. Not having faith, or not knowing Jesus very well, doesn't mean a person isn't working with Jesus.

Jesus asked the boy's father, "How long has he been like this?" "From childhood," he answered. "It has often thrown him into fire or water to kill him. But if you can do anything, take pity on us and help us." "'If you can'?" said Jesus. "Everything is possible for one who believes." Immediately the boy's father exclaimed, "I do believe; help me overcome my unbelief!"

When Jesus saw that a crowd was running to the scene, he rebuked the impure spirit. "You deaf and mute spirit," he said, "I command you, come out of him and never enter him again." The spirit shrieked, convulsed him violently and came out. The boy looked so much like a corpse that many said, "He's dead." But Jesus took him by the hand and lifted him to his feet, and he stood up. After Jesus had gone indoors, his disciples asked him privately, "Why couldn't we drive it out?" He replied, "This kind can come out only by prayer and fasting" (Mark 9:21–29).

When people do not have a strong faith or when they are not praying or associating with Christ, they cannot solve their problems, even when they are not actively involved in the Devil's kingdom and the Devil's work. Amanda's parents may not have been pressing into spiritual truths, but they weren't actively positioning themselves against Christ either. Jesus said these kinds of people can still be welcomed to His side because they are not against him.

"Teacher," said John, "we saw someone driving out demons in your name and we told him to stop, because he was not one of us." "Do not stop him," Jesus said. "For no one who does a miracle in my name can in the next moment say anything bad about me, for whoever is not against us is for us. Truly I tell you, anyone who gives you a cup of water in my name because you belong to the Messiah will certainly not lose their reward (Mark 9:38–41).

Amanda's parents weren't trying to be evil. They didn't hate God's house, His people, and His plans and purposes as Nathanial did, and Jesus doesn't and never has turned away imperfect people who themselves need to be healed and delivered from their oppressor, who has tried to steal from them and take from them all their lives. God's family is full of imperfect people. Heaven will be full of humans who didn't deserve to be there, but they are there anyway because they took Jesus's gift of salvation and grace.

Nathanial pretended to be holy and righteous. He wanted the world to believe he was someone that he wasn't. He was never honest with himself or with others around him. He hated God, His word, and His Church, and Nathanial made it his mission to destroy it. For whatever reason, he decided that he was going to turn against God and betray Him despite all of His love that He had shown him in his life. Nathanial decided that he would rather drown and die alone and miserable, full of hatred and lies, than turn to his Savior who would restore his life and return his dignity.

The Church is full of imperfect people, but Amanda finally understood, as she stared at his corpse lying in the casket, that there was a difference between him and her. She loved God and Nathanial hated Him. She wanted to turn from her sin, live a different life, and be loving, kind, and truthful, but he didn't want any of those things. Amanda tried to please the Lord, listen for His wisdom, and build His kingdom, but Nathanial didn't care about God, His ways, His wisdom, or His kingdom. He made it his mission to align himself against the Church. He made it his mission to destroy the thing that God had commanded him to build up: his Christian wife.

Proverbs 18:22 says," *He who finds a wife finds what is good and receives favor from the LORD."* And in Proverbs 19:3 we learn, *"A person's own folly leads to their ruin, yet their heart rages against the LORD."* Some people love folly. They love the sin they pursue and chase. And Nathanial's favorite verse to use against his wife was Proverbs 19:13, which says, *"A foolish child is a father's ruin, and a quarrelsome wife is like the constant dripping of a leaky roof."* But the truth was, she wasn't a quarrelsome wife. She was a loving one. A wife who continued to forgive, love, and give her heart to a man who quarreled with her constantly day and night.

The quarreling wasn't natural. It wasn't normal. It was supernatural. It was a war that was raging in the unseen realm, deep in the world of the spirit, where the forces of good and evil oppose one another. A place where there are sides and alliances. A place where good cannot coincide peacefully with evil because good and evil have nothing in common, and that is why the Lord commanded His people to never become unequally yoked.

Do not be yoked together with unbelievers. For what do righteousness and wickedness have in common? Or what fellowship can light have with darkness? What harmony is there between Christ and Belial? Or what does a believer have in common with an unbeliever? What agreement is there between the temple of God and idols? For we are the temple of the living God. As God has said: "I will live with them and walk among them, and I will be their God, and they will be my people." Therefore, "Come out from them and be separate, says the Lord. Touch no unclean thing, and I will receive you." And,

"I will be a Father to you, and you will be my sons and daughters, says the Lord Almighty" (2 Cor. 6:14–18).

"Goodbye, Nathanial," Amanda said as she looked over the casket. This chapter of her life was over. This season of captivity was coming to an end. She knew that she wasn't innocent in the pain she had caused herself or her children. She did marry someone God told her to never marry, but because God is loving and because He is good, He was going to keep His promise to Amanda. God was going to restore everything to her, bring her back to fullness of life, and restore her future because she humbled herself, prayed, and sought forgiveness from God for all her sins, something Nathanial was never willing to do.

Amanda was now dependent on God for everything. She and her children were going to need Jesus today more than ever. Amanda was going to walk in her faith. She was going to have to prove that she believed what she said she believed. She was going to have to trust the Lord with all her heart and lean not on her own understanding. She was going to have to believe that God would make all her paths straight as she put her faith in Him alone for her provision and protection.

Blessed are those who find wisdom, those who gain understanding, for she is more profitable than silver and yields better returns than gold. She is more precious than rubies; nothing you desire can compare with her. Long life is in her right hand; in her left hand are riches and honor (Prov. 3:13–16).

Godly wisdom was going to lead her way. A Christian life full of divine favor and protection was going to pave her path. God's Spirit was going to go before her, protecting her and guiding her in all her ways, and angels were going to surround her and bring her the things she needed but couldn't get from the natural resources on the earth. Amanda and her children were going to be more than all right, whether people partnered with her ministry and her work or not. God was going to take care of Amanda. He was going to keep the covenant that He made, one way or another.

"My son, do not let wisdom and understanding out of your sight, preserve sound judgment and discretion; they will be life for you, an ornament to grace your neck. Then you will go on your way in safety, and your foot will not stumble. When you lie down, you will not be afraid; when you lie down, your sleep will be sweet. Have no fear of sudden disaster or of the ruin that overtakes the wicked, for the LORD will be at your side and will keep your foot from being snared.

Do not withhold good from those to whom it is due, when it is in your power to act. Do not say to your neighbor, "Come back tomorrow and I'll give it to you"—when you already have it with you. Do not plot harm against your neighbor, who lives trustfully near you. Do not accuse anyone for no reason—when they have done you no harm. Do not envy the violent or choose any of their ways. For the LORD detests the perverse but takes the upright into his confidence.

The LORD's curse is on the house of the wicked, but he blesses the home of the righteous. He mocks proud mockers but shows favor to the humble and oppressed. The wise inherit honor, but fools get only shame" (Prov. 3:21–35).

{ 10 }

Dressed in White

Most people display their grief and mourning for months or years after the death of a loved one. Many people wear black, especially to funerals, because they want the world to know they are mourning a death. In some cultures and situations people choose to wear the black attire for up to two years, and today there are people who refuse to move on from a death and continue to mourn and live in a state of depression until they themselves die and go into the eternal world.

What a person wears says a lot about them. Amanda knew that all too well. There was a day when Amanda dressed provocatively and enticingly to lure men to her. She would use her appearance and skill at dressing up to charm others. When she dressed like a prostitute, she got a lot more attention. And that is why she kept doing it, at least for a while, because she wanted people to pay attention to her. She wanted people to notice her.

For a long time any attention was good attention in Amanda's eyes. She would rather be seen, heard, and acknowledged than neglected, ignored, and alone. One of her biggest fears had always been being alone. She didn't want to be. She hated the thought of it, and she was willing to do anything to make sure she wasn't alone, including entertaining people who were not worthy of her entertainment.

One of the best things that Nathanial did for Amanda was policing her outfits and appearance. In an effort to keep Amanda to himself, he constantly criticized her dress. He hated that other people liked how Amanda looked. He didn't want her to be looked at or valued at all, especially not by other people who could threaten his place with her. So, he schooled Amanda on her clothes. He told her she needed to cover up, dress better, and stop looking like such a hoe.

"Why are you dressed like that?" he would ask. "Take them shorts off. You can't wear that." At first this seemed kind of controlling to Amanda. She didn't think it was right for a man to tell her what to wear and how to look. But then she realized that God didn't want her dressing like that either. She realized that she didn't want any attention. She just needed the focus of the right people, like Nathanial.

Through the years Amanda started dressing better. She changed the most after she had their daughter and realized the impact her clothes could have on her young daughter's mind. Amanda took out her belly button ring because she felt convicted by it after her daughter saw it. She stopped wearing two-piece bathing suits, too, because she didn't want her daughter to want to wear the same and also be sexualized and treated like an object. She wanted her daughter to be valued and loved for who she was, not what she looked like.

Amanda went through a phase in high school where she was overweight. During this time her boyfriend cheated on her, and she determined that since they were a match in every other way, her weight must have been the reason why. This high school heartbreak caused Amanda to work out excessively at the gym and obsess over her appearance. She made up her mind that no man would ever cheat on her again because she was going to be hot and fun.

From an immature 16 to 17-year-old's brain this would make total sense. Her parents had been divorced because of lust and cheating. Her serious high school boyfriend, as well as the boys she had dated before, were also guilty of cheating. It was only logical to assume that if she was the other chick, the one who everyone wanted, then she wouldn't have to deal with being cheated on. She could just avoid the pain entirely. She could elevate herself above it.

Amanda wanted to believe she could look a certain way on the outside and change someone else's heart. She thought her femininity and beauty could fix someone by drawing them in and convincing them that she was enough. However, Amanda discovered that she was wrong and incapable of this very complex job. It isn't a woman's job to fix a man, stop his bad behavior, or change his corrupt heart. A woman and her beauty, whether inside or out, cannot stop an evil man from doing evil things. His choices are his responsibility entirely, and they have absolutely nothing to do with her.

Romans 14:12 says, "*So then, each of us will give an account of ourselves to God.*" It isn't wise to compare ourselves with others. God doesn't want us looking around at the behavior of other people to determine if we are in right standing with Him. Someone else's sin or lack of sin can't transfer to our account. The only man who has been given permission to trade places with another, removing their sin and their shame, is Jesus, and we should keep this job reserved for Him alone.

John 14:6–7 teaches, "*Jesus answered, 'I am the way and the truth and the life. No one comes to the Father except through me. If you really know me, you will know my Father as well. From now on, you do know him and have seen him.'*" It is possible to walk with God, know Him personally, and hear directly from Heaven's throne. People don't have to wait to get to Heaven to hear from God, talk with Him, and receive divine protection and love. So many things are available to us through our union with Christ, but if we want to receive them, we must be willing to put on the righteousness of Christ and remove the former dirty rags we once proudly wore.

The angel said to those who were standing before him, "Take off his filthy clothes." Then he said to Joshua, "See, I have taken away your sin, and I will put fine garments on you." . . . "This is what the LORD Almighty says: 'If you will walk in obedience to me and keep my requirements, then you will govern my house and have charge of my courts, and I will give you a place among these standing here" (Zech. 3:4,7).

God wants to give us a special place in His house. He wants us to look different from the world, dress differently from the world, and carry His name. A good wife wants to represent her husband well. She wants to make him happy in her attire and in her actions. Good wives tell the world they are married, not only through the wedding band on their fingers, but through their lifestyles and representations of respect, dignity, and love for their husbands.

Amanda had heard women in the hair salon, the nail salon, or even at church making fun of their husbands. She knew there were women who gossiped, talked bad about, and made fun of the men who loved them, trusted them, and cared for them with sincerity and passion. This wasn't the kind of woman Amanda wanted to be. She hated it when she heard women mocking their husbands or making fun of them. She knew this behavior was beyond wrong, so she went to the other extreme and stopped talking about her husband at all unless she had something nice to say.

What Amanda didn't know, though, was that her silence was breaking her down. Her silence was a weapon her enemy wanted to harness against her and her future. Her silence was allowing her enemy to continue to dominate her life and keep her in a state of control and domination. God never wanted Amanda to be quiet. He never wanted her to bow down and quit. He wanted Amanda to stand up to her enemy, fight for her voice, and for the truth to be made clear. Jesus died to establish truth in the world, and as His people we are called to do the very same thing.

Sometimes the world, especially the world who has aligned itself against the gospel message, wants to suffocate the message. Just like Nathanial tried to do that day in the early part of the marriage, the Devil wants to stop the voice of the believer from speaking another word. Devils want to keep the Christian quiet and weak. Psalm 81:10 commands us, *"I am the LORD your God, who brought you up out of Egypt. Open wide your mouth and I will fill it."*

Life and death are in the power of the tongue. What we speak matters. How we act toward others matters. When words are destructive and abusive, they become weapons that the enemy uses to destroy lives. Conversely, when a Christian obeys God and opens their mouth wide, refusing to side with the lies of the enemy, the Lord will put His word in their mouth. He will use their mouth to bring forth His plans for the world and for their life.

God wants to use wives. He wants women to be impactful in their homes, in their communities, and in the Church. God never intended for women to be locked in the house, shamed, afraid, and unable to make a difference in the lives of others. God doesn't want women chained by a man who struggles with fear and hatred because he is afraid to put down his false gods and the demons he has befriended.

Speak up for those who cannot speak for themselves, for the rights of all who are destitute. Speak up and judge fairly; defend the rights of the poor and needy. A wife of noble character who can find? She is worth far more than rubies. Her husband has full confidence in her and lacks nothing of value. She brings him good, not harm, all the days of her life. She selects wool and flax and works with eager hands. She is like the merchant ships, bringing her food from afar. She gets up while it is still night; she provides food for her family and portions for her female servants.

She considers a field and buys it; out of her earnings she plants a vineyard. She sets about her work vigorously; her arms are strong for her tasks. She sees that her trading is profitable, and her lamp does not go out at night. In her hand she holds the distaff and grasps the spindle with her fingers. She opens her arms to the poor and extends her hands to the needy. When it snows, she has no fear for her household; for all of them are clothed in scarlet. She makes coverings for her bed; she is clothed in fine linen and purple.

Her husband is respected at the city gate, where he takes his seat among the elders of the land. She makes linen garments and sells them, and supplies the merchants with sashes. She is clothed with strength and dignity; she can laugh at the days to come" (Prov. 31:8–25).

When a woman puts her faith in God, she will laugh without fear of the future, and she will be successful in all that she does. The right man will see her talents. He will appreciate her unique strength and love that she can bring into his life. Wise men don't tear down women, and good men don't destroy what God has explicitly commanded them to construct.

God didn't ask men if they wanted to love their wives and build them up. He commanded them, too, saying: *"Husbands, love your wives, just as Christ loved the church and gave himself up for her to make her holy, cleansing her by the washing with water through the word, and to present her to himself as a radiant church, without stain or wrinkle or any other blemish, but holy and blameless. In this same way, husbands ought to love their wives as their own bodies. He who loves his wife loves himself. After all, no one ever hated their own body, but they feed and care for their body, just as Christ does the church—for we are members of his body"* (Eph. 5:25–30).

Anything worth having in life takes work. To present your own body or the body of another person to God isn't a light responsibility. It is very possible to disobey the Lord's commands in marriage and lose your authority and headship over a woman. God doesn't owe anyone a wife. A man gets blessed with one. When the truth is revealed and the light shines into a home and into a dark situation, people can see what was behind the curtains, behind the scenes. Only when the light comes in does the dark get driven out.

Ephesians 5:8–13 teaches, *"For you were once darkness, but now you are light in the Lord. Live as children of light (for the fruit of the light consists in all goodness, righteousness and truth) and find out what pleases the Lord. Have nothing to do with the fruitless deeds of darkness, but rather expose them. It is shameful even to mention what the disobedient do in secret. But everything exposed by the light becomes visible—and everything that is illuminated becomes a light."*

Amanda didn't hate Nathanial. She had always loved him. For so many years she believed in him and wanted him to be the man she knew he could have been if he had turned to Christ and trusted

Him as his spiritual leader. But when the light was turned on and the curtains pulled back Amanda was horrified by what she saw. God showed her a man who had never been honest with her, never loved her, and never treated her like the bride she was.

Nathanial may have seemed like a good man to all who lived outside of his house. He looked like he was doing many of the right things, but deep in his heart, down into the inner layers of the soul, Nathanial was corrupt and rotten. He was a man who refused to turn from evil and do good. Nathanial hurt those whom he was called to love. He brought fear, shame, and sorrow to the people who trusted him with their lives. And just like the New Year's Eve party at the beginning of the relationship, Nathanial promised to take care of Amanda when indeed he didn't.

Nathanial was too caught up with the sins of the world. He was too focused on the party and the worries of life. Amanda tried to warn him, like Noah warned the people of the impending flood. She tried to take him into the ark with her. She tried to offer him a lifeboat, but he didn't want it. He laughed at her and called her crazy. He said that he had never seen rain and that she was an idiot and a fool who had no clue what she was talking about. That was his choice, but the rain did come.

Who is going to harm you if you are eager to do good? But even if you should suffer for what is right, you are blessed. "Do not fear their threats; do not be frightened." But in your hearts revere Christ as Lord. Always be prepared to give an answer to everyone who asks you to give the reason for the hope that you have. But do this with gentleness and respect, keeping a clear conscience, so that those who speak maliciously against your good behavior in Christ may be ashamed of their slander.

For it is better, if it is God's will, to suffer for doing good than for doing evil. For Christ also suffered once for sins, the righteous for the unrighteous, to bring you to God. He was put to death in the body but made alive in the Spirit. After being made alive, he went and made proclamation to the imprisoned spirits— to those who were disobedient long ago when God waited patiently in the days of Noah while the ark was being built. In it only a few people, eight in all, were saved through water, and this water symbolizes baptism that now saves you also—not the removal of dirt from the body but the pledge of a clear conscience toward God. It saves you by the resurrection of Jesus Christ, who has gone into heaven and is at God's right hand—with angels, authorities and powers in submission to him" (1 Pet. 3:13–22).

Amanda sat in her living room, wondering out loud whether she could have done more. "Should I have been a better wife to him? Could I have changed his future and his fate if I had just tried a little more and done a little more?" Then, she heard the Spirit of the Lord say to her, "No. You can only witness, love, and live out the gospel in front of others, hoping they will choose to turn and receive, but not all people make a good decision, even in the perfect conditions."

God was a perfect parent operating in pure love. The original family, consisting of God, Adam, and Eve, was healthy and in harmony, but Satan was still able to deceive Adam and Eve and get them to sin against God. So, who are you to think you can do enough, be enough, and become enough to save another person's soul from the traps of the enemy? Perfectionism, beauty, including inner beauty aren't enough to turn back a determined soul set for Hell.

1 Peter 3:1–5 explains, *"Wives, in the same way submit yourselves to your own husbands so that, if any of them do not believe the word, they may be won over without words by the behavior of their wives, when they see the purity and reverence of your lives. Your beauty should not come from outward adornment, such as elaborate hairstyles and the wearing of gold jewelry or fine clothes. Rather, it should be that of your inner self, the unfading beauty of a gentle and quiet spirit, which is of great worth in God's sight. For this is the way the holy women of the past who put their hope in God used to adorn themselves."*

Amanda had done that. She had submitted herself to her husband. She had adorned herself with God's beauty and Spirit. Amanda spent many years working to behave in a way that would appeal to the man she loved and shared her life with, but in all that she did it wasn't enough. Just like for some cold and heartless people, the sacrifice of Christ will never be enough. His behavior and His love for them couldn't change them. His submission to death on the cross couldn't drive them back from the grave.

So in everything, do to others what you would have them do to you, for this sums up the Law and the Prophets. "Enter through the narrow gate. For wide is the gate and broad is the road that leads to destruction, and many enter through it. But small is the gate and narrow the road that leads to life, and only a few find it" (Matt. 7:12–14).

As far as Amanda was concerned, her conscience was clear. She knew God wasn't displeased with her. She knew that the Lord was in fact very proud of her because she walked with Him in front of her husband. She demonstrated God to him for years before he died. Amanda had changed a lot, and she was an entirely different person from the person she was in high school when she met Nathanial. That Amanda was dead and gone, and the new Amanda was alive and well and had been for quite some time.

Amanda had never been more alive in her life. As Nathanial's life ended, hers was just beginning to blossom. God wasn't done with her life or her story. She never imagined that her life would be lived out without him. She didn't foresee that he would be removed from her in 2026 just as quickly as he had emerged in her life in 2015. And Amanda wouldn't be witnessed wearing black for years, moping around, and mourning the past. She would be witnessed walking confidently and forward into her future, because her years of crying were behind her, and the best days were yet to come.

Amanda was going to dress and perform like a respectful Christian woman, even after Nathanial was gone and no longer monitoring her attire. She wanted to please God, and one thing was for sure, she definitely didn't want to draw the attention of men like Nathanial into her life. Her whoredom clothes were what got her into this situation to begin with. He liked her when she dressed like that. He just didn't want anyone else to like it because it threatened his ego and his place as her possessor.

Jesus said that the Saints will be dressed in white. He tells us that He removes our sin and makes us as white as snow. In a world where people wear filthy rags, Amanda was thankful to be wearing a robe of luxury and honor. She was thankful that her God wanted to clothe her and help her to be loved and treated with respect, and He didn't have an alternative motive. Jesus isn't threated by a person's choices to dress immodestly. Jesus had always accepted Amanda, but He wasn't going to allow her to stay that way because He loved her.

You turned my wailing into dancing; you removed my sackcloth and clothed me with joy, that my heart may sing your praises and not be silent. LORD my God, I will praise you forever. For the director of music. . . . In you, LORD, I have taken refuge; let me never be put to shame; deliver me in your righteousness. Turn your ear to me, come quickly to my rescue; be my rock of refuge, a strong fortress to save me. Since you are my rock and my fortress, for the sake of your name lead and guide me. Keep me free from the trap that is set for me, for you are my refuge. Into your hands I commit my spirit; deliver me, LORD, my faithful God.

I hate those who cling to worthless idols; as for me, I trust in the LORD. I will be glad and rejoice in your love, for you saw my affliction and knew the anguish of my soul. You have not given me into the hands of the enemy but have set my feet in a spacious place. Be merciful to me, LORD, for I am in distress; my eyes grow weak with sorrow, my soul and body with grief. My life is consumed by anguish and my years by groaning; my strength fails because of my affliction, and my bones grow weak. Because of all my enemies, I am the utter contempt of my neighbors and an object of dread to my closest friends—those who see me on the street flee from me. I am forgotten as though I were dead; I have become like broken pottery. For I hear many whispering, "Terror on every side!" They conspire against me and plot to take my life.

But I trust in you, LORD; I say, "You are my God." My times are in your hands; deliver me from the hands of my enemies, from those who pursue me. Let your face shine on your servant; save me in your unfailing love. Let me not be put to shame, LORD, for I have cried out to you; but let the wicked be put to shame and be silent in the realm of the dead. Let their lying lips be silenced, for with pride and contempt they speak arrogantly against the righteous.

How abundant are the good things that you have stored up for those who fear you, that you bestow in the sight of all, on those who take refuge in you. In the shelter of your presence you hide them from all human intrigues; you keep them safe in your dwelling from accusing tongues. Praise be to the LORD, for he showed me the wonders of his love when I was in a city under siege. In my alarm I said, "I am cut off from your sight!" Yet you heard my cry for mercy when I called to you for help. Love the LORD, all his faithful people! The LORD preserves those who are true to him, but the proud he pays back in full. Be strong and take heart, all you who hope in the LORD. . . . Blessed is the one whose transgressions are forgiven, whose sins are covered. Blessed is the one whose sin the LORD does not count against them and in whose spirit is no deceit. When I kept silent, my bones wasted away through my groaning all day long. For day and night your hand was heavy on me; my strength was sapped as in the heat of summer.

Then I acknowledged my sin to you and did not cover up my iniquity. I said, "I will confess my transgressions to the LORD." And you forgave the guilt of my sin. Therefore let all the faithful pray to you while you may be found; surely the rising of the mighty waters will not reach them. You are my hiding place; you will protect me from trouble and surround me with songs of deliverance (Ps. 30:11–Ps. 32:7).

{ 11 }

Forever Family

The last Christmas that Nathanial and Amanda shared together wasn't a good one. Nathanial didn't want to have anyone over. He didn't want to do Christmas with anyone outside of his house. Nathanial wanted Amanda to feel bad that her parents and grandmother wanted to see her and the children. "I hate these people and can't wait for them all to be dead," he would say. "I am not going to go over to their house. I am not going to be a part of anything that they are doing," he had made clear throughout the years.

When the two first started dating, Nathanial went over to her parents' house for the holidays. He would visit her grandparents with her. He pretended that he was okay with her family's involvement in her life, at least for a little while. The gradual poisoning of the characters and intents of Amanda's family was a scheme of isolation. It was a way of controlling and owning Amanda and her children. Nathanial's family was terrible. He didn't come from a good home. Meanwhile, Amanda's family had always treated him well and welcomed him in like a son.

"They are not my family. That is your family," he began to say a few years in. "If you want to see them, do it when I am not around. I don't have time for that." For a little while, Amanda did try to manage seeing her family and still making time for Nathanial. She didn't want to hurt him and make him feel bad that he didn't have a good relationship with his family. At the same time, it didn't seem right that they couldn't have anything to do with her family because he didn't have anything to do with his.

"If you are going to let your mom see the kids, why don't you let mine see them?" he would ask. But Nathanial already knew the answer to that pointed question. His mom didn't see the children because she didn't want to, and she wasn't a safe person either. His mom didn't come to their wedding, she didn't come to the baby shower, and she rarely showed up for any Christmas event, Thanksgiving, or other family party they tried to host. His mom was constantly hiding in her bedroom, ignoring phone calls and texts, and coming and going out of their lives, only talking to them a few days out of the year.

She also had mental problems. She had even been locked up in a mental institution for a few years because she was a danger to herself and to others. And his dad, who raised him, but was really his stepdad, constantly minimized his mom's problems and used prescription pills inappropriately so he could cope with the chaos at their house. "Your mom put bleach into our son's sippy cup and gave it to him to drink, Nathanial. Don't you remember that?" Amanda asked him. "And besides, she doesn't want to come around. She doesn't even talk to you! I am not keeping them from her. She is keeping herself from them."

Nathanial knew that. He knew the truth about his mom. He only said he wanted her to be involved because he didn't want Amanda to see her mom or dad. "I hate my mom. She is dead to me. She has been dead to me since I was a teenager. My kids won't ever know her. She is a b**** and she is insane. After I saw her crawling around on the floor in the mental institution, I will never look at her the same again. She is a liar," he would say when they were alone and it wasn't time for a family get-together with Amanda's family.

The truth was, he didn't want to see his mom, dad, or siblings. He didn't want to be a part of their lives. He wanted to be alone, but he also didn't want Amanda to have anyone because he didn't. Over the years it got more and more intense. If Amanda tried to see her parents, he would start making jokes about her. "You are just a mommy's girl (or a daddy's girl). You have been spending too much time doing things that you shouldn't be doing, and you are doing a bad job taking care of things at home. Why am I working and you're playing all the time?" he would say.

Amanda was definitely not playing. In fact, she only saw her parents on rare occasions, usually for an hour or two to get lunch, or at the holidays. But she didn't want to hear her husband's condemning remarks. She didn't want to deal with any turmoil. It was way easier to just appease him and stay home. It was way easier to just tell her parents no and handle the things she needed to handle at home. Nathanial was right. She had a lot to do at home. She didn't have time for much else anyway because he didn't help her at all at home. He made her do everything.

Nathaniel would sit on his computer playing video games and talking to his friends while Amanda ran around the house, making dinner, changing diapers, and trying to help her children finish their schoolwork. She would be doing laundry, making a grocery list on her phone, and trying to make sure the bills were paid all at the same time. From sunup until sundown most days Amanda was busy. She had no time to rest, but Nathanial had plenty.

"HAHAHA dude! Let's get this motherf*****! God damn!" he would be screaming from the living room. All the while, Amanda was struggling, overwhelmed, and trying to do the things that needed to be done. After dinner it was common for Nathanial to sit on the couch or get back on his computer while she did all the cleanup, washing dishes, sweeping the floor, and trying to get the children ready for their baths. He didn't notice. He didn't care, and if she dared ask him for a little help he would yell, "I am not helping you. I have worked all day. This is YOUR job, not mine."

On the weekends, even when Nathanial wasn't working, he would stay up all night getting drunk and talking to his friends on his games, and then he would sleep in until eleven or twelve o'clock in the afternoon of the following day. He didn't get up, he didn't help Amanda, and he never let her sleep in or have a day off. Seven days a week Amanda worked and handled everything. And on the rare occasions that Nathanial would chip in a little bit by sweeping the floor or carrying his dishes to the sink, he would make sure everyone knew he wasn't happy with helping.

"Why am I even doing this anyway? This is not my job," he would say. Nathanial wanted Amanda to know that her job was to please him. Her job was to make sure he had to do as little as possible, and if she failed at this job, or if she tried to take any time off, even for a lunch date with her parents or for a holiday, he was going to make sure she heard about it. He was going to guilt-trip her and make her think she was a bad wife, homemaker, and mother. "You have it so easy! What is wrong with you? Why do you need time off? You don't do anything," he proclaimed.

Amanda knew his words weren't true. She did things . . . constantly. She never had time off. She worked far more hours than he ever did. She took care of everything, except for the financial realm, and even in that realm she helped him so much. She would load his truck and trailer, help him organize his shop, advertise, go pick up supplies, and do anything else he asked her to do. She was at his beck and call. She was his employee, at home, at his business, and at any other time. The relationship wasn't a relationship of teamwork and common love and respect. It was a boss and employee situation, and she had a very demanding and cruel boss.

Nathanial was far nicer to his actual employees, who were men. He would give them extra time off and extra pay, and he would permit them to do whatever they wanted to do at work. Some of his employees would smoke weed on the job, and this was totally fine with him as long as they were still working. Amanda noticed that things were unfair. She noticed that she was being slighted and treated in a way that was less than, but what was she going to do? After all, she wanted to stay home with her children, so she decided to just grin and bear it.

The Bible addresses these kinds of situations because God knew that slavery and unfair relationships would be formed on the earth. God was not endorsing or advocating for slavery, or for situations that arise similar to slavery, but He was addressing the situation because the situation would present itself. Amanda did what Jesus said. She worked hard, day after day as her husband's slave, and she did her best not to complain because she knew God was watching her. She knew that Jesus was going to reward her for what she had done.

Obey them not only to win their favor when their eye is on you, but as slaves of Christ, doing the will of God from your heart. Serve wholeheartedly, as if you were serving the Lord, not people, because you know that the Lord will reward each one for whatever good they do, whether they are slave or free. And masters, treat your slaves in the same way. Do not threaten them, since you know that he who is both their Master and yours is in heaven, and there is no favoritism with him (Eph. 6:6–9).

Amanda didn't think her parents understood. She was sure that they were hurt by her actions, but she didn't feel like she had a choice. She didn't want to upset her "master" because if she did, he would be cruel to her and maybe even the children. She wanted peace to remain in the house, so she tried to work hard and take no time off because this is what he expected her to do. Nathanial had no clue that his behavior toward Amanda was being recorded by God. If he did, he likely wouldn't have treated her with such harsh treatment and high standards. He didn't meet these standards himself—a truth he would be judged for now.

Matthew 7:2 explains, *"For in the same way you judge others, you will be judged, and with the measure you use, it will be measured to you."* If Nathanial had known that he was going to be judged for his treatment of Amanda, maybe he would have worked with her and helped her. Maybe he would have treated her with more love and kindness. He could have easily allowed her to sleep in sometime. He could have helped with the cooking, cleaning, and housekeeping, but he didn't because he wanted to play and be served like the king he thought he was. Matthew 23:12 states, *"For those who exalt themselves will be humbled, and those who humble themselves will be exalted."*

Oftentimes, when people are treating others in malicious and cruel ways, they assume they will get away with it. Throughout history, men have been unkind to women, and some women unkind to their children. Masters of slaves have treated their slaves with contempt, and bosses have treated employees with disrespect. Kings and other rulers have killed people, used people, and been incredibly inhumane toward the lives of others, but the truth is, these people won't get away with what they have done. God is measuring. And He is watching every person who has judged others' actions with a high standard, a standard they themselves would never be able to attain.

This life isn't all that there is. There is a kingdom that lies beyond us. There is a King who knows every word, every action, and every failure. But the good news is that this King also knows every good word, work, action, and success. God sees when we are working diligently, even when our work isn't respected by those we work for. God sees when we are being treated unfairly, unkindly, and with contempt and disrespect, and God will make sure people get justice. He will make sure they are paid back for what they have done, both good and bad.

Romans 12:19 teaches, *"Do not take revenge, my dear friends, but leave room for God's wrath, for it is written: 'It is mine to avenge; I will repay,' says the Lord."* Amanda knew God was going to repay Nathanial for what he had done, and really, she felt sorry for him because he wasn't going to be repaid well. He was not going to get what he thought he deserved: a crown, a place of honor, a castle, or a throne. He was going to get a lowly place, a place of suffering, a place of humility, because he hadn't lived his life in accordance with God's standards, but he had expected his wife to do far more than he ever could have.

Sometimes strength comes through doing hard things, and what Nathanial didn't know at the time was that he was building Amanda's resilience through his absence. Amanda was already a single mom, aside from the financial provision. She did everything for her children. She took them to their classes, she helped with their schoolwork, and she cooked, shopped, and cleaned. She gave them baths and took them to all of their appointments. And her life was going to be far easier now, far more than it was before, because she would be freed up from the time she had been spending pampering him.

Amanda wouldn't have to pick up his dirty clothes off the floor and wash them. She wouldn't have to spend her Saturday morning cleaning up the kitchen from his partying the night before. Amanda wasn't going to have to help her husband run his business, and she wasn't going to have to listen to him gripe and complain about his day, sitting patiently at the kitchen table, knowing she had so many things she needed to do for the house and children. The truth was, Amanda was being freed through Nathanial's death. Would she have to make money? Of course, but she was going to have far more time than she had before because she wasn't going to be serving him.

Amanda was already operating like a single mother, but on top of that role, she was also operating as a man's slave, and this was far harder than being a single mom. When Nathanial wanted the family to ride with him to get his work materials, and when he wanted them to help him to finish a job, she always did it, even when it took her away from her other work. But each and every time she helped him, she got further behind in what she needed to do, and he never returned the favor. He just watched her struggle and take on more and more, piling more onto her back and then criticizing her for weakness.

When someone does resistance training, they will become stronger through muscle fatigue and pain. The pain and the hardship it takes to do the hard work and push yourself beyond what you imagined you could do ultimately brings a new level of strength. Nathanial thought he was breaking Amanda down. He thought he was tearing her apart, keeping her working sunup to sundown with no break, but what he was really doing was giving her resilience and strength. He was giving her a toughness that no one could ever take away from her.

Romans 13:7 says, *"Give to everyone what you owe them: If you owe taxes, pay taxes; if revenue, then revenue; if respect, then respect; if honor, then honor."* The Scriptures affirm that people deserve to be paid for what they have done, and Jesus was always clocking her hours. Month after month, day after day, and year after year, He saw that she was being stolen from and not properly compensated or assisted. Amanda knew Jesus had been watching her pain and her work, and He was going to repay her for what she had done. Money was not going to be a problem for her or her children. She had been working unpaid for years, so payday was on the way.

Trouble pursues the sinner, but the righteous are rewarded with good things. A good person leaves an inheritance for their children's children, but a sinner's wealth is stored up for the righteous. An unplowed field produces food for the poor, but injustice sweeps it away. (Prov. 13:21–23)

Financial prosperity and blessing are a part of the covenant rights of God's children. Sometimes, evil people try to steal the blessings and the benefits of God's covenant with his children. Men like Laban thought he was harming Jacob and keeping Jacob from succeeding in life. He thought that his business would continue to thrive and prosper and that he could continue mistreating Jacob indefinitely. But God saw all that was done to Jacob. He saw the hard work, the respect, and the diligent hand that Jacob had, just like he saw the stealing, the lying, and the unpaid wages that were held back from Jacob.

"Give me my wives and children, for whom I have served you, and I will be on my way. You know how much work I've done for you." . . . Jacob said to him, "You know how I have worked for you and how your livestock has fared under my care. . . . And my honesty will testify for me in the future, when-

ever you check on the wages you have paid me. Any goat in my possession that is not speckled or spotted, or any lamb that is not dark-colored, will be considered stolen" (Genesis 30:26, 29, 33).

God was blessing Laban's business and life because of Jacob. Laban wouldn't have had what he had if Jacob had not been working for him. People within Laban's household and family, including Laban himself, felt that Jacob was stealing from them and that he was taking from them, but the truth was that Laban was the thief. He was the one who had been exploiting Jacob, stealing his wages, and not giving him the honor and the respect that he deserved as a faithful man and employee.

Jacob heard that Laban's sons were saying, "Jacob has taken everything our father owned and has gained all this wealth from what belonged to our father." And Jacob noticed that Laban's attitude toward him was not what it had been. Then the Lord said to Jacob, "Go back to the land of your fathers and to your relatives, and I will be with you" (Gen. 31:1–3).

God wanted people to know and to recognize that Jacob's wealth was not due to his association with Laban. He wanted to bless Jacob far beyond what he had been blessed before, and this was proof that Jacob was blessed, not Laban. As Jacob separated himself from Laban in business, he did nothing but prosper all the more. Laban was holding Jacob back, and he wasn't aiding in his business endeavors either. A wise man can easily discern that.

Amanda was in awe of God and His word as she resonated these Biblical truths within her heart. "God is going to bless me more than I have ever been blessed before. He is going to fulfill His covenant in my life. He is going to continue to multiply all that I have," she realized. "Being separated from Nathanial isn't a curse. It is a blessing. God was helping me even when I was associated with a bad man. He was blessing his business and his endeavors on my behalf."

The only reason Amanda and Nathanial hadn't failed and tanked in all their financial endeavors was that God was helping him because of her. Nathanial was not prospering because he was worthy, hardworking, or exceptionally intelligent. He wasn't any of those things. Nathanial was prospering because God's hand was on his wife, and his wife was associated with him for a season. Genesis 31:7, 9 says, *"Yet your father has cheated me by changing my wages ten times. However, God has not allowed him to harm me. . . . So God has taken away your father's livestock and has given them to me."*

There are times when a forever family is the goal. Laban didn't want Jacob to leave and separate himself from him. He didn't want Jacob to take what was rightfully his because he wanted to profit financially from Jacob's exploitation. Jacob was only a part of Laban's life and finances for a season, but his wealth and blessings were eternal. His future of financial prosperity and success was assured, not because of Laban, but because of God.

But Laban said to him, "If I have found favor in your eyes, please stay. I have learned by divination that the Lord has blessed me because of you." He added, "Name your wages, and I will pay them." Jacob said to him, "You know how I have worked for you and how your livestock has fared under my care. The little you had before I came has increased greatly, and the Lord has blessed you wherever I have been. But now, when may I do something for my own household?" (Gen. 30: 27–30).

Jacob knew it was time to rest as a member of the household of God. God's family was his forever family. Jacob didn't belong to the house of a man who served foreign gods. He didn't have Laban's name. He was only in Laban's life for a little while because he had allowed fear to drive him into a house he didn't belong in. A house with a man who didn't serve his gods or deserve his labor. But God was faithful to Jacob through it all. He continued to help him and multiply him, even throughout his struggle, but there was a time to end the relationship with a foreign family, a foreign man who didn't believe in the God he believed in.

Being in business or an intimate relationship with corrupt people isn't a virtue. Thieves are not good people to work for or to be married to. God made a promise to Jacob, and He was making a promise to Amanda. "Leave this place and go back to the country of your family. Get away from the man who has served foreign gods. And as you go, I will be with you. I will multiply you and bless your work and your hand. I will give you far more than you have had before."

Genesis 30:43 tells us, *"In this way the man grew exceedingly prosperous and came to own large flocks, and female and male servants, and camels and donkeys."* If Laban or Nathanial had known that their prosperity was linked to the people they were cheating and mistreating, I am sure they would have tried a little bit harder to appease and care for the people God had allowed into their lives. But ungodly people have to learn the hard way. Things aren't always what they seem, and before you know it your season of prosperity will be cut off if you aren't a child of God.

{ 12 }

Preparation

There was a time between Jacob's departure from Laban and God's command for separation. God told Jacob he was going to be leaving Laban and taking his wives and children to a new destination, but God gave Jacob a heads-up, so he could properly prepare himself for the new life God was forming for him. In the in-between season, Jacob had work to do to prepare himself, and God gave Jacob clear instructions, a plan and a goal, so when the time of departure came, he was not going to struggle or be negatively impacted in his business or life.

The angel of God said to me in the dream, "Jacob." I answered, "Here I am." And he said, "Look up and see that all the male goats mating with the flock are streaked, speckled or spotted, for I have seen all that Laban has been doing to you. I am the God of Bethel, where you anointed a pillar and where you made a vow to me. Now leave this land at once and go back to your native land" (Gen. 31:11–13).

The angel told Jacob to depart "at once," but he also told Jacob to do something that was going to take time. For the goats to mate, give birth, and be given to Jacob as his share, the goats would have needed at least two to three months. God wanted Jacob to know that he was to go, and quickly, but the going needed to be calculated. There needed to be a plan, a controlled goal and a method of operation, so that things went smoothly for Jacob and his family.

Jesus also told the disciples ahead of time that He was going to be going soon, and He also gave them time to prepare for His departure. He told them what was going to happen, and then in a little while, after a time of preparation, the departure occurred. Jesus also assured His disciples, as God did for Jacob, of their positive future. He wanted them to know that things were going to be okay, even if it seemed like a death or separation had occurred.

Jesus went on to say, "In a little while you will see me no more, and then after a little while you will see me." At this, some of his disciples said to one another, "What does he mean by saying, 'In a little while you will see me no more, and then after a little while you will see me,' and 'Because I am going to the Father'?" They kept asking, "What does he mean by 'a little while'? We don't understand what he is saying."

Jesus saw that they wanted to ask him about this, so he said to them, "Are you asking one another what I meant when I said, 'In a little while you will see me no more, and then after a little while you will see me'? Very truly I tell you, you will weep and mourn while the world rejoices. You will grieve, but your grief will turn to joy (John 16:16–20).

At the beginning of the year before the death of Amanda's husband, God told her to go back to school and get her license. She needed to do professional counseling. If she was going to open up her own practice and work as a counselor, she needed four more courses. For years, Amanda thought she was going to stay home and raise her children. She didn't think she needed to pursue the classes and take steps to secure her license because she had no intention of leaving her current occupation at home.

God had told Amanda to homeschool her children. He had told her that she was going to be a mother who was responsible for them, so why would He tell her to go back to school now? She thought to herself, *God, are you the one telling me to go back to school? Why would that be?* That is when the Lord told her the news about her husband: "Amanda, your husband is going to die. You are going to become a widow, and you are going to need a way to continue doing the things I have called you to do."

To be honest, it took a few days for Amanda to process what God had said to her. Like Gideon, Amanda felt unprepared. She didn't know how to make money and provide for herself, much less for her entire household. She had never been fully independent and alone. She had never worked and sustained herself, much less others, financially. "God, I need you to tell me for sure that this is true. I need you to confirm this. This doesn't make sense," she prayed.

But God continued to assure her and tell her the same message. The message wasn't changing. "You are going to need to build up your ministry this year. You are going to need to get those classes and begin working toward your licensure. You need to do this right now, but don't worry because you have a little time before the departure will occur," the Holy Spirit assured her. "Okay, God. If this is what you want me to do, I will trust you and do it, even though I am not sure how this will work out," she responded.

Amanda knew that her husband couldn't find out she was going back to school. She knew that he wouldn't help pay for it, and she knew that he wasn't going to be happy about it either. Nathanial always made fun of Amanda's education, telling her that her education was pointless and that she should have never gone and gotten a master's degree to begin with. "You are a stay-at-home mom, Amanda. Why did you need to go and get a degree? What was the point? You made such a dumb decision that has costed us thousands of dollars," he would say.

Maybe he is right, Amanda began to think. *Maybe I did make a mistake going to college, but I know God was with me then. I know He made a way for me and helped me. So if I shouldn't have gone to college, then why did God walk with me through it? Why did He help me and support me during it? There must be a reason I went to school. God must want to use it somehow, someway,* she would reason within herself.

She had thought maybe one day, when her children were grown, or maybe during her ministry, that she would continue. She even thought at one point, *Or maybe I shouldn't have gone to school at all.*

This was something Amanda said a few times to others, even on her Facebook, because she thought she had made a mistake pursuing her education. Some of her friends would comment on her post and say things like, "It will help you one day. An education is never a bad thing." Amanda wasn't so sure. She reasoned, *Yeah, but I am not going to need it. I am only a stay-at-home mom.*

"Education means nothing. Hahaha! I make way more money than you would ever make, and I don't even have the education you have," Nathanial would say. "I am smarter than you. I make more money than you. You don't even know how to do basic things. What good is an education when you can't even cook properly?" He would complain, "I am so tired of eating this same menu anyway. Can't this restaurant change its s***** menu?"

These words hurt Amanda, but she didn't know what to say. She was doing her best. She was trying to cook healthy meals for her family. She wanted to help financially, too, but God had told her to stay home, just like He had told her to get her degree. She was trying to do what God said. So why didn't Nathanial understand? Why didn't he care about the things she did for him?

For many years Amanda would have to make more than one dish or meal. She would make one for her and the children that was healthy, and then she would make one for him that had what he liked. On one occasion he asked her, "Why didn't you make me biscuits?" To which she responded, "Um, well, I didn't think we needed any. We have lima beans, corn, mac and cheese, and steak." Nathanial retorted, "Are you dumb? Who makes a steak dinner without biscuits? And I don't like this mac and cheese anyway. I want my kind of mac and cheese."

Amanda prepared, and she prepared a lot. She would buy his and her groceries at the store, and then she would spend hours preparing the food before her family could eat. Making sure Nathanial had the food he wanted was a challenging task because sometimes he would be thankful and other times enraged by the same effort she put in.

The time she spent preparing and anticipating his reaction to her cooking was immense. In fact, she had to make her entire day around their dinner, because if she didn't have dinner on the table when he was ready to eat, she would pay for it.

"I need three hours to set the table, get the food ready, and make sure the food is hot for when he gets here sometime between five and six o'clock," she would say. But after a while, Amanda realized she had gotten good at having dinner ready when he arrived home. Except of course on the nights that she would spend hours preparing their food, and he would come in and say, "I am not eating with y'all tonight. I am going to be drinking and turning up tonight. So I am going to wait to eat until later."

"Well, we have waited to eat, and I was hoping we could all eat together as a family tonight. I have been working on this all day," Amanda would remind him. "Don't you want to eat with us? Can't you not drink tonight or drink after you eat?" "No. I already told you I am not eating with you tonight. What the hell is wrong with you? Why are you trying to control when I eat? Let a man do what he wants to do," Nathanial said. "Okay. Whatever," Amanda responded. "I guess me and the kids will just eat by ourselves then, and I'll put your plate in the microwave."

Amanda was never quite sure when Nathanial was going to come in, starving and demanding his dinner, or when he was going to come in and tell her to leave him the f*** alone and to stop pestering him to eat with her and the children. But she did her very best to ensure he had dinner and so did the children because she didn't want to set off the mine explosion and have him tell her that she was doing a s***** job for not having his food prepared for him. "I work all damn day and come home and you can't even have biscuits. No one gives a f*** about me. You don't love me," he would tell her.

One thing was for sure, if Amanda and her children had gone to the pool or the library, she needed to be home in time to make the family's dinner, even if she'd later find that Nathanial wasn't going to eat it right then. Her entire day often revolved around ensuring the food was going to meet his standards and expectations. Working around him and his schedule and requirements for the evening was often very inconvenient.

"Kids, we are going to have to leave the playground," Amanda would call out. "Aww, but mom, we just got here. Can't we stay a few more minutes?" She would shake her head and say, "No, we can't, y'all. I have got to get home and make sure I have time to get dinner ready." "Okay, mom," they would say. Amanda hated the life she had created for her children. She hated that they couldn't stay and play or have a good time because their dad would be mad if they weren't in the house, doing what he said for them to do, especially when he got home from work.

The ingredients she used were also highly monitored. "Why do you always buy all this organic bulls***? This costs too much money. Don't buy this s*** again. I don't want you to buy this. You are an idiot to be paying more for grass-fed beef. This is just fine. Buy the cheaper s***. Don't spend all of my money. All you and these kids do is waste my money. All you do is eat eat eat. These kids shouldn't even be eating steak. Steak is a luxury. It is an expensive food. They don't need f****** steak, Amanda."

"Nathanial, they are kids. They need to eat healthy food," she would remind him. "They can just have mine. No worries. I would rather them eat steak, and I will eat something else." "Well, that is why they think they deserve it. That is their problem. You are spoiling them, Amanda. You are making them into brats who think they are entitled to whatever the hell they want. My kids aren't going to be raised how you were raised. They aren't going to think that they are going to have whatever they want," he yelled.

Amanda looked over at her children. She saw their innocence, their beauty, and their sweetness. She loved them so much, and she hated that their dad would talk about them like they were dogs. "I hope they know how much You love them, God. I hope they know how much I love them. God, please help us. Please help them, Lord," she would pray. Even when it seemed like nothing changed, and when everything looked exactly the same, Amanda knew that God was hearing her prayers. She knew that her prayers were preparation for their future. They were heard, registered, and received in Heaven, and God was going to do something for her, for them.

Sometimes when we are in the gap or the in-between between where we are going and where we currently are it doesn't look like anything has happened on the outside. There are times when you have to do another workout, cook another healthy meal, say another prayer, and prepare yourself for your future, even when it doesn't seem like anything that you are doing is working. When Jesus cursed the fig tree, the tree withered up and died at its roots, but the change wasn't immediately evident to everyone else. It wasn't magic, and it didn't happen without a period of time or an in-between.

The next day as they were leaving Bethany, Jesus was hungry. Seeing in the distance a fig tree in leaf, he went to find out if it had any fruit. When he reached it, he found nothing but leaves, because it was not the season for figs. Then he said to the tree, "May no one ever eat fruit from you again." And his disciples heard him say it.

On reaching Jerusalem, Jesus entered the temple courts and began driving out those who were buying and selling there. He overturned the tables of the money changers and the benches of those selling doves, and would not allow anyone to carry merchandise through the temple courts. And as he taught them, he said, "Is it not written: 'My house will be called a house of prayer for all nations'? But you have made it 'a den of robbers.'" The chief priests and the teachers of the law heard this and began looking for a way to kill him, for they feared him, because the whole crowd was amazed at his teaching.

When evening came, Jesus and his disciples went out of the city. In the morning, as they went along, they saw the fig tree withered from the roots. Peter remembered and said to Jesus, "Rabbi, look! The fig tree you cursed has withered!" "Have faith in God," Jesus answered. "Truly I tell you, if anyone says to this mountain, 'Go, throw yourself into the sea,' and does not doubt in their heart but believes that what they say will happen, it will be done for them. Therefore I tell you, whatever you ask for in prayer, believe that you have received it, and it will be yours'" (Mark 11:12–24).

Jesus was hungry and ready to eat, and the tree's refusal to have His food ready when He wanted it was what caused Him to curse it. Jesus didn't like that a tree that had been created to produce fruit wasn't producing it. God does want food to be ready and prepared on time, but this story wasn't only talking about dinner. It was talking about the people of the world who should be ready to serve God and to have fruit in their lives, but they don't because they have been lazy, unconcerned, and unfruitful in their faith and in their relationships with others and with God.

People like Nathanial, who demand that other people serve them and bow down to them, think that they are going to get away with their deeds. They think that the world revolves around them, but the truth is, the world revolves around Jesus Christ. This world was created by God, and He is the One who determines which fruit is acceptable and which isn't. People who think they are something will soon discover that their unfruitfulness in Christ will be their demise.

A decision to ignore Jesus and not plan for His arrival will prove problematic when they are faced with the reality of His coming. Jesus has the ability to say: Be cursed, be removed, be thrown into the sea, and it comes to pass. He can tell people that your life is no more, and only a fool wouldn't prepare food for a King. We see this contrast in the lives of Abigail and her husband Nabal. Abigail prepared food for David. She recognized his coming and took the necessary precautions to prepare. Nabal didn't, and it cost him his life.

A certain man in Maon, who had property there at Carmel, was very wealthy. He had a thousand goats and three thousand sheep, which he was shearing in Carmel. His name was Nabal and his wife's name was Abigail. She was an intelligent and beautiful woman, but her husband was surly and mean in his dealings—he was a Calebite.

While David was in the wilderness, he heard that Nabal was shearing sheep. So he sent ten young men and said to them, "Go up to Nabal at Carmel and greet him in my name. Say to him: 'Long life to you! Good health to you and your household! And good health to all that is yours! "'Now I hear that it is sheep-shearing time. When your shepherds were with us, we did not mistreat them, and the whole time they were at Carmel nothing of theirs was missing. Ask your own servants and they will tell you. Therefore be favorable toward my men, since we come at a festive time. Please give your servants and your son David whatever you can find for them.'"

When David's men arrived, they gave Nabal this message in David's name. Then they waited. Nabal answered David's servants, "Who is this David? Who is this son of Jesse? Many servants are breaking away from their masters these days. Why should I take my bread and water, and the meat I have slaughtered for my shearers, and give it to men coming from who knows where?" David's men turned around and went back. When they arrived, they reported every word.

David said to his men, "Each of you strap on your sword!" So they did, and David strapped his on as well. About four hundred men went up with David, while two hundred stayed with the supplies. One of the servants told Abigail, Nabal's wife, "David sent messengers from the wilderness to give our master his greetings, but he hurled insults at them. Yet these men were very good to us. They did not mistreat us, and the whole time we were out in the fields near them nothing was missing. Night and day they were a wall around us the whole time we were herding our sheep near them. Now think it over and see what you can do, because disaster is hanging over our master and his whole household. He is such a wicked man that no one can talk to him."

Abigail acted quickly. She took two hundred loaves of bread, two skins of wine, five dressed sheep, five seahs of roasted grain, a hundred cakes of raisins and two hundred cakes of pressed figs, and loaded them on donkeys. Then she told her servants, "Go on ahead; I'll follow you." But she did not tell her husband Nabal. As she came riding her donkey into a mountain ravine, there were David and his men descending toward her, and she met them. David had just said, "It's been useless—all my watching over this fellow's property in the wilderness so that nothing of his was missing. He has paid me back evil for good. May God deal with David, be it ever so severely, if by morning I leave alive one male of all who belong to him!"

When Abigail saw David, she quickly got off her donkey and bowed down before David with her face to the ground. She fell at his feet and said: "Pardon your servant, my lord, and let me speak to you; hear what your servant has to say. Please pay no attention, my lord, to that wicked man Nabal. He is just like his name—his name means Fool, and folly goes with him. And as for me, your servant, I did not see the men my lord sent. And now, my lord, as surely as the LORD your God lives and as you live, since the LORD has kept you from bloodshed and from avenging yourself with your own hands, may your enemies and all who are intent on harming my lord be like Nabal. And let this gift, which your servant has brought to my lord, be given to the men who follow you.

"Please forgive your servant's presumption. The LORD your God will certainly make a lasting dynasty for my lord, because you fight the LORD's battles, and no wrongdoing will be found in you as long as you live. Even though someone is pursuing you to take your life, the life of my lord will be bound securely in the bundle of the living by the LORD your God, but the lives of your enemies he will hurl away as from the pocket of a sling. When the LORD has fulfilled for my lord every good thing he promised concerning him and has appointed him ruler over Israel, my lord will not have on his conscience the staggering burden of needless bloodshed or of having avenged himself. And when the LORD your God has brought my lord success, remember your servant."

David said to Abigail, "Praise be to the LORD, the God of Israel, who has sent you today to meet me. May you be blessed for your good judgment and for keeping me from bloodshed this day and from avenging myself with my own hands. Otherwise, as surely as the LORD, the God of Israel, lives, who has kept me from harming you, if you had not come quickly to meet me, not one male belonging to Nabal would have been left alive by daybreak" (1 Sam. 25: 2–34).

You see, if it had been up to Nabal, or to men like Nathanial, their entire household would have been destroyed. The children, the wife, the husband, and all that they had would have been erased, cursed, and removed because of the foolishness of their hearts and minds. Abigail knew she needed to make preparations. She knew she needed to bow down to a man who was powerful, holy, and anointed. She gave honor and respect to the right person, and this is a picture of our relationship with Christ.

People who don't prepare for Jesus or find value in His name or His mission won't honor him. They won't prepare for Him, and they won't serve Him out of honor and respect. But these kinds of men will be wiped from the face of the earth. Their names will be remembered, but only with the association of the title of fool. But women like Abigail, women of character, love, and admiration toward God and His kingdom, will go down in history as women of honor. They will live, and their lives will demonstrate the covenant between God and His people. A love story—the best love story to ever be written.

Then David accepted from her hand what she had brought him and said, "Go home in peace. I have heard your words and granted your request. When Abigail went to Nabal, he was in the house holding a banquet like that of a king. He was in high spirits and very drunk. So she told him nothing at all until daybreak. Then in the morning, when Nabal was sober, his wife told him all these things, and his heart failed him and he became like a stone. About ten days later, the LORD struck Nabal and he died (1 Sam. 25:35–38).

Evil men don't need to be dealt with by the sword. They don't need to be taken out by force by those around them. Their evil deeds will chase them down. Their failure to honor God will destroy them. God is in control. He is the One who says, "Be prepared or be cursed and dried up at the root." He is the One who says, "No one will ever eat from you again." Money can't save you. Pride can't save you. Human strength and wisdom can't save you. These things have never saved anyone. There is only One way to salvation.

There is only one door that leads to life. His name is Jesus Christ, and He is the Son of God.

Then I saw "a new heaven and a new earth," for the first heaven and the first earth had passed away, and there was no longer any sea. I saw the Holy City, the new Jerusalem, coming down out of heaven from God, prepared as a bride beautifully dressed for her husband. And I heard a loud voice from the throne saying, "Look! God's dwelling place is now among the people, and he will dwell with them. They will be his people, and God himself will be with them and be their God. 'He will wipe every tear from their eyes. There will be no more death or mourning or crying or pain, for the old order of things has passed away."

He who was seated on the throne said, "I am making everything new!" Then he said, "Write this down, for these words are trustworthy and true."

He said to me: "It is done. I am the Alpha and the Omega, the Beginning and the End. To the thirsty I will give water without cost from the spring of the water of life. Those who are victorious will inherit all this, and I will be their God and they will be my children. But the cowardly, the unbelieving, the vile, the murderers, the sexually immoral, those who practice magic arts, the idolaters and all liars—they will be consigned to the fiery lake of burning sulfur. This is the second death" (Rev. 21:1–8).

Your Word or His?

Often when women, particularly those who are involved in domestic or sexual violence situations, report what has been done to them people do not believe them. This same phenomenon happens for children who have been violated or abused by people around them. The American criminal justice system often wants the abused party to prove that they are telling the truth. They want a substantial amount of evidence if what they are saying is indeed true.

Many women or children do not come forward or tell others about their abuse for this very reason, and abusers will often use this fact against their victims as well. "No one would believe you. Don't tell anyone about what I have done. This is a secret," they will say. Abusers work hard at creating images or lives that say one thing but are not genuinely that thing. Abusers are willing to go to great measures to avoid being detected. They are willing to create entire schemas and skits that lead people astray and cause them to side with an abuser over the abusee.

How people could ever justify or come up with good reasons for abuse and mistreatment, the ultimate disdain and hatred toward other humans, is beyond hard to imagine. Unfortunately there will be and always have been people who accuse the victim of wrongdoing and insinuate or openly say that these women or children who have been abused must have done something to deserve it. "Did you entice him? You must have been wearing something, or you must have said something that made him act that way," they will say.

"I know him. He would never do something like that!" deceived people will proudly assert. "She was a terrible wife and mother. What you are hearing about him isn't true. That is my son, and he is a good person," says the mother who finds herself on the news after a domestic violence incident that took the life of a woman and her children. *What is wrong with these people?* Amanda wondered as she listened to another news report about domestic homicide. *I can't believe these people are testifying against innocent victims of a crime. Why would they go on TV and say that this guy was a good person after he just killed everyone in his house?*

Absolutely crazy! Amanda thought. *But people are going to believe what they want to believe . . . I guess. Validity and truth must have nothing to do with their opinions. They must want to believe a lie.* Wait a minute. Didn't Jesus say something about this? Didn't He say that liars want to believe the lies that they believe?

The coming of the lawless one will be in accordance with how Satan works. He will use all sorts of displays of power through signs and wonders that serve the lie, and all the ways that wickedness deceives those who are perishing. They perish because they refused to love the truth and so be saved. For this reason God sends them a powerful delusion so that they will believe the lie and so that all will be condemned who have not believed the truth but have delighted in wickedness (2 Thess. 2:9–12).

The ways of God seem silly to unbelievers. The truth sounds like a bunch of gibberish, because God has given some people over to ignornace and folly, so they will believe the lies they want to believe.

Sometimes Amanda would read in the news about domestic violence cases, where a father, brother, or friend went and killed their loved one's attacker after the crime. Even though she understood why they felt like they needed to avenge the situation, she also knew that this was another spirit pretending to be good. It was a demon spirit manifesting itself as a spirit of truth and justice. Some demons do present themselves as good. Some do act like they are righteous.

2 Corinthians 11:14–15 says, *"And no wonder, for Satan himself masquerades as an angel of light. It is not surprising, then, if his servants also masquerade as servants of righteousness. Their end will be what their actions deserve."* There are times when demons lure people to do seemingly good acts that are indeed wrong. Two wrongs never will make a right, and when one of these lying devils presents itself, it will tell a person that they are right for the wrong they are doing. It will lie and say, "This is noble, good, and just. God wants you to do this." When in fact, He does not.

When someone kills another person to avenge a wrong done to someone they love, their actions are still wrong. God doesn't want us to use physical weapons and violence to kill people. He doesn't want us to try to fight our battles without the spiritual weapons He has given us. Peter, one of Jesus's disciples, although well-intentioned, tried to stand up for the truth and for Jesus when the guards were coming to take Him away to crucify Him. Peter got out his sword and chopped off a guard's ear, thinking this would please Jesus, but it wasn't what Jesus wanted Peter to do.

With that, one of Jesus' companions reached for his sword, drew it out and struck the servant of the high priest, cutting off his ear. "Put your sword back in its place," Jesus said to him, "for all who draw the sword will die by the sword. Do you think I cannot call on my Father, and he will at once put at my disposal more than twelve legions of angels? But how then would the Scriptures be fulfilled that say it must happen in this way?" (Matt. 26:51–54).

Jesus was in control of the entire situation. He could have stopped the men from taking Him in that moment. He wanted Peter to know: "Peter, I am in control. This is going to end the way God wants it to end." Don't worry, and don't try to do things in a different way than God wants them done. God has a plan. He has a way that He wants to execute justice. Don't take matters into your own hands! Sometimes people think they are helping God or doing God's will by using physical violence in a life-or-death situation, but we must know God doesn't need our help.

When we try to avenge or bring justice ourselves, we are in disobedience to God. He wants to be the One to dictate the terms and determine the fate and outcome of the person who is opposing Him or those who love Him. He wants to be the One to decide and carry out the judgment process. In gang movies or shows we often hear the boss say, "This one is mine" or "This one is personal." Their followers will step out of the way when the boss is going to take out someone who is a personal enemy or betrayer.

Like a mob boss, God wants to be the One to "do it." He wants to be the One that executes justice. When the police do their part and arrest a criminal they bring the perpetrator to the judge for sentencing. Then the judge handles the situation and does whatever needs to be done. If the police had killed the criminals before they were given the opportunity to stand before the judge, they would be in disobedience to the criminal justice system that was in place for a reason.

Amanda's stomach was in knots thinking about telling her parents the truth about her and Nathanial's marriage. She could hardly even eat. "I really hope my parents don't worry about me. I hope they understand that I am okay and that God is with me. They don't have anything to worry about. Me and the kids are okay, but I still want them to know what is happening in my life. I want them to hear it from me before anything happens and Nathanial is gone. Then they will know that God is working in my life. They will be able to testify that I told them ahead of time."

Amanda was the most concerned about her dad. She knew that her dad was a man of law, order, and justice. His entire life and career had revolved around bringing criminals into the courtroom where they could get justice. He had even written a book about his experience, titled *Bearing Witness to Evil*. Her dad had seen some bad dudes and chicks. He had locked up many people and helped many victims of crimes. But this crime was different. This crime was personal because the crimes that had been committed had been committed against his daughter.

"I need to tell my dad, but I am going to warn him about the demonic spirits that will present themselves to him as just spirits," Amanda said in prayer. "Please, God, help my dad to listen. Help him to trust You and to let You handle this. Don't let him take things into his own hands. Don't let him be deceived and go off course doing something that You don't want him to do. Give him strength, God. Give him wisdom to know that You are with me and that You are good."

"God, I trust you to handle this. I know you are going to work everything out. Just let my dad know that too. Let him know that he doesn't need to avenge me or the kids. Let him know that You want to handle this!" she prayed. Romans 12:21–13:1 says, *"Do not be overcome by evil, but overcome evil with good. Let everyone be subject to the governing authorities, for there is no authority except that which God has established. The authorities that exist have been established by God."*

"Help my dad know that he is the good guy," Amanda prayed. "He has always been the good guy, and he doesn't need to change sides now. He was the one who trusted the system. He was the one who let the system handle those who were wrong. Let him understand that he needs to do the same in this situation. Let him know that he can't change sides now. God, please don't let his emotions get the best of him. Give him the strength to control his anger. Give him power to resist the enemy's temptation to sin and handle this without you."

All throughout life people are given a choice to listen to two very different voices. Some voices sound sweet, but indeed they are not. But God's voice is always steady. It is always trustworthy, and we can trust what God says. If God says He is going to handle it, and He says that He doesn't want you to handle it, then you must trust that He knows what He is doing. That is the lesson that Jesus was trying to teach Peter.

Let them look like they are winning. Let them think they have the last word. When the time comes, I am going to handle it. Soon the truth will come out. Just be patient, just wait.

Patience is the thing we need when we are confronted with anger. Anger roars and wants us to act now. Anger causes people to do foolish things. *"In your anger do not sin": Do not let the sun go down while you are still angry, and do not give the devil a foothold"* (Eph. 4:26–27). Amanda knew that her dad would be angry. She just hoped he could be angry and not sin. That he could control himself and allow justice to be served God's way.

Just then, God spoke back to Amanda. He told her to tell her dad that this demon spirit was going to come to him and pretend to be good. He told Amanda to warn her dad of the Devil's attempt to steal his dignity and honor as the good guy. "Amanda, give him the information I have given you. Explain to him that we are on the same team. We both want to take out this dude. We both want our daughter to be protected and safe. We have the same mission. We are on the same team, but just stand down and let me handle it. Don't try to take this into your own hands."

Was he going to heed her warning? She sure hoped so. Now her husband wasn't listening to her warnings at all. He was making fun of them and saying she was crazy. Would her dad do the same? "The choice is up to him now," God said. "All you can do is warn people. All you can do is tell them and then hope that they make the right choice." Amanda nodded, "Okay, God. I am going to turn this over to you. I am going to trust you with my dad."

Amanda obeyed the Lord. She told her dad about the things that God had been showing her about her husband. She shared with him the truth about her life over the last ten years. Then, she gave her dad some of the Scriptures that the Lord had given her and explained how He told her that He was going to be angry and that another spirit was going to visit him and tell him to do something that God didn't want done. Now she just had to wait. She had to hope and pray that her dad would listen to her warnings. She had to trust that he was going to make the right decision and heed God's warning and command.

When Moses saw an Israelite being attacked by an Egyptian he got angry and killed the man who was harming the innocent man. Then, because Moses acted out of anger, he had to run away because he knew he had done something outside of God's command. After a little while, the Lord spoke to Moses and told him to go back to Egypt and to lead the people out. He gave Moses the same mission he had many years before: Free the oppressed people. When Moses went under God's direction and command, he didn't have to take matters into his own hands. He just needed to trust God to handle it.

Moses and God were on the same team. They were both mad that God's people were being abused, and they wanted the abuse to stop. God was going to handle the abuse. He was going to bring judgment on Egypt, but the way that He did it was not the way Moses did it. God wanted Moses to trust him and be patient. He wanted him to do it God's way, not his own way. In the end God wiped out the pursuing Egyptians. Moses couldn't have done that level of damage against the enemy, not even close.

One day, after Moses had grown up, he went out to where his own people were and watched them at their hard labor. He saw an Egyptian beating a Hebrew, one of his own people. Looking this way and that and seeing no one, he killed the Egyptian and hid him in the sand. (Ex. 2:11–12).

Moses gave the Egyptians an excuse to label him as evil. He gave them an opportunity to call him a bad man or an evil man when indeed he was not. That is what happens when people try to take things into their own hands. They give their enemies a reason to look down on them and say, "Look at you and what you've done. You are bad. You are the criminal, not us." And that is not what God wants at all. God wants us to stay pure and just and trust Him with the battle.

The next day he went out and saw two Hebrews fighting. He asked the one in the wrong, "Why are you hitting your fellow Hebrew?" The man said, "Who made you ruler and judge over us? Are you thinking of killing me as you killed the Egyptian?" Then Moses was afraid and thought, "What I did must have become known" (Ex. 2:13–14).

Moses was only afraid because he was not in the perfect will of God. When you are doing things that are just and pure you are bold and confident. You are sure that you are on the right side. Murder, even when we feel like it is justified, really isn't in the eyes of God. God doesn't need us to use our weapons to handle things. When God is involved, He can do things all by Himself.

Proverbs 28:1 teaches, *"The wicked flee though no one pursues, but the righteous are as bold as a lion."* Our boldness comes from the assurance of doing the right thing and being on the side of justice. The enemy wants us to get mad. He wants us to think we are doing the right thing when we aren't, because our conscience has been skewed by our emotions. Yet we must always remember that God isn't moved by emotions. He makes just and fair decisions that are rational and controlled, and that is why sometimes His judgment seems to take a little longer.

Child experts will tell parents not to discipline a child when they are angry. They tell parents to calm down before they issue a consequence for poor behavior. This guidance is wise and biblical because we shouldn't ever try to bring forth punishment, consequences, or judgment toward another when we are not in total self-control. Doing so can cause us to hurt people when we shouldn't. It can cause us to make mistakes that God doesn't want us to make.

If a parent has ever acted out of emotion and disciplined a child because they were angry, then they know the guilt they felt when they calmed down and realized that the child hadn't deserved to be treated the way they were treated. As a Father and a wise man of war, God thinks and waits to do what He is going to do. He is controlled. He is full of strength, not emotional vulnerability and weakness.

Proverbs 28:5 says, *"Evildoers do not understand what is right, but those who seek the LORD understand it fully."* Amanda realized that she really was a prophet. She could see into the future and see the various spirits around her. Her ability to see and decipher what was happening in the spirit world was improving by the day. She was finally at a place where she could warn others of what was coming. She could tell people what God wanted them to do step by step, and she could tell them what the enemy was going to try to do too.

You may say to yourselves, "How can we know when a message has not been spoken by the LORD?" If what a prophet proclaims in the name of the LORD does not take place or come true, that is a message the LORD has not spoken. That prophet has spoken presumptuously, so do not be alarmed" (Deut. 18:21–22).

God wants us to test prophecy. He wants us to determine what is true and what isn't based on His word. When a prophet speaks, it should be aligned with the Scriptures. Prophets should be able to tell you and prove to you that they have really heard from God. When a prophet works for God what they say does come to pass. Sometimes, the prophecy may take a little while to be fulfilled, because God is the One who sets the dates on the fulfillment of the message spoken, but a true prophet's prophecies can be tested and believed because their words will always lead you to God's word and they will always come true.

In the end there should be a clear determination made. Who is telling the truth? Whose word do you believe, and who deserves to be locked up and acquitted? In the law enforcement and justice arena hard decisions must be made. People need to be sure they are always operating on the side of justice and they are not acting out of emotion or out of a heart of revenge. God doesn't want us to be unforgiving, harsh, and emotionally driven. He wants us to trust Him and do our part by bringing the criminal to His courtroom. Then we must let go and let God take it from there.

He will do the right thing at the right time. He knows exactly what has been done and what the future is for all the parties in the room. Do you trust His word, or do you trust the word of a lying spirit pretending to be something it isn't? There is always a liar, and there is always someone who is telling the truth. Liars don't want to be discovered. They want to remain covert, but a good detective can tell who is really responsible and who is lying. They can decipher good from evil and truth from lies, and they can make wise judgment calls.

For the LORD is our judge, the LORD is our lawgiver, the LORD is our king; it is he who will save us (Isa. 33:22).

{ 14 }

Songs of Rejoicing—Dancing &
Prayer

Fast-forward into the future and it is now the year 2030. Amanda and her children were happier, healthier, and richer than they've ever been. They didn't have to worry about buying organic because God made a way for them to afford to eat the best of the land. Amanda and her children ate dinner in peace, saying grace and thanksgiving before they enjoyed their meal. Her children knew that God had provided for them. They knew that they had experienced something supernatural.

When they finished eating dinner, they walked into their living room and put on praise and worship music on the TV. They'd laugh, play, and work together to clean up the kitchen mess. Amanda didn't have to stop homeschooling. They were now free to go to church on Wednesday nights or Sunday nights and not have to rush home or worry about Nathanial being mad at them for "messing everything up and making life hectic for someone else."

No one was yelling at them anymore. No one was telling them how stupid they were or that he was going to hit them. And they didn't have to listen to drunken laughter and banter from their living room when they were trying to lie down and sleep at night. The days were peaceful, and so were the nights. The love and the joy of Jesus radiated through the walls and rooms of their home. Their home had been blessed by the Lord. Their home had the Holy Spirit's protection and anointing.

Sometimes they would all remember the former season. They would say, "Do you remember when dad would play his game or when he would sleep in on the weekends, and we would have to ask if we were allowed to wake him up?" But then they remembered the truth, that their dad had always acted like they were a burden to him. He had always acted like he didn't want them around or to mess with him. They didn't have to hear him say, "Go play and get away from me." They didn't have to face the daily rejection of the person who was called to love them.

The family went on vacations and had fun together, which was something Nathanial resented doing He always said that vacations were a waste of his money. He said that they were pointless and that he only agreed to go on a trip because Amanda wouldn't stop nagging him about it. Plus, the family's vacations were so much more enjoyable now anyway. It was much easier not to hear about the financial burden the trip had caused, or to hear that one of the people on the trip would rather be at home than here.

Overall, their life was better. It was stronger. Things had changed, and they had changed drastically. But the changes weren't bad changes. In fact, they were good. Sometimes when Amanda or the children would tell people that they had lost their dad or her husband, they would look at her with such pity and such pain. "Oh, I am so sorry to hear that. I didn't know. That must be hard," they would say. But the truth was, it wasn't hard. It wasn't hard to serve God and live in His love. It wasn't hard to experience authentic freedom, joy, and peace.

Life wasn't harder after Amanda got sin and evil out of her home. Life was much, much better. Do you want to know what was hard? It was hard to be around someone who served the Devil. It was hard to tolerate living with someone who hated himself and hated the world he lived in. It was hard to be abused every day of your life and pray to God to save you while the rest of the world thought everything was perfect and okay.

It was much harder to hear people tell you how lucky you were to stay home and to have others assume you were married to a loving and honest man. It was far harder to live a lie. To pretend that you had a picture-perfect family when the truth was, you didn't. "I would rather live in the truth, tell the truth, and let people know about what happened and is happening in my life than live a lie," Amanda said. "It is so funny that everyone assumes I am struggling. Everyone assumes I am having a hard time now, but before no one was concerned about my health and well-being."

This is what we speak, not in words taught us by human wisdom but in words taught by the Spirit, explaining spiritual realities with Spirit-taught words. The person without the Spirit does not accept the things that come from the Spirit of God but considers them foolishness, and cannot understand them because they are discerned only through the Spirit. The person with the Spirit makes judgments about all things, but such a person is not subject to merely human judgments, for, "Who has known the mind of the Lord so as to instruct him?" But we have the mind of Christ (1 Cor. 2:13–16).

When you have the mind of Christ you don't look at things the same way as everyone else. The mind of Christ permits you to look at things honestly. It permits you to see the truth and live in the truth, even when others around you think you are crazy. Yet Amanda knew that it didn't matter what other people thought about her. What mattered was what God thought because God was right, and everyone else, if they didn't agree with God, was wrong.

What would be crazy would be to continue living a lie just so others could justify your story or make sense of your truth. It would be crazy to continue to tolerate the opinions of others just because someone else disagreed with you. Amanda spent many years being quiet and allowing someone who didn't even love her to alter her story and manipulate her plans. One thing she learned through it all was that persecution for her faith would come, but when it did it would eventually be removed from her.

God doesn't like persecution, whether it comes from within the house or outside of it. God wants families to work together. He wants people to be on the same team and operating in one accord, but unfortunately, some people don't want to love and honor those they are called to love and honor. Some people don't want to treat others with human decency and respect because they have been deceived and bought into the demonic kingdom's lies. And God's kingdom and the Devil's kingdom cannot be equally yoked.

The righteous will always triumph over the unrighteous. The wicked will always fall when they position themselves against the Church. One Christian is a part of the body of Christ. One Christian has power, authority, and dominion over the powers and the forces of Hell. When there is a dispute or a disagreement, and the Devil or anyone who works for him thinks it is your word against mine, he will discover that isn't the case at all. God has plenty of evidence. He has been building a case.

God may wait and watch for a season. He may let people persecute others and treat them with contempt for a little while, but that season will come to an end. God will have the final word. He will ensure that the victims of crimes perpetrated against them are given justice. Psalm 37:13–15 tells us, *"But the Lord laughs at the wicked, for he knows their day is coming. The wicked draw the sword and bend the bow to bring down the poor and needy, to slay those whose ways are upright. But their swords will pierce their own hearts, and their bows will be broken."*

If you or someone you know is in the in-between and they are waiting for God's judgment, be patient. God knows what He is doing. He has a perfectly detailed and orchestrated plan. Just like the abuser spends hours, months, and even years planning their attack against their unsuspecting victims, the Lord in His justice does the same. God is a man of war. Sometimes He hits people when they don't see it coming. That is what soldiers do. They plan an attack, and before you know it their enemy has no idea what hit them.

The LORD is a warrior; the LORD is his name. Pharaoh's chariots and his army he has hurled into the sea. The best of Pharaoh's officers are drowned in the Red Sea. The deep waters have covered them; they sank to the depths like a stone. Your right hand, LORD, was majestic in power. Your right hand, LORD, shattered the enemy (Ex. 15:3–6).

As the Egyptians chased those they had oppressed for years into the freedom God had for them the enemy destroyed each and every one. When God gives someone a warning He isn't playing. He isn't just talking tough and blowing smoke. When God says stop you'd better stop. If God says that you need to leave His people alone, then leave them alone. Because if you have been given a warning by God and He has told you to stop and you continue, you will find out that God is a man of war who defends His people. You will discover that God is more strategic than you.

"In the greatness of your majesty you threw down those who opposed you. You unleashed your burning anger; it consumed them like stubble. By the blast of your nostrils the waters piled up. The surging waters stood up like a wall; the deep waters congealed in the heart of the sea. The enemy boasted, 'I will pursue, I will overtake them. I will divide the spoils; I will gorge myself on them. I will draw my sword and my hand will destroy them.' But you blew with your breath, and the sea covered them. They sank like lead in the mighty waters. Who among the gods is like you, LORD? Who is like you— majestic in holiness, awesome in glory, working wonders? "You stretch out your right hand, and the earth swallows your enemies" (Ex. 15:7–12).

Amanda remembered Nathanial's voice. "You will never be anything. You are so crazy. God isn't real! You think you are a prophet! HAHAHHA! You are no prophet. I should lock you up in the insane asylum. Do you think people know how effin' crazy you really are or is it just me?" he would shout at her.

"Oh, Nathanial, if you only could see us today. If you could only see what God has done. If you only knew the Lord is real and He does what He says. If you could only see I am a prophet, a prophet who was sent to help you, to warn you, and to teach you how to hear from

God and obey Him," Amanda would lament. But then she heard God say, "He knows, Amanda. He knows now I am God and I am working in your life."

"It is written: 'As surely as I live,' says the Lord, 'every knee will bow before me; every tongue will acknowledge God.'" So then, each of us will give an account of ourselves to God" (Rom. 14:11–12).

Memories are sometimes painful. As Amanda remembered the past and remembered her late husband, she had pain, but her pain at least had a purpose. Nathanial looked back, too, but he had to look back from a place of torment that didn't provide relief. He looked back and couldn't change a thing or do anything about his past because nothing that he did now meant anything to God or His kingdom. When Amanda tells her story now, she builds the kingdom of the Lord, but as he tells his, no one listens or cares.

"Once again, the kingdom of heaven is like a net that was let down into the lake and caught all kinds of fish. When it was full, the fishermen pulled it up on the shore. Then they sat down and collected the good fish in baskets, but threw the bad away. This is how it will be at the end of the age. The angels will come and separate the wicked from the righteous and throw them into the blazing furnace, where there will be weeping and gnashing of teeth" (Matt. 13:47–50)

"Repent and be baptized. Turn from your sin and follow God," Amanda preached to the people standing before her. "God has anointed me to bring the good news. He has called me to teach and preach to you today, so you have a chance to turn from your sin and come to Jesus. Jesus is real. He is a protector, a provider, a restorer, and a redeemer. Jesus loves you, and He wants to save you from your sins. Heed the words I am telling you today. Let today be the day of your salvation before it is too late."

"God wants you to receive His free gift of salvation," she would tell them. "He died on the cross and rose from the grave on the third day so you could live and be forgiven for all of your sins. The Bible tells us that all are born sinners. One day I was the worst sinner. I did all kinds of terrible things, but when I gave my life to Jesus everything changed for me. Jesus forgave me and gave me a place in His house. He will do the same for you. He will forgive you for anything you have ever done. He will make room for you if you will only believe!"

"I am going to do an alter call," Amanda informed them. "If you have never given your life to Jesus before come to the front and we will pray to a real God who hears you. When you say this prayer you will receive new life. You will become new and Jesus will forgive you for all of your former sins. He will help you, teach you, and give you the things you need so you can change every part of your life and live an abundant life full of happiness, joy, and peace." And many people went forward and gave their lives to Christ because of her ministry. Many people were set free from the captivity of Satan, and they came into the household of faith.

Peter replied, "Repent and be baptized, every one of you, in the name of Jesus Christ for the forgiveness of your sins. And you will receive the gift of the Holy Spirit. The promise is for you and your children and for all who are far off—for all whom the Lord our God will call. With many other words he warned them; and he pleaded with them, "Save yourselves from this corrupt generation" (Acts 2:38–40).

The Sinner's Prayer

God, I come before You today as a sinner in need of Your grace. I repent of my sin, and I am sorry for the things I have done. Please forgive me and come into my heart today. Allow me to partake in Your kingdom and in Your house. I promise to serve You with my whole heart. I promise to do my best to follow You. I ask now for the gift of the Holy Spirit. I ask for Your help to follow You. I believe Jesus died on the cross and after three days rose from the dead. I believe Jesus Christ is the Son of God and He died to forgive me for my sins. Thank you, God, for all You did for me while I was still living in bondage to sin. Thank you for setting me free from my enemy. From this day forward I vow to be Your bride. I leave my former life behind and I walk confidently into the future with You. I believe that You have given me a new name and that my name is now found in the Lamb's book of life. It is in Jesus's name I pray. Amen.

"If you just said this prayer, then welcome to the family of God," Amanda announced. "You are now a child of God. You just made the best decision of your life. I will give you a Bible and some other resources. And it is important to get plugged into a local church where you can learn about your new family and your new life as a Christian," she told the people standing in front of her at the altar. "Congratulations!" she shouted.

Angels dance when they see someone give their life to Christ. All of Heaven rejoices when a victory is won in the Spirit. God wants us to dance. He wants us to sing. God wants us to be happy. He wants us to win in life, now and forever. God rejoices with His people. He gives His people a good life, full of sweet things. And the good news is it is all free. All of this is free. If you accept the gift and only believe. *"In the same way, I tell you, there is rejoicing in the presence of the angels of God over one sinner who repents"* (Luke 15:10).

{ 15 }

A Prophet's Predictions

"Daddy, who is your favorite Bible character?" Nathanial's children asked him one night when they got home from church. "Samson," he answered. "WHAT!!!!!!!" Laughter erupted from the table. "Why would you choose Samson, daddy? That isn't a good Bible character to choose. Don't you know what happened to Samson?" they replied in loud voices. "Yeah, my favorite character is Samson because he proves that b***** ain't s***," Nathanial jeered. "You can't trust these women out here."

The children really didn't know what their dad meant. They thought he was joking because Nathanial often used comedy to express himself. "Daddy, you're joking!" their daughter yelled at him. "No, I am not," he said back to her with a smile. "I am serious. It is Samson." "That is silly, daddy. You shouldn't choose Samson!" they said with urgency. Then, their oldest son said, "My favorite Bible character is Jesus." Their daughter said, "Mine is Moses!" And the family continued eating their dinner, laughing and discussing different Bible characters.

Nathanial's children talked to him about Jesus a lot. His oldest son prayed for him, and he told his mom, "Mommy, I don't want daddy to go to Hell. I have been praying to Jesus for him." Amanda nodded and assured him, "That is good, son. Your dad needs your prayers. I don't want him to go to Hell either. Neither does God."

One of the things that Amanda was going to miss about Nathanial was his humor. He could make Amanda and her children laugh sometimes. Not all times with abusers are bad. In fact, there are some fun times, happy times, and moments of bonding. If there weren't some fun, laughter, and joy in the relationship then people wouldn't be bonded and torn by their relationship with their abusers. "They aren't that bad of a person," people will often tell themselves. "We have had good times. We have had fun."

"I love comedy. Comedy has always been my way of coping with life. You know that in all comedy there is some truth," Nathanial would frequently say. "Some of the saddest people are people who make others laugh. Look at people like Robin Williams." And it was definitely true. Nathanial could make people laugh, but did he mean what he said about there always being truth in what comedians say? Was he being serious that he meant the things he joked about?

One night, after a bad fight lasting a few days, Nathanial followed Amanda around the house while pointing their son's Nerf gun at her neck and head. He smiled and glared at her like he had a real weapon. On other occasions he would tell her that he was going to kill himself, saying things like, "I should just blow my brains out, pow. Or I will go and jump off a cliff. What is the effin' point of any of this?" His jokes were often very morbid. They could also be threatening toward himself and others.

"That isn't funny," Amanda would tell him. "Yeah, I am not trying to be funny," he would reply. "God would be doing me a favor to get me out of here. This place effin' sucks. I would love to not have to deal with any of this anymore." Was Nathanial joking? Was he letting off some steam or using comic relief? Amanda often wondered. *I really don't know. None of this seems good. It doesn't seem normal, but maybe he is only joking.*

One day God revealed to her that her husband's jokes, remarks, and actions that oftentimes were presented as jokes were indeed not jokes at all. He meant what he was saying. The things he was saying were being said because they resided somewhere deep in his heart. When someone keeps saying the same message, and they keep on insisting that something is how they feel, even when they smile at you, lift their hand to tickle your side, or wink at you while they are saying it, that message is their message. It is their truth.

Luke 6:45 tells us, *"A good man brings good things out of the good stored up in his heart, and an evil man brings evil things out of the evil stored up in his heart. For the mouth speaks what the heart is full of."* Whether you know it or not, some people's truth is morbid. Some people's truth is not of God, and the words they speak are not of Him either, because their hearts have stored up evil. *"Each tree is recognized by its own fruit. People do not pick figs from thornbushes, or grapes from briers"* (Luke 6:44).

Proverbs 6:24 tells us that people with demonically inspired agendas will use their tongues to flatter others. *"Keeping you from your neighbor's wife, from the smooth talk of a wayward woman."* Evil people can make their messages, appearance, and approach seem harmless when in fact they aren't harmless at all. The intent of the heart is to destroy the person they are speaking to. To lead the vulnerable and naive astray while insinuating that they don't have bad intentions.

"Do not lust in your heart after her beauty or let her captivate you with her eyes. For a prostitute [whore] can be had for a loaf of bread, but another man's wife preys on your very life" (Prov. 6:25–26). Here God warns us not to look at people's outward appearances alone when we are making our observations. Christians can be deceived by looking with their physical eyes and not with their spiritual eyes. Whores, both male and female, can look appealing in the natural realm. They can cause you to think you are safe in their presence when indeed you are not.

When God describes a whore, he is not only referring to women. God considers someone a whore if they have turned to false gods, served foreign things, and have refused to commit themselves wholly to Him. When a person is unfaithful to God, regardless of the circumstances, they are a whore. God wants us to love Him more than anything else. He wants us to recognize Him in all we do.

A married woman or man should be mindful when they are interacting with others. They should ensure they aren't giving off vibes that they are interested in someone other than their spouse, even through what some would call innocent flirting. God doesn't want us to flirt with the world. He doesn't want us to entertain the world, laugh with the world, and act like the world is something special. God is a jealous God. He commands all who serve Him and make a vow to Him to be faithful, and if people can't do this, then He considers them a whore.

Sometimes people who are wholeheartedly committed to the Lord will be made fun of. "You are so obsessed with God. You are too extreme. That isn't normal." How many people have been made fun of for their faithfulness and commitment to God? How many people know what it is like to be made fun of for being true to God's word regardless of the influence of others around them? This spirit is the spirit of lust, a spirit that tries to pull you away from God, promising you a life outside of Him. It is a spirit that wants you to cheat on God and make light of your commitment to Him, so it can lure you into worldliness or outright sin and disobedience to God.

One of the seven angels who had the seven bowls came and said to me, "Come, I will show you the punishment of the great prostitute, who sits by many waters. With her the kings of the earth committed adultery, and the inhabitants of the earth were intoxicated with the wine of her adulteries" (Rev. 17:1–2).

This spirit gets people drunk with a disobedience toward God. People are intoxicated into a place of ignorance, stupidity, and foolishness because they are living a life outside of God, and they don't even know it. People prop this spirit up through their unfaithfulness to God. They give it power and elevate it to a place where it shouldn't be permitted to sit. *"Then the angel said to me, 'The waters you saw, where the prostitute sits, are peoples, multitudes, nations and languages'"* (Revelation 17:15).

For the antichrist to rise and have power, a man must serve Satan. Then, the multitudes that continue to aid in his power will strengthen his mission. The devils couldn't continue their mission if people didn't associate themselves with devils. The Devil and all devils need people to do what they want to do. Demons need submission and worship to continue their quest. Christians are called to starve and refuse wine to the demonic realm. We are called to tell demons what to do and where to go. We are given the authority to evacuate them from people, places, and things.

But what happens when a person willingly gives themselves to evil? Can the prayers of another person change them, save them, and make them receive the salvation of Christ? The answer to that question is a resounding no. *"Jesus said to them, 'A prophet is not without honor except in his own town, among his relatives and in his own home.' He could not do any miracles there, except lay his hands on a few sick people and heal them. He was amazed at their lack of faith. Then Jesus went around teaching from village to village"* (Mark 6:4–6).

When people don't believe in Jesus or trust the prophets in their lives they cannot receive from the prophets. Only when people receive the prophet can they receive the blessing of the prophet. Matthew 10:41 states, *"Whoever welcomes a prophet as a prophet will receive a prophet's reward, and whoever welcomes a righteous person as a righteous person will receive a righteous person's reward."*

Some people want demons to continue in their lives. As bizarre as it is, some people like demonic power and demonic manifestations. They align themselves with the forces of evil, and they don't want to be removed from the course they are on. These people will continue to disregard the prophet's messages from God because they are listening to other prophets, the demonically inspired ones. Jeremiah 23:10 says, *"The land is full of adulterers; because of the curse the land lies parched and the pastures in the wilderness are withered. The prophets follow an evil course and use their power unjustly."*

Not everyone who calls themselves a prophet is one, but prophets are very real. Their ministries, whether good or evil, are around, and people side with messages from the prophets in their lives. A prophet's written or spoken word has power and authority, whether people acknowledge it or not. Like all authorities, some authorities are godly and some aren't. *"So Christ himself gave the apostles, the prophets, the evangelists, the pastors and teachers to equip his people for works of service, so that the body of Christ may be built up"* (Eph. 4:11–12).

Not everyone is a prophet, but prophets are for everyone in the Church, and they are called to speak to the Church and edify it. God gave us prophets so we can determine ahead of time what is going to happen in our lives, our countries, or the lives of others. He gave us prophets to make us stronger. Godly prophets inform people of impending danger. They tell people what is going to happen ahead of time so people can prepare, change, or decide if they are going to listen to the word of the Lord.

"But when he, the Spirit of truth, comes, he will guide you into all the truth. He will not speak on his own; he will speak only what he hears, and he will tell you what is yet to come" (John 16:13). The widow who fed Elijah was told ahead of time to prepare for him, but she was not a prophet herself. How could this be? How could someone do what God wants them to do but not know why they are doing it? The Holy Spirit wants to guide everyone. He wants to help believers know right from wrong, but some people have a special gifting from God. This gift is the gift of a ministry prophecy.

When Elijah was going to go to the widow's house, God gave him clear, in-depth instructions. He couldn't have found this woman without the information from God. Elijah had a very keen understanding of what was going to happen, like he was looking at a picture or movie ahead of time. The widow, on the other hand, knew how to prepare for something. She knew what God wanted her to do, but she wasn't receiving the same level of revelation.

Then the word of the Lord came to him: "Go at once to Zarephath in the region of Sidon and stay there. I have directed a widow there to supply you with food." So he went to Zarephath. When he came to the town gate, a widow was there gathering sticks. He called to her and asked, "Would you bring me a little water in a jar so I may have a drink?" As she was going to get it, he called, "And bring me, please, a piece of bread" (1 Kings 17:8–11).

We know the widow didn't see into the future, even though she was still obeying God, because of her response in the following scriptures. 1 Kings 17:12 continues, *"'As surely as the Lord your God lives,' she replied, 'I don't have any bread—only a handful of flour in a jar and a little olive oil in a jug. I am gathering a few sticks to take home and make a meal for myself and my son, that we may eat it—and die.'"* A prophet with a prophetic gift wouldn't have thought she was going to die when she was going to live. This woman, if she had the gift of prophecy, would have known ahead of time what her life was going to be like.

Jesus was a prophet, but not all of his disciples were. Consider when Jesus told his disciples what to do and how things were going to happen in detail. This gift was operating in Jesus's ministry, but it wasn't in the other men's skill set to do so. Jesus will go to great lengths to ensure the words of His prophets come to pass. He will make sure that if a prophet is speaking in accordance with the will of Heaven, then the things they speak will happen as they said.

As they approached Jerusalem and came to Bethphage on the Mount of Olives, Jesus sent two disciples, saying to them, "Go to the village ahead of you, and at once you will find a donkey tied there, with her colt by her. Untie them and bring them to me. If anyone says anything to you, say that the Lord needs them, and he will send them right away." This took place to fulfill what was spoken through the prophet: "Say to Daughter Zion, 'See, your king comes to you, gentle and riding on a donkey, and on a colt, the foal of a donkey'" (Matt. 21:1–5).

Prophets must understand the authority that they carry so they can properly administer justice when justice is necessary. A prophet who doesn't see themselves as an authority figure and an instrument of God's justice through their proclamations will not use their gift properly for the kingdom. There are times when God tells the prophet to speak or write what they see so the words they speak can be carried out, sometimes in the here and now and other times in the future.

Nathanial constantly made fun of Amanda's proclamation that she was a prophet. He thought it was funny that she considered herself a spokesperson from Heaven. "Yeah, Ohhhkay!" he would say. Amanda knew that he didn't understand spiritual things. She knew that he was ignorant of his submission to demonic voices, demonic prophets, and demonic messages. He loved listening to music, watching movies, and playing video games. These were some of his favorite things, alongside comedy, but what he didn't understand was that all of these things were associated with prophecy.

Nathanial was following prophets. He was listening to them and allowing them to shape his future. Things like music, movies, and other forms of entertainment have the authority and power to move people into new futures and destinations. They have the power to transform a person's actions when the person hears the prophecy and then receives it into their heart. Nathanial worshipped the prophets of Baal. He thought they were super cool! "Babe, listen to this song!" he would say, as he brought her some garbage music straight out of the Devil's camp.

"Come on, why don't you give a f*** about what I am into? Why don't you want to listen to anything or watch anything I ask you to listen to or watch? You are too serious. What is wrong with this? There is nothing wrong with it," he would say. "You are so overboard with God. You cannot even have fun. What is wrong with you, Amanda?" he asked in sincerity. "Nathanial, I don't hate music, movies, or any of that stuff. I just don't want to listen to that kind of music or watch that kind of movie. I know what is behind it. I know what it is," she would tell him.

"These people are not evil! If they are going to Hell, then I am going to go too! Some of the best music was written by people who were tormented. Can't you feel their pain? Can't you resonate with their struggle?" he would ask. Amanda tried to be understanding. She knew that he didn't see what she saw. He didn't get that what he was joining himself to was a demonic world propped up by his worship. He didn't see that these prophets were drinking his blood, so the demons could drink theirs.

"These people are leading people to Hell, Nathanial. They are prophesying into people's futures. They are not good people. No one is worth going to Hell over. I don't get why you are obsessed with this stuff so much," she would say. Many of their fights were about music and movies. "I love movies, and you won't ever watch a movie with me!" he would complain. "Well, I just am not interested in watching certain things, Nathanial. If it is a good movie I will watch it, but I know the power of these things, and I am not willing to involve myself in it," she would explain.

Nathanial regularly put on music in the house. He loved having his children watch EDM festivals and dance along to the catchy beats. Sometimes his children would say that it didn't sound very good, and they would pick up on the deception in the music. But sometimes they thought the beat sounded catchy and their dad seemed to like it, so they tried to dance along too. Amanda hated that her children were watching these festivals and listening to these lyrics, but she couldn't make Nathanial turn his music off without a huge fight.

So, Amanda prayed. She just kept praying, week after week, month after month, for the future and safety of her children. She believed that what she was doing in their life was far more powerful. She knew that the power of the Holy Spirit could override the power of the Devil. Even if they were exposed to some things through demonic media and messaging, they wouldn't be overtaken by these messages because there is more power in a godly prophet's proclamation than there is in a prophet of Baal.

Elijah knew this truth very well. When he went up against the prophets of Baal in a contest to prove whose god was stronger, he challenged the weaker prophets, even when he thought he was outnumbered.

Then Elijah said to them, "I am the only one of the Lord's prophets left, but Baal has four hundred and fifty prophets. Get two bulls for us. Let Baal's prophets choose one for themselves, and let them cut it into pieces and put it on the wood but not set fire to it. I will prepare the other bull and put it on the wood but not set fire to it. Then you call on the name of your god, and I will call on the name of the Lord. The god who answers by fire—he is God." Then all the people said, "What you say is good" (1 Kings 18:22–24).

Elijah was confident in his prophecy. He was confident in the future. He knew that if there were 450 prophets and only one of God's prophets that God would still be the supreme power in the competition. Elijah was sure that God was going to prove Himself to be true, and he knew that the devils' weaker counterparts were going to involve themselves in a battle they couldn't win.

Elijah said to the prophets of Baal, "Choose one of the bulls and prepare it first, since there are so many of you. Call on the name of your god, but do not light the fire." So they took the bull given them and prepared it. Then they called on the name of Baal from morning till noon. "Baal, answer us!" they shouted. But there was no response; no one answered. And they danced around the altar they had made (1 Kings 18:25–26).

Demons can and do answer people. They do have power, but their power is rendered useless when a higher power steps in. In all military ranks and in all systems where there is authority, when a higher-ranking leader makes an order, calls a command, or gives a directive, those who are in a lower position of authority must obey the order even when they don't want to do so. The kingdom of God is above the kingdom of the Devil. God's people have authority over the Devil's people. We can say go and things must go. We can say stop and they must stop.

Elijah thought that their failure to get an answer from their false gods was funny. He mocked them and their inferior prophecies and proclamations. He mocked their ability to prove and alter the future when he was present and standing before them dictating the terms of the relationship. *"At noon Elijah began to taunt them. 'Shout louder!' he said. 'Surely he is a god! Perhaps he is deep in thought, or busy, or traveling. Maybe he is sleeping and must be awakened'"* (1 Kings 18:27).

When a prophet is working for the Lord they aren't concerned about the opinions of others around them, including the opinions and words of prophets who are working for Satan. God's people laugh at the prophets of Baal. They laugh at their foolishness to think they could alter what God has said is going to come to pass. Elijah went the extra mile to show out for God. He poured water on the altar before it was lit. He proved that God could light up an altar even when water had drenched it. There is nothing too hard for God. He holds all power and authority, and then He delegates His authority to His prophets so the world can see who He is.

Prophecies can be written, or they can be spoken, acted out, or sung. People who work in the arts, making music, writing books, performing in movies or live shows, and doing other similar jobs, are prophets who are conveying a message to others. People who watch, hear, or receive the message can have their futures altered by the prophet's proclamations or demonstrations. And that is why prophets have authority and power, and God tells us not to misuse it.

People who make demonic music will continue to lead people into Hell far beyond the grave. Likewise, people who write books for Jesus will continue to save souls when they are no longer living on the earth. Some of the prophets from the Bible have yet to see their prophecies in full demonstration and manifestation. Not all prophecies occur when they are given, but if a prophet speaks, the things they speak do make a difference. Prophecies set things into motion.

The idols speak deceitfully, diviners see visions that lie; they tell dreams that are false, they give comfort in vain. Therefore the people wander like sheep oppressed for lack of a shepherd. "My anger burns against the shepherds, and I will punish the leaders; for the LORD Almighty will care for his flock, the people of Judah, and make them like a proud horse in battle. From Judah will come the cornerstone, from him the tent peg, from him the battle bow, from him every ruler. Together they will be like warriors in battle trampling their enemy into the mud of the streets. They will fight because the LORD is with them, and they will put the enemy horsemen to shame.

"I will strengthen Judah and save the tribes of Joseph. I will restore them because I have compassion on them. They will be as though I had not rejected them, for I am the LORD their God and I will answer them. The Ephraimites will become like warriors, and their hearts will be glad as with wine. Their children will see it and be joyful; their hearts will rejoice in the LORD. I will signal for them and gather them in. Surely I will redeem them; they will be as numerous as before. Though I scatter them among the peoples, yet in distant lands they will remember me. They and their children will survive, and they will return." (Zech. 10:2–9).

When God's prophets refuse to tell people what the Lord has told them to tell, they leave the people without a shepherd to properly guide them. The job of a prophet is to guide. Prophets are to see and then inform people about what they are to do or not to do if they are going to be in the Lord's plans for the upcoming situation, time, or season in life. Amanda knew she was a prophet. She knew that God had told her to warn Nathanial and to tell others that he was going to die before he died, so they could believe that the Lord was truly the Most High.

Witches and people who believe in luck, fortune, or other divinations like horoscopes are often deceived because they think the prophet's word toward them will come to pass. At the beginning of the year many people make New Year's proclamations. They say, "This is going to be a good year for us. This is going to be the best year we have had yet." Nathanial loved fortune cookies and New

Year's Eve proclamations and assertions. He loved horoscopes and a plethora of other demonic propaganda. But he didn't like the prophecies that his wife tried to give him.

Nathanial hated those kinds of prophecies, the prophecies that told him to change or face the consequences of his disobedience toward the Lord God. "Shut up! I am so tired of hearing this s***! Blah Blah Blah. Doom and gloom. Spooky vibes!" he would exclaim. "You are just a negative person. Why are you always talking about Jesus? You are so obsessed. This is not normal. You need to get mental help, Amanda."

"Nathanial, I am serious! Please just listen to me. God isn't going to be patient forever. He isn't going to continue giving you time to change. Something changed the other day. Everything is so different. I have been in mourning thinking that you are not going to repent and turn to God. It is hard to accept this. You have to change or you are going to die soon," she said again as they sat in a parking lot with their children in the backseat. "I am just fine," he replied firmly. But those words meant nothing to her.

Amanda knew that the word God had given her about her husband was going to come to pass. She knew that she was going to have to stand before people one day and tell them the truth about her husband's death and her foresight of it. The thought of all of this was hard to process. It was hard to see, hear, and experience, but Amanda knew that if Nathanial didn't change he would soon be gone forever from her life. She knew that it was only a matter of time until she didn't see him lying beside her in the bed. What would she do with his cell phone, his computer, or his clothes? What was she going to do with all his tools and his truck?

She realized one day, "I am going to have to continue to love him and be kind to him until he dies. I will keep trying to warn him, and I will keep trying to convey the message from Heaven. But I think I am going to be the only wife that he will ever know. I think the majority of his life is going to be with me, but he is only a small fragment and part of mine. How tragic. How awful." Her heart felt like it was breaking. And now she understood why God said not to join yourself to unbelievers, as He knew that it would end in heartache. He foresaw and told His people that if you do, you will hurt for it and wish you had adhered to the prophecy you were formally given.

{ 16 }

Where Does Your Strength Come From?

In this chapter we will discuss some of the ways that Christians can get their strength from God.

Iron sharpens iron.

Being around other believers who are on fire for God matters. When we are around dull people, we cannot grow in the way that God wants us to grow. Being around on-fire Christians changes our lives. It changes our destinies. It changes our future. Sometimes we can look around at the world and think that things are so bad and that no one loves God. The prophet Ezekiel, after defeating the prophets of Baal and going against Jezebel, felt alone and asked God why he was alone. Then God said, "You aren't alone. Go anoint people for ministry."

This tells us that God is calling new people into ministry. It tells us that we have a part to play in bringing the next generation into their places as leaders and anointed servants for Christ. It also tells us that we need other believers to help us stay on fire and do the work of the Lord. Proverbs 27:17 says, *"As iron sharpens iron, so one person sharpens another."*

Not all people are the same. Some knives and swords are sharper than others. We need to watch the company we keep. We need to be intentional about our close spiritual relationships. In the book of Revelation, God addresses a church that is lukewarm (a church that isn't on fire for Him). He warns this church that they need to rekindle their fire. They need to desire Him more than anything else, or they are in danger of being cast out from God's presence.

Having the joy of the Lord.

Then Nehemiah the governor, Ezra the priest and teacher of the Law, and the Levites who were instructing the people said to them all, "This day is holy to the LORD your God. Do not mourn or weep." For all the people had been weeping as they listened to the words of the Law. Nehemiah said, "Go and enjoy choice food and sweet drinks, and send some to those who have nothing prepared. This day is holy to our Lord. Do not grieve, for the joy of the LORD is your strength" (Neh. 8:9–10).

The first thing we can see from this scripture is who you have as your leader matters, even though we cannot blame our leaders and fail to take personal responsibility. This leader properly instructed the people in righteousness. He told them what God wanted them to do, and then they obeyed and respected the leadership God had appointed in their life. God wants His people to be happy when they are committed to serving Him. He wants people to be joyful and strong. A good leader will help people to know this about God. They will help to equip people with the joy of the Lord.

Our perspective on life matters.

If we have a sad and dejected outlook on life, we will not have the joy of the Lord, and we will feel weak and defeated. Do you think your enemy is stronger than you? Do you believe a lie? Sometimes we think Satan is more powerful than he is. Sometimes we allow him to dictate the terms of our lives when God said we have been given authority to trample over all the power of the enemy.

When the Israelites were in the wilderness and approaching the promised land God had for them they believed Satan's lie that they were incapable and weak. They believed they didn't have enough strength to do what God had called them to do. It was their unbelief in God and His power in their life that caused them to fail. If they had only believed they could have moved forward and conquered their enemies. Numbers 13:33 says, *"We saw the Nephilim there (the de-*

scendants of Anak come from the Nephilim). We seemed like grasshoppers in our own eyes, and we looked the same to them."

Don't believe Satan's lies that you aren't capable of doing what God has called you to do. Don't listen to the enemy. Goliath wanted David to think he was more powerful than he was, but David knew his covenant with God was going to give him the victory. Joshua and Caleb knew the same thing David knew: Yes, there are giants, but we can take them because our God is with us. Numbers 14:24 tells us, *"But because my servant Caleb has a different spirit and follows me wholeheartedly, I will bring him into the land he went to, and his descendants will inherit it."*

Presenting our requests before God.

Philippians 4:6–7 says, *"Do not be anxious about anything, but in every situation, by prayer and petition, with thanksgiving, present your requests to God. And the peace of God, which transcends all understanding, will guard your hearts and your minds in Christ Jesus."*

This scripture tells us anxiety and worry steal our strength. Being afraid and worried about the future keeps people in bondage. Fear is a different spirit from faith. That is why God told us Joshua had a "different" spirit from those who were around him. Fear will keep you weak and keep you from doing what God has commanded you to do. 2 Tim. 1:7 says, *"For the Spirit God gave us does not make us timid, but gives us power, love and self-discipline."* When you have power, you are not weak. Power makes you strong. God has given us a Spirit of power.

Hearing a prophecy from God reminds us God knows everything and He has everything under control.

Knowing God is with us and He wants us to be doing what we are doing emboldens and strengthens us. God wants to give us words unique to us, because when we get a unique and personal word from God, we will believe He cares about us and our lives, and we will do the thing He has told us to do with assurance and confidence God used the prophet Isaiah to give Hezekiah—a king who was faced with a great battle with his enemy—a word of victory in the battle. God told Isaiah to reassure Hezekiah and to tell him God had heard his prayers and would be with him through the battle.

Then the commander stood and called out in Hebrew, "Hear the words of the great king, the king of Assyria! This is what the king says: Do not let Hezekiah deceive you. He cannot deliver you! Do not let Hezekiah persuade you to trust in the Lord when he says, 'The Lord will surely deliver us; this city will not be given into the hand of the king of Assyria.'

"Do not listen to Hezekiah. This is what the king of Assyria says: Make peace with me and come out to me. Then each of you will eat fruit from your own vine and fig tree and drink water from your own cistern, until I come and take you to a land like your own—a land of grain and new wine, a land of bread and vineyards.

"Do not let Hezekiah mislead you when he says, 'The Lord will deliver us.' Have the gods of any nations ever delivered their lands from the hand of the king of Assyria? Where are the gods of Hamath and Arpad? Where are the gods of Sepharvaim? Have they rescued Samaria from my hand? Who of all the gods of these countries have been able to save their lands from me? How then can the Lord deliver Jerusalem from my hand?" (Is. 36:13–20).

The enemy wants people to believe a lie. He wants them to think they are not going to win the battles against him and they must submit to his ways and plans if they are going to live. Satan knows by submitting to an enemy, through fear and doubt of God's protection and promise for your life, you can lose your strength. At times we need God to tell us exactly what to do and how to do it because we cannot do it without His help and insight. His assurance and guidance is what gives us the fuel we need for the battle. His personal spoken revelation is the key to our victory.

Hezekiah needed to know God was with him. He needed a prophecy from Heaven reassuring him that God was with him and he would be victorious if he continued to stand strong against his enemy. Others in the Bible have also asked God for reassurance and confidence. David asked God if he should pursue the enemy troops when they had stolen his wives and children. He wanted God to give him a prophecy about his situation.

Gideon also inquired of God on multiple occasions to ensure he was on the right path. Judges 6:17 tells us, *"Gideon replied, 'If now I have found favor in your eyes, give me a sign that it is really you talking to me.'"* Later on, in verses 36–37, we read, *"Gideon said to God, "If you will save Israel by my hand as you promised—look, I will place a wool fleece on the threshing floor. If there is dew only on the fleece and all the ground is dry, then I will know that you will save Israel by my hand, as you said."* Gideon didn't feel strong enough to do what God was saying to do. Feelings cannot determine what Christians do. Christians need to hear from God, then ignore their personal feelings! Personal feelings can be wrong, but God is always right.

Pardon me, my lord," Gideon replied, *"but if the Lord is with us, why has all this happened to us? Where are all his wonders that our ancestors told us about when they said, 'Did not the Lord bring us up out of Egypt?' But now the Lord has abandoned us and given us into the hand of Midian."* *The Lord turned to him and said, "Go in the strength you have and save Israel out of Midian's hand. Am I not sending you?"* **"Pardon me, my lord,"** **Gideon replied, "but how can I save Israel? My clan is the weakest in Manasseh, and I am the least in my family." The Lord answered, "I will be with you, and you will strike down all the Midianites, leaving none alive"** (Judg. 6:11–16, emphasis added).

Don't trust outsiders or strangers. Don't assume everyone is your friend.

Samson didn't listen to God's command to keep foreign women away from him. He thought he could trust someone he couldn't, and she ended up stealing his strength and his life. Delilah was not someone to be trusted. She was an enemy who pretended to care about him. Judges 16:5–6 says, *"The rulers of the Philistines went to her and said, 'See if you can lure him into showing you the secret of his great strength and how we can overpower him so we may tie him up and subdue him. Each one of us will give you eleven hundred shekels of silver.' So Delilah said to Sam-*

son, *'Tell me the secret of your great strength and how you can be tied up and subdued.'*"

The enemy forces were persistent. At first Samson resisted them and didn't share everything with them, but then he began to trust them when he shouldn't have! One of the commands of God for our lives is for us to be separate from unbelievers. This doesn't mean we can't be kind to people in the community or offer them the chance to receive from God, but it does mean that when we are interacting with people outside of the faith household, we need to be on guard about who they are, what they want, and what their purposes are in our lives.

Satan sometimes puts people in the lives of others to take them out or destroy them. We see this happen to Hezekiah, that after being strong at first, standing against the Assyrian army, he was later in life defeated by his enemies because he allowed them close and trusted them when he shouldn't have. The Bible tells us to be as wise as serpents but as harmless as doves. Many Christians think anyone who calls themselves a Christian is one. They think that all people are good and that they can trust people whom God doesn't want them to trust. Some unbelievers are villains, and so are some who call themselves Christians.

God will reveal the truth about people to His children when they are looking, searching, and asking Him to tell them the truth. God wants us to be set free. He wants us to know what is true. John 8:31–32 says, *"To the Jews who had believed him, Jesus said, 'If you hold to my teaching, you are really my disciples. Then you will know the truth, and the truth will set you free.'"* If people want to be ignorant, blind, and trusting, or even disobedient to Him, then God will allow them to choose that path. People are free to choose, but they are not free from the consequences of their choices.

The Bible commands us to resist the Devil, and when we resist him then he will flee. Christians have a job to do. We are called to resist evil. We are called not to play around with our enemy or permit him a place within our lives. What we do or don't do impacts our lives and the lives of others. Christians must obey God and resist the enemy and all who are a part of his kingdom. Not all people are good. Not everyone is on our team.

John 8:44–45 tells us, *"You belong to your father, the devil, and you want to carry out your father's desires. He was a murderer from the beginning, not holding to the truth, for there is no truth in him. When he lies, he speaks his native language, for he is a liar and the father of lies. Yet because I tell the truth, you do not believe me!"* It is often easier to believe a lie that all people love you and want your best interests, but some people don't and won't. Some people have the Devil as their father.

There are people who are unbelievers and outside of the Church, and they will blatantly tell you they are not on the same mission and team. Then, there are others who are more sly and cunning. These people will pretend to be part of the Christian faith when they aren't. Judas wasn't really Jesus's friend. He wasn't friends with the other disciples either. Judas pretended to be a Christian. He lied to the people who thought he was their friend.

God commands us to test the spirits. He commands us to pay attention. Are you listening? Are you testing? Or are you willfully blind because you want to believe the lie that everyone around you is your friend? 1 John 4:1 says, *"Dear friends, do not believe every spirit, but test the spirits to see whether they are from God, because many false prophets have gone out into the world."* Jesus said in Matthew 23:15, *"Woe to you, teachers of the law and Pharisees, you hypocrites! You travel over land and sea to win a single convert, and when you have succeeded, you make them twice as much a child of hell as you are."*

Not everyone who calls themselves a Christian or a good person is one. Some people wear masks and wear them well. Some people live their entire lives as a character under a false premise and guise. Sure, it hurts, sometimes deeply, when you discover the truth about these people, but you can't change them. You can only admit the truth that has been revealed to you and trust God with their fate and outcomes.

We must be committed to not losing our strength for anyone or anything. God wants us to be healthy. He wants us to be strong. Are you willing to do what He has told you to do? If so, you will enter the promised land. If not, you can't and won't enter it, not because God didn't want you to, but because you didn't believe. It is possible for people to limit the power of God. It is possible for them not to allow Him to do what He wants to do in their life.

Again and again they put God to the test; they vexed the Holy One of Israel. They did not remember his power— the day he redeemed them from the oppressor, the day he displayed his signs in Egypt, his wonders in the region of Zoan. He turned their river into blood; they could not drink from their streams. He sent swarms of flies that devoured them, and frogs that devastated them. He gave their crops to the grasshopper, their produce to the locust. He destroyed their vines with hail and their sycamore-figs with sleet. He gave over their cattle to the hail, their livestock to bolts of lightning. He unleashed against them his hot anger, his wrath, indignation and hostility—a band of destroying angels. He prepared a path for his anger; he did not spare them from death but gave them over to the plague. He struck down all the firstborn of Egypt, the firstfruits of manhood in the tents of Ham.

But he brought his people out like a flock; he led them like sheep through the wilderness. He guided them safely, so they were unafraid; but the sea engulfed their enemies. And so he brought them to the border of his holy land, to the hill country his right hand had taken. He drove out nations before them and allotted their lands to them as an inheritance; he settled the tribes of Israel in their homes. But they put God to the test and rebelled against the Most High; they did not keep his statutes. Like their ancestors they were disloyal and faithless, as unreliable as a faulty bow. They angered him with their high places; they aroused his jealousy with their idols. When God heard them, he was furious; he rejected Israel completely.

He abandoned the tabernacle of Shiloh, the tent he had set up among humans. He sent the ark of his might into captivity, his splendor into the hands of the enemy. He gave his people over to the sword; he was furious with his inheritance. Fire consumed their young men, and their young women had no wedding songs; their priests were put to the sword, and their widows could not weep. Then the Lord awoke as from sleep, as a warrior wakes from the stupor of wine.

He beat back his enemies; he put them to everlasting shame. Then he rejected the tents of Joseph, he did not choose the tribe of Ephraim; but he chose the tribe of Judah, Mount Zion, which he loved. He built his sanctuary like the heights, like the earth that he established forever. He chose David his servant and took him from the sheep pens; from tending the sheep he brought him to be the shepherd of his people Jacob, of Israel his inheritance. And David shepherded them with integrity of heart; with skillful hands he led them.

O God, the nations have invaded your inheritance; they have defiled your holy temple, they have reduced Jerusalem to rubble. They have left the dead bodies of your servants as food for the birds of the sky, the flesh of your own people for the animals of the wild. They have poured out blood like water all around Jerusalem, and there is no one to bury the dead. We are objects of contempt to our neighbors, of scorn and derision to those around us.

How long, LORD? Will you be angry forever? How long will your jealousy burn like fire? Pour out your wrath on the nations that do not acknowledge you, on the kingdoms that do not call on your name; for they have devoured Jacob and devastated his homeland. Do not hold against us the sins of past generations; may your mercy come quickly to meet us, for we are in desperate need. Help us, God our Savior, for the glory of your name; deliver us and forgive our sins for your name's sake.

Why should the nations say, "Where is their God?" Before our eyes, make known among the nations that you avenge the outpoured blood of your servants. May the groans of the prisoners come before you; with your strong arm preserve those condemned to die. Pay back into the laps of our neighbors seven times the contempt they have hurled at you, Lord. Then we your people, the sheep of your pasture, will praise you forever; from generation to generation we will proclaim your praise. (Ps. 78:41–79:13)

God has given humanity breath and life to be a part of His world. A Christian's life should demonstrate God's power and strength. A believers sole job is to know God and to trust Him in faith to continue doing what He has always done— protected and provided for His people. Do we believe it? Or are we limiting Him and testing Him through our lack of faith?

Remain holy before God. Don't compromise!

The angel of the LORD went up from Gilgal to Bokim and said, "I brought you up out of Egypt and led you into the land I swore to give to your ancestors. I said, 'I will never break my covenant with you, and you shall not make a covenant with the people of this land, but you shall break down their altars.' Yet you have disobeyed me. Why have you done this? And I have also said, 'I will not drive them out before you; they will become traps for you, and their gods will become snares to you'" (Judg. 2:1–3).

When Christians do the same detestable things the world does, then they will lose their strength. Christians who drink alcohol because the world says alcohol is normal need to develop in their understanding of holiness. Christians shouldn't be living with or sleeping with people they aren't married to. Christians should be separate, set apart, and distinct in all their doings. A failure to be separate puts believers in danger of falling to the false gods and their total domination.

Christians must remain pure. They must keep the commands of God regardless of the actions or the thoughts about their choices from those around them. The Bible tells us we are a peculiar people. Christians are people who seem strange to the people who are around us. God didn't call us to do the things the world does. He does not give a free pass to sin, permitting the church to do all the same sins everyone else is going to Hell for— chiefly the sin of unbelief and doubt.

To be strong, defeat your enemies, and continue to remain a powerful force in God's house you must never compromise. You must learn what God's word expects of you and then fulfill it—every single part of it through faith.

"So I tell you this, and insist on it in the Lord, that you must no longer live as the Gentiles do, in the futility of their thinking. They are dark-

ened in their understanding and separated from the life of God because of the ignorance that is in them due to the hardening of their hearts. Having lost all sensitivity, they have given themselves over to sensuality so as to indulge in every kind of impurity, and they are full of greed.

That, however, is not the way of life you learned when you heard about Christ and were taught in him in accordance with the truth that is in Jesus. You were taught, with regard to your former way of life, to put off your old self, which is being corrupted by its deceitful desires; to be made new in the attitude of your minds; and to put on the new self, created to be like God in true righteousness and holiness.

Therefore each of you must put off falsehood and speak truthfully to your neighbor, for we are all members of one body. "In your anger do not sin": Do not let the sun go down while you are still angry, and do not give the devil a foothold. Anyone who has been stealing must steal no longer, but must work, doing something useful with their own hands, that they may have something to share with those in need.

Do not let any unwholesome talk come out of your mouths, but only what is helpful for building others up according to their needs, that it may benefit those who listen. And do not grieve the Holy Spirit of God, with whom you were sealed for the day of redemption. Get rid of all bitterness, rage and anger, brawling and slander, along with every form of malice. Be kind and compassionate to one another, forgiving each other, just as in Christ God forgave you" (Eph. 4:17–32).

Christians are expected to be different. We are called to stand out and to say no to the things that the world doesn't say no to. When Baalam, a traitor prophet, was asked to put a curse on God's people, he found that he couldn't do it. God wouldn't allow His people to be cursed when they were walking in full obedience to Him, following His ordinances and commands. No matter what, God protected the integrity and lives of His people as they continued to do what He told them to do and served Him with their whole hearts.

It was only when Baalam was able to introduce unholy practices into God's people's camps that he was able to get God to turn His back on the people He once protected. Sin will bring a curse. It will cause God to turn away from people, even those that He at one time protected, talked to, and was intimate with. No one is exempt from holiness. All of us must go before God daily and ask Him if we have any sin in our lives, because only a pure and just man in the eyes of God continues to walk with Him into the future.

When we see the world doing evil we shouldn't be surprised. They are not a part of the Church. Sinners need to be witnessed to, taught, and told the truth so they can have a chance to repent. A conversion to Christianity is something that should change us. We got washed in the blood of Christ, and we should stop sinning and be different from how we were before. This also calls us to understand the suffering and captivity of sinners because we ourselves were once sinners, too, but because we found Christ, we are no longer in bondage to our sin.

Do you not know that wrongdoers will not inherit the kingdom of God? Do not be deceived: Neither the sexually immoral nor idolaters nor adulterers nor men who have sex with men nor thieves nor the greedy nor drunkards nor slanderers nor swindlers will inherit the kingdom of God. And that is what some of you were. But you were washed, you were sanctified, you were justified in the name of the Lord Jesus Christ and by the Spirit of our God (1 Cor. 6:9–11).

However, we must note that God classifies sinners differently from how He classifies those within the Church who have formally been forgiven but continue to do wrong when they know the truth. Sometimes God will remove people from the earth so their souls can be saved if they do not stop sinning, even when they claim to know God and His word. Some deaths occur because if they didn't, other people in the Church could be led astray by associating with a little bit of old yeast. If we know what we need to do, we will be accountable for doing it. God doesn't want us to sin against Him. He doesn't want us to go to Hell. God says, *"If anyone, then, knows the good they ought to do and doesn't do it, it is a sin for them"* (James 4:17).

It is actually reported that there is sexual immorality among you, and of a kind that even pagans do not tolerate: A man is sleeping with his father's wife. And you are proud! Shouldn't you rather have gone into mourning and have put out of your fellowship the man who has been doing this? For my part, even though I am not physically present, I am with you in spirit. As one who is present with you in this way, I have already passed judgment in the name of our Lord Jesus on the one who has been doing this. So when you are assembled and I am with you in spirit, and the power of our Lord Jesus is present, hand this man over to Satan for the destruction of the flesh, so that his spirit may be saved on the day of the Lord.

Your boasting is not good. Don't you know that a little yeast leavens the whole batch of dough? Get rid of the old yeast, so that you may be a new unleavened batch—as you really are. For Christ, our Passover lamb, has been sacrificed. Therefore let us keep the Festival, not with the old bread leavened with malice and wickedness, but with the unleavened bread of sincerity and truth.

I wrote to you in my letter not to associate with sexually immoral people—not at all meaning the people of this world who are immoral, or the greedy and swindlers, or idolaters. In that case you would have to leave this world. But now I am writing to you that you must not associate with anyone who claims to be a brother or sister but is sexually immoral or greedy, an idolater or slanderer, a drunkard or swindler. Do not even eat with such people. What business is it of mine to judge those outside the church? Are you not to judge those inside? God will judge those outside. "Expel the wicked person from among you" (1 Cor. 5:1–13).

Compromises in the Church are dangerous. We must be sure to be on guard for people who want us to compromise or change and alter God's word. When Moses went to get a word from God for the people, Aaron compromised and allowed the people to begin to worship false gods. As Moses came back down, he had to intervene and ask the Lord not to destroy the people. If Moses had not prayed to God and interceded on behalf of the people, they would have been destroyed for their idol worship.

When leaders permit compromise, as Aaron did, people will be in danger of losing everything. Leaders must never compromise and must be strong like Moses. Not everyone is the same in the Spirit. Some people train, hear from God, and walk in full obedience to God and His word. These people will be distinct, different, confident, and bold. They will prove themselves to be followers of God. They will show the world through the demonstration and supernatural signs and wonders that God is with them. These people will lead others to be closer to God. They will teach people to live a holy life.

God did extraordinary miracles through Paul, so that even handkerchiefs and aprons that had touched him were taken to the sick, and their illnesses were cured and the evil spirits left them. Some Jews who went around driving out evil spirits tried to invoke the name of the Lord Jesus over those who were demon-possessed. They would say, "In the name of the Jesus whom Paul preaches, I command you to come out." Seven sons of Sceva, a Jewish chief priest, were doing this. One day the evil spirit answered them, "Jesus I know, and Paul I know about, but who are you?" Then the man who had the evil spirit jumped on them and overpowered them all. He gave them such a beating that they ran out of the house naked and bleeding (Acts 19:11–16).

Devils can be domestically violent, and Christian leaders need to be violent back. We can drive out devils and win if we have the Holy Spirit. Domestic violence is a demonically inspired religious institution and practice. For domestic violence to continue, people must bow down before a demanding, degrading, and despicable spirit that hates them and wants them to be dejected, defeated, and weak. Victims are often sacrificed and lose their lives. This isn't godly. This isn't of our Lord Jesus.

Domestic abusers come as friends. They come as Delilahs inquiring, "Where does your strength come from? Tell me, please, if you love me, so I can steal it." Do we recognize when we are with a Delilah? Do we stand against her or him and stand strong for our covenant with God? Can we see when a loved one is unequally yoked with these spirits? Are we willing to intervene and help them?

The Lord will bring victory if we are willing to fight. God delivers His people. If Samson had stood strong against Delilah she wouldn't have been able to capture him and lead him to his demise and his death. God wants His people to be strong. He will give His people the chance to have the last word, the last victory, the last manifestation of power over their enemies. God will allow us to shape the story, to detect the enemies in our lives, and to drive them out with His power. So let us determine ahead of time, before their final attack, that we are going to resist them. We are going to stand with God no matter what.

Samson could have continued to resist his enemy. He could have recognized Delilah as a threat after the Lord told him that she was one. His failure to believe God's report about his enemy was what caused him to be captured and taken into captivity. His failure to stand against the Devil presenting itself as a friend was what caused his demise. I warn you today, friend. Don't be like Samson. Don't allow the enemy to take you captive. Believe the word of the Lord when He tells you the truth about a person. Trust God. He will always tell you the truth, even when it is hard to accept.

We can't tell people to blindly trust an abuser. We can't, with a good conscience, think that they don't know what they are doing. Don't believe they are not being compensated and paid by the Devil to do what they are doing. The Devil often offers people a powerful position, as he offered to Delilah, because he wants people to side with him to defeat God's anointed people. To be honest, I hope Delilah and all who worked with her were destroyed that day in the temple. I hope they saw the power of God coming down on their lives as they took their last breath. These people weren't good people. They were people who worshiped devils and gave human sacrifices to their gods.

They were people who wanted to taste the blood of the Saints and destroy their ministry. These people don't deserve pity. They don't deserve tears. Wicked people who do the work of devils don't deserve to be praised and remembered as great men and women. All of the people who openly mock God, mock God's people, and make fun of them will be stopped by God Himself. God will always have the last laugh. He will always have the last word, and when His people work with Him, they will demonstrate His continual and eternal power today.

When we are willing to be bold and go forward in faith with God, believers and unbelievers alike will see that there is a God who exists and refuses to compromise with devils. Do you want God to use you in this way? Do you want Him to show the world that He is the Most High and He is not one to be played with?

Now the rulers of the Philistines assembled to offer a great sacrifice to Dagon their god and to celebrate, saying, "Our god has delivered Samson, our enemy, into our hands." When the people saw him, they praised their god, saying, "Our god has delivered our enemy into our hands, the one who laid waste our land and multiplied our slain." While they were in high spirits, they shouted, "Bring out Samson to entertain us." So they called Samson out of the prison, and he performed for them."

When they stood him among the pillars, Samson said to the servant who held his hand, "Put me where I can feel the pillars that support the temple, so that I may lean against them." Now the temple was crowded with men and women; all the rulers of the Philistines were there, and on the roof were about three thousand men and women watching Samson perform. Then Samson prayed to the Lord, "Sovereign Lord, remember me. Please, God, strengthen me just once more, and let me with one blow get revenge on the Philistines for my two eyes."

Then Samson reached toward the two central pillars on which the temple stood. Bracing himself against them, his right hand on the one and his left hand on the other, Samson said, "Let me die with the Philistines!" Then he pushed with all his might, and down came the temple on the rulers and all the people in it. Thus he killed many more when he died than while he lived (Judg. 16:23–30).

We must ask ourselves challenging questions to grow. If you are in an abusive relationship, or you know someone who is, do you want the deceived, manipulated person to die with the Philistines? Do you want to give them the ability to capture you and take you to your total demise? Or do you want to obey God and resist the devil of domestic abuse in your life or the life of someone you love? Are you willing to believe God when He says that He hates injustice and corruption, and that He will deliver His people when they are mistreated by devils and those who serve them?

If you are a minister, I challenge you today to train others how to fight the domestic devil in their lives. Choose to confront, address, and drive out the evil in the household in front of you. Of course you can compromise. But will you knowingly turn a blind eye to those who are hurting and in need of your help? A part of the job of a pastor or a spiritual leader is deliverance and restoration. If we are truly God's people we cannot turn our backs on injustice and pretend that it isn't there. Christian leaders, we need to speak up for the voiceless. We need to help those who need help by partnering with them and standing with them in faith for their total deliverance.

Don't tell people that God wants them to be abused. Don't tell them that God hates divorce and that they must live with a devil over their head. Pray and ask God to give you wisdom. Pray and ask God to give them the spiritual armor and spiritual strength they will need, because all Christians are empowered to take out devils. All Christians can win this battle, but they must be trained on how. *"Praise be to the LORD my Rock, who trains my hands for war, my fingers for battle. He is my loving God and my fortress, my stronghold and my deliverer, my shield, in whom I take refuge, who subdues peoples under me"* (Ps. 144:1–2).

Whose word do you believe anyway? Is there really "truth" in everyone's story, or is that something that worldly people say as a cliché statement that hides responsibility and accountability for abusers? God will show you the truth if you want to know. He showed Solomon, a wise leader, which woman was lying about her baby. God is not a respecter of persons. He will do the same thing today for ministers, wives, children, husbands, or anyone else who wants to know what God's perfect will is for their life. Ask and you will receive. Seek and you **will** find.

Are you a Christian who believes the giants are too big? Do you believe God wants a Goliath to win the battle? Are you so naive that you think God wanted Samson to be overrun and overtaken by Delilah? Or do you believe that God will give His people a way out of captivity? Do you believe that God can do supernatural things at the hands of His people who put their trust in Him? The choice is yours to believe or not to believe, serve or not to serve, but for me and my house, we will serve the Lord.

But if serving the LORD seems undesirable to you, then choose for your-selves this day whom you will serve, whether the gods your ancestors served beyond the Euphrates, or the gods of the Amorites, in whose land you are liv-ing. But as for me and my household, we will serve the LORD (Josh. 24:15).

Martin Luther King, Jr. once said, "In the End, we will remember not the words of our enemies, but the silence of our friends."

{ 17 }

Not Mad, Just Misunderstood

In the days following her husband's death many people thought Amanda was bitter, especially as they learned the truth about her abusive marriage. "She must hate him. He sounds like he was awful," whispered the people all around her. They didn't get it. They didn't understand at all. Amanda didn't hate her former husband. She had loved him very much, probably more than most people will ever love anyone. Amanda had done all she could to love him and to help him. She had tried her best to change things for them, so their story didn't end the way that it did.

Amanda understood how God felt. People think that God is bitter, angry, and glad to be separated from people for an eternity, but the truth is, God doesn't feel that way at all. God hates being separated from His creation who He wants to help and save from. It isn't God's plan for people to choose to rebel against Him and force Him to take their lives from them.

The truth is, the world would be better without demonically inspired men and women leading others to Hell. Some people don't give God another option. It is either let them live and permit more people to be led into darkness, or get rid of them so they can't continue to spread their filth and disease to others. *"This is what the LORD Almighty says: 'Look! Disaster is spreading from nation to nation; a mighty storm is rising from the ends of the earth.' At that time those slain by the LORD will be everywhere—from one end of the earth to the other. They will*

*not be mourned or gathered up or buried, but will be like dung lying on the
ground"* (Jer. 25:32–33).

Sin spreads like a plague. Sin is a form of sickness. It is spiritual
decay. Out of a love for people, the Lord will remove certain people
from the earth, because if they aren't removed they will cause others
to go to Hell. Headship, when abused, puts those under the headship
in danger. And in this particular situation, if God didn't remove
Nathanial, his wife and children would not abide in the good, safe
pastures that He had promised them in His word. They wouldn't have
the same life or opportunities. When a place is full of filth, it cannot breed health. If something is going to be pure, the filth must be
purged.

King Hezekiah's father was an evil man who worshipped false
gods and set up altars for evil. He shut the temple doors and allowed
the worship of God to lie dormant, and even sacrificed his own child,
Hezekiah's brother, to the demons he worshipped. People who serve
demons cannot have loyalty or lead their children into a loving relationship with God. They also can't lead others with whom they are
associated or in authority over them into one.

We aren't sure how Hezekiah ended up serving God and hating
evil. The Bible doesn't recount how he was endowed with the passion,
love, and fervent desire to please God and trust Him, but we know
that he did the opposite of his father. He chose to hate evil and cut
ties with it. Hezekiah cut down all the foreign altars. He reopened the
temple, gave offerings, and encouraged God's people to follow him
and remove evil from their lives and their families.

*At the king's command, couriers went throughout Israel and Judah with
letters from the king and from his officials, which read: "People of Israel, return to the LORD, the God of Abraham, Isaac and Israel, that he may return to you who are left, who have escaped from the hand of the kings of
Assyria. Do not be like your parents and your fellow Israelites, who were unfaithful to the LORD, the God of their ancestors, so that he made them an
object of horror, as you see. Do not be stiff-necked, as your ancestors were;*

submit to the LORD. Come to his sanctuary, which he has consecrated forever. Serve the LORD your God, so that his fierce anger will turn away from you. If you return to the LORD, then your fellow Israelites and your children will be shown compassion by their captors and will return to this land, for the LORD your God is gracious and compassionate. He will not turn his face from you if you return to him" (2 Chr. 30:6–9).

To restore the temple, Hezekiah had to remove all the foreign gods. If God was going to be supreme in the lives of the people of this land, and He was going to be given the proper position of authority, then the evil had to be eradicated from their presence. Cleansing, cleaning, removing, and reestablishing the proper authority in the houses and places of worship was a requirement for their salvation. It was the only reason they weren't destroyed by their enemies as some of their family members had been.

When all this had ended, the Israelites who were there went out to the towns of Judah, smashed the sacred stones and cut down the Asherah poles. They destroyed the high places and the altars throughout Judah and Benjamin and in Ephraim and Manasseh. After they had destroyed all of them, the Israelites returned to their own towns and to their own property (2 Chr. 31:1).

In addition, they distributed to the males three years old or more whose names were in the genealogical records—all who would enter the temple of the LORD to perform the daily duties of their various tasks, according to their responsibilities and their divisions. And they distributed to the priests enrolled by their families in the genealogical records and likewise to the Levites twenty years old or more, according to their responsibilities and their divisions. They included all the little ones, the wives, and the sons and daughters of the whole community listed in these genealogical records. For they were faithful in consecrating themselves (2 Chr. 31:16–18).

Hezekiah was given the opportunity to choose a different course from his father as his life had been spared. He was raised in a time when the full wrath of God was not manifest in people's lives. In the middle of the prophecies, the people made a different decision, and it changed the future of the next generation and those who wanted to make a different choice. If the people had chosen to continue in their evil practices, then everyone would have been destroyed. Everyone, including the children, would not have been given a choice to change their futures.

At the end of sin there is death. In the early stages of sin, it often seems like things are manageable or that they can be dealt with, but when sin has taken its full course in a life, death is impending and knocks on the door. Later in Hezekiah's life he would face this exact thing. He was heading toward death. It was nearing him, and he was given a prophecy that he was going to die soon. 2 Kings 20:1 says, *"In those days Hezekiah became ill and was at the point of death. The prophet Isaiah son of Amoz went to him and said, 'This is what the LORD says: Put your house in order, because you are going to die; you will not recover.'"*

This prophecy was given by the prophet who simply reported what he saw coming in Hezekiah's life. However, the prophecy was then reversed shortly after because of Hezekiah's actions. He asked God to heal him, and He did.

Hezekiah turned his face to the wall and prayed to the LORD, "Remember, LORD, how I have walked before you faithfully and with wholehearted devotion and have done what is good in your eyes." And Hezekiah wept bitterly. Before Isaiah had left the middle court, the word of the LORD came to him: "Go back and tell Hezekiah, the ruler of my people, 'This is what the LORD, the God of your father David, says: I have heard your prayer and seen your tears; I will heal you. On the third day from now you will go up to the temple of the LORD. I will add fifteen years to your life. And I will deliver you and this city from the hand of the king of Assyria. I will defend this city for my sake and for the sake of my servant David'" (2 Kings 20:2–6).

Scripture affirms to us that prophecies can sometimes be changed if the people involved in the prophecy abruptly turn and make a different choice. God will sometimes give prophecies for this precise reason. He wants people to see their future if they don't change. He wants them to fear what is coming so they will turn from their sin and spiritual decay and change to serve Him and continue to live.

A few months before God revealed to Amanda that her husband was going to die and leave her as a widow, she had written a book as a part of her ministry. In this book she prophesied for her husband's success and prosperity. She prophesied Nathanial would hear the Lord's voice, follow it, and win in the races of life. She was at times hopeful for the prophecy over his life about restoration, healing, and deliverance— asserting God could help anyone, even the most unsuspecting, if they would hear His voice and follow it.

The book was a gift to her husband, and she surprised him with it on their ten-year anniversary. The book was about a horse. The horse could win, regardless of what anyone else thought about him, if he trusted his trainer and adhered to the teachings. The problem was her husband didn't believe these prophecies. He didn't believe the good news, and he didn't want to follow the trainer.

Today, you can still look at the publication she created out of a place of love and belief in his success and triumph. When the book was written she still believed that God's restorative power would manifest in his life if she only believed enough. It was only when Amanda finally realized that it wasn't her belief that could set him free that she was free from misplaced guilt. There was nothing else that Amanda could do, say, or proclaim. Her prophecies of success or failure couldn't come to pass in his life unless he heard them and accepted them as his own.

God's promises can only be accessed through belief in the promise. If someone doesn't believe they can't receive. If someone wants to remain sick they will. After all it wasn't Amanda's words of prophecy that caused things to come to pass. It was Nathaniel's own words and disbelief in God that brought about his demise. Amanda was just a prophet, so she saw it coming on the horizon in the realm of the spirit as Isaiah had seen what was coming to Hezekiah.

Like she was watching a movie in her mind, Amanda saw everything coming toward Nathanial, and then she recounted the things she saw both to him and to others through her writing. Prophets don't create or cause things to happen. They see the things that are going to happen and then recount them or speak and record them so others can see them too. The events are already going to happen. They have already been set in motion, like a movie on a movie screen that has already begun to play, because of the script that is behind the movie.

Prophets see the end before the movie has completed because God permits them to see the person's script. Prophets can see the finale, but they have nothing to do with the script that caused it to occur. If a person changes the script, God can grant them a different future, but most people don't realize the power of the script that they are writing. Most don't believe the Bible when it says, *"For by **your words** you will be acquitted, and by **your words** you will be condemned"* (Matt. 12:37, emphasis added).

People write their own scripts. They come up with their own stories and then they act them out with their words and actions. The scripts of our lives are personal to us. They are something no one else can ever take away from us. God gave us all the power to control our destinies and our lives. He gave us the ability to make choices that impact everything. When Isaiah saw that Hezekiah was going to die he spoke the prophecy to him. Then, Hezekiah realized he didn't want the prophecy to come to pass, so he begged God to change the future on his behalf.

It was his position toward his future and toward God that altered his destiny and gave him another fifteen years of life. Isaiah could see the change of direction in the spirit. He could proclaim a different future for Hezekiah, not because of his own word, desires, or plans, but because of the relationship that was taking place between God and the man before him. When someone chooses to repent and turn to God, He often does change their future. A prophet doesn't *make* the change; they just report it when they see it change.

In the early part of Hezekiah's life he changed the future for the people around him because he went to God for help. Isaiah saw that Hezekiah's position with the Lord was going to position him for victory over his enemies. He saw that God was going to help Hezekiah win a battle he could never have won on his own, because **Hezekiah's words and actions** were honest and just toward God. The military force that was advancing against Hezekiah was positioned for failure with the Lord because of **their actions toward God** too. As they taunted God, and Hezekiah exalted Him, the two were bound to clash, and someone had to be taken out of the equation.

When two armies are going toward one another someone is going to win. One side must lose and the other must win. That is a part of war. Nathanial and Amanda didn't realize that this was what was happening in their marriage. They didn't know that this exact situation was playing out before their eyes. As Nathanial marched toward God and His people, mocking God with his actions and words, and Amanda positioned herself toward God, presenting her requests before Him in honesty and sincerity for help for herself and for her children, the two were headed toward a collision, a war, and one side would have to lose the battle. One side was going to have to surrender or be taken out.

Then Isaiah son of Amoz sent a message to Hezekiah: "This is what the LORD, the God of Israel, says: I have heard your prayer concerning Sennacherib king of Assyria. . . . Who is it you have ridiculed and blasphemed? Against whom have you raised your voice and lifted your eyes in pride? Against the Holy One of Israel! By your messengers you have ridiculed the Lord . . ." (2 Kings 19:20, 22–23).

"'But I know where you are and when you come and go and how you rage against me. Because you rage against me and because your insolence has reached my ears. I will put my hook in your nose and my bit in your mouth, and I will make you return by the way you came'" (2 Kings 19:27–28).

When the King of Assyria taunted God and said things like, "Where is your God? He won't save you. He won't help you. I will overtake you. I will destroy you, and your God can't help you." God heard it and took it personally. And when Nathanial said, "God isn't real, Amanda! He isn't going to help you! You are crazy for serving Him!" he was doing the same exact thing the King of Assyria had done. Amanda prayed to God for mercy and took the words of her husband to the throne of God. She humbled herself before Him, just as Hezekiah had done when he laid the letters and words spoken out before the Lord in the temple.

Hezekiah received the letter from the messengers and read it. Then he went up to the temple of the Lord and spread it out before the Lord. And Hezekiah prayed to the Lord: "Lord, the God of Israel, enthroned between the cherubim, you alone are God over all the kingdoms of the earth. You have made heaven and earth. Give ear, Lord, and hear; open your eyes, Lord, and see; listen to the words Sennacherib has sent to ridicule the living God. "It is true, Lord, that the Assyrian kings have laid waste these nations and their lands. They have thrown their gods into the fire and destroyed them, for they were not gods but only wood and stone, fashioned by human hands. Now, Lord our God, deliver us from his hand, so that all the kingdoms of the earth may know that you alone, Lord, are God" (2 Kings 19:14–19).

Therefore this is what the LORD says concerning the king of Assyria: "'He will not enter this city or shoot an arrow here. He will not come before it with shield or build a siege ramp against it. By the way that he came he will return; he will not enter this city, declares the LORD. I will defend this city and save it, for my sake and for the sake of David my servant.'" That night the angel of the LORD went out and put to death a hundred and eighty-five thousand in the Assyrian camp. When the people got up the next morning—there were all the dead bodies! So Sennacherib king of Assyria broke camp and withdrew. He returned to Nineveh and stayed there. One day, while he was worshiping in the temple of his god Nisrok, his sons Adrammelek and Sharezer killed him with the sword, and they escaped to the land of Ararat. And Esarhaddon his son succeeded him as king (2 Kings 19:32–37).

Sometimes when we think we are writing a personal letter to another person or a group of people, we are in fact writing it to God.

God sees what we speak and what we write. He watches over the words of our mouths, and He watches over the work of our hands. He sees all we do. Hezekiah thought he was reading a letter from an opposing king written to him, but what he was reading was a letter from another king addressed to God. The same was true for the King of Assyria, because as Hezekiah refused to back down to his enemy and quoted his love for God, he sent a personal message to God, showing Him he loved Him and cared for Him.

Amanda and her children were going to be more than all right. The Lord was their protector and provider. Her children weren't going to serve the false gods of their father. They weren't going to be invaded and taken over by enemy forces and have their homes and security stripped from them. They were going to live. They were going to be preserved because of their mothers' decision to align with the truth. But Nathanial, in his refusal to honor his creator, would know there is a God, and His name isn't Ashur, Ashera, or that of any other foreign god. God's name is Jehovah. His son's name is Jesus. He is the God of Abraham, Issac, and Jacob, and there is no other God higher than Him.

God doesn't even need to come down from Heaven to destroy 150,000 soldiers. He can send one angel and defeat an entire powerful army that was known for its devastation, conquering, and war. Don't you know how big God is? Don't you see that God is powerful, strong, and able to deliver His people from anything that the enemy tries to throw at them? Don't limit the Holy One of Israel. Don't assume He can't do mighty miracles, works, and healings today. He does and always has helped His people when they call on Him for help.

Amanda didn't want people's sympathy. She didn't want them to give her alms and act like she was a weak and pitiful woman. Because the truth is, she wasn't even close to that. She was a Christian and the Spirit of Almighty God was within her. She had the help of legions of angels. She could call down fire from Heaven and see the altar light up. Can't you hear it? Can't you perceive it, you of little faith?

Jesus called his twelve disciples to him and gave them authority to drive out impure spirits and to heal every disease and sickness (Matt. 10:10).

{ **18** }

Tombstone

"Put it on my tombstone. I didn't care about the church. I know God. God isn't who you people think He is," Nathanial said one evening as the family was in the kitchen preparing to eat dinner. "Come with me to Church tomorrow," Amanda suggested. "You will get to see your grandpa since it is his church. God is letting me preach there tomorrow because the pastor is sick. You should come! You and the kids come!" "No, thank you," he said. "The Church has nothing for me. I am just fine."

Amanda accepted the news, but she didn't want to. *Why doesn't he just come to church? If he could come hear me preach then maybe he would change his mind,* she thought to herself. *I want him to know the truth. I want him to be saved. It isn't too late.* But Amanda had just finished writing the book of the prophecy God had given her. She thought that things couldn't change. "It looks hopeless. He isn't going to change. This is just the way it is, I guess," she told herself.

But deep inside her spirit Amanda kept wondering and talking to God. "God, is this really how it has to end? Does he really have to die and go to Hell? Isn't there something I can do? Isn't there something You can do? I don't want him to die not knowing You. I don't want to live a life without him. I really do love him. The kids love him. They need a dad. Is there a way to turn this situation around? Or is this Your plan? God, I will do whatever You think is best. I will do whatever You want me to do. Let Your plan happen. Please. I will even stay with him and keep doing what I have been doing, even though I know what kind of man he has been."

After dinner Amanda went into her bedroom where she had a bookcase. The spinning bookcase had been moved, and she saw the Holy Spirit draw a circle around the book, *The Praying Wife*. At first she told herself, "What is the point of praying? Why would I pray? He doesn't care, God. Look at everything he is saying. Look at what he is doing." But she heard the Holy Ghost say to pick the book up, open it up, and pray for her husband. "Okay, God, I will open it," and she did. When she saw the page, she opened her mouth and gasped.

The first page was a page with a prayer for her husband's mind. It addressed the demonic forces attacking his thinking and mindset. The page said: "I command the spirits attacking my husband's mind to be gone from him. I pray that my husband has a sound mind as You promised us we could have in the Scriptures. I pray now in the name of Jesus that the devils after his thinking be removed. I pray that he will see the truth and it will set him free. Let my husband know what is right. Let him walk in the truth and walk toward You and Your salvation."

Once she had completed the first prayer she flipped to another page. This page addressed the sexual relationship of the couple. Sex was the start of their big fight because Nathanial wanted her to have oral sex with him when she didn't want to. The oral sex debate was what had begun their last fight and caused him to say he would find what he needed somewhere else. That comment was what caused God to be angry at him and place the death sentence over his head.

"Whoa!! You must really want me to pray this, God," Amanda said. "Okay, here we go. God, I pray for our marriage's sexual relationship. I pray that we will meet each other's needs but remain holy and pure. I pray that the marriage bed will remain pure. I pray that we will respect each other and what we want. I pray that we won't push each other to do anything, but that we will work together and be one flesh as you intended."

Amanda wondered why God would have her pray this prayer. He had already said Nathanial was going to die. He had already told her that he was a dead man. Why in the world would God have her praying these prayers for their marriage and for her husband's well-being? Amanda thought it was strange, but she was obedient. She prayed the prayers, got everyone ready for bed, and went to sleep. She needed to be up early to preach at Nathanial's grandpa's church.

During the night Amanda had a dream where God showed her talking to another minister, where they talked about a soda. When she woke up she prayed and asked God to tell her the meaning of the dream and what she was supposed to preach that day. Just then, God told her to read Joshua 8:34–35. She opened up her Bible app and read: "*Afterward, Joshua read all the words of the law—the blessings and the curses—just as it is written in the Book of the Law. There was not a word of all that Moses had commanded that Joshua did not read to the whole assembly of Israel, including the women and children, and the foreigners who lived among them.*"

So that was the scripture God wanted Amanda to read and preach on. She got up and went outside to do her workout as she did in the mornings before she took her shower or got ready for the day. It was during her workout time that she would get quiet and alone with God. She would separate herself from her family and hear what He wanted to say to her. Amanda loved listening to sermons when she worked out, and today she knew which minister she needed to listen to. She typed into YouTube the minister's name and the word "soda."

A message popped up and she clicked on it in faith, believing the message was going to have what she needed in it. No sooner had the minister started preaching his message than she heard him say something about Joshua. As he went into his message, he also mentioned the Kentucky Derby. A horse racing book was the book that God had given her to dedicate to her husband. She had the book themed to be like the Kentucky Derby. He went on about horses for at least five minutes, but horses were the thing that God had been speaking to her about her husband.

For their ten-year anniversary a few months prior they had visited Mount Vernon, the home of America's first president, George Washington. When they were there, she said, "Look, horses!" as she saw the horse gifts in the gift shop. "I know there is something to the horse thing because God told me to give you this horse book." After the couple finished walking around the estate and having a beautiful time together, they decided to get a take-home present to remember their anniversary.

"My parents didn't make it ten years," Amanda said. Her parents had divorced when she was a young girl, and she didn't know what it was like to grow up in a house with a mom and dad who loved each other. That is one of the reasons she always wanted to be married and believed that marriage was sacred. Amanda knew that marriage was supposed to be forever. She knew that divorce was far too prevalent in her society. "I don't want to ever get a divorce," they agreed. "Marriage is important."

The take-home present they finally settled on was an ornament that had a horse and carriage with George Washington and his wife, Martha, sitting inside. "This is perfect! It is so cute. It has the horse and us in a carriage together. It will remind me of giving you the horse book and of our date at Mount Vernon. I want this one!" Amanda said. Her husband nodded and replied, "Okay, whatever you want. I'll get it for you. That one is cool."

As the couple went to put up their Christmas tree that Christmas season, they proudly got out their ornament from the box and hung it on the tree. Their first-year anniversary ornament was broken. "It is old. Maybe we could get another one that still says the same thing," Nathanial suggested. "No, that would be silly. It is just missing a few jewels. The point of the ornament is that it was for our first Christmas. Who cares if it's broken? It is ours," Amanda said.

As Amanda listened to the preacher speak about horses, the Kentucky Derby, and flavor, which was the title of his message, she noticed God was speaking to her directly about what was going on in her life. "God, why did You tell me to write the horse book? Why did You tell me to write down the prophecy of Nathanial's death, and what does this have to do with the message I am preaching today? Explain, please!" she said to God. The pastor got to the end of his message and said, "Pray for those who persecute you and be good to those who have done wrong to you. There is a higher way than praying for the demise of your enemies. You can pray for their good."

Amanda remembered how the night before God had told her to pray for her husband. Despite his outward condition, she knew God wanted her to pray over him. Now God was talking to her about praying for her husband once again. He was saying, *"But I tell you, love your enemies and pray for those who persecute you"* (Matt. 5:44). Amanda got off her treadmill, headed inside, and got in the shower. Before she got in, she looked over at her husband, who was asleep in bed, and he looked dead. He wasn't moving as he lay on his back, just motionless.

Amanda was startled. Now that God had told her he was going to die she was worried about when he would be gone. She was watching his every move to see if he was still okay and breathing. Then the Spirit of God said, "Everyone must die if they are going to live. All people are sinners. All people deserve to go to Hell. No one is worthy, not one. For a man to live they must first die to themselves. If people are going to ever be alive, then they must die, not physically, but spiritually."

"God, what are you saying to me?" Amanda asked God as she was taking her shower. "Are you saying that he is spiritually dead, and the death I am seeing could be his carnal nature? His human desire is to live apart from you? Are you saying that you are going to save my husband and he is going to die, but not literally, just spiritually, he is going to die to himself?"

Then God reminded Amanda of the man on the cross who was dying in his sins, but he asked Jesus to forgive him and Jesus said He would. God also reminded her of Jesus's words on the cross, "Father, forgive them for they know not what they do." God reminded her for thirty minutes that people must die to themselves if they are going to be saved. He kept on telling her that death is a part of spiritual rebirth, and that all things are possible to those who believe.

Amanda left the house and headed to church to preach to the people at Nathanial's grandfather's church. When she got there one of the men was talking to Nathanial's grandpa and said, "I saw your last name on one of the tombstones when we went to a funeral this week. I wondered if you were related." Amanda's ears perked up. God had been talking to her about tombstones, and he had been talking to her about her husband's name being on one.

Amanda prepared her ministry table for people to learn about her ministry, then she got up before the people and preached the message God had given her out of Joshua. She spoke about how God wants all people, regardless of their age or background, to hear the full counsel of His word. Then she went on to tell them that God loves all of us, and that we have a job to do to ensure people don't go to Hell. She said, "Each one of us is responsible for ministering to the people in front of us. If we don't, who will? We will know people in eternity. We must tell them about Jesus."

She also spoke about the difference in leadership. Some leaders, like Moses, hear from God and intercede for others, and others, like Aaron, do what people want them to do, but they don't confront people in love and with the full sword of the word, because they are afraid that they won't be liked. "A real leader must tell people the truth even when they don't want to hear it. They must not care if they are liked by the people they are called to minister to, because sometimes people don't like to hear what they need to hear. Some foods are harder to digest than others. But we must help people mature and grow up. We must feed them the whole word."

"All people of all ages deserve to be told the truth," she told them. "Joshua tells us that God wants all people, even the foreigners, to hear the message. We must take the message. We must tell people the truth, so they don't go to Hell. God has called us to do this work. He has called us to heal the sick, cast out devils, and trample on the enemy. He has called us to do the work of the ministry. Jesus said, 'Greater works than I do will you do also.' Are you doing greater works than Jesus? Are you seeing what God says can be manifested in your life? If not, press into the word. Study the word. Devour the word as you would food."

Amanda released everyone with a prayer of power, strength, and ability. She prayed a prayer exalting God's kingdom, noting that Jesus told us to pray like this: "Your kingdom come, your will be done, on earth as it is in Heaven." Amanda prayed over the people for them to be strong and to go forth with boldness and power over the enemy, so they could do God's work and help to save the lives of those around them. As Amanda started driving home she realized that the message was for her and her husband.

"Is it that You want me to rise in authority and command the Devil to get away from my husband?" she asked herself and God. "Is it that he will be saved, and that is why I saw him as a dead man, because he was going to die to his old nature and his former self? I remember hearing Kenneth Hagin preach a message one time where he said that he claimed his brother's salvation. Can I claim my husband's salvation and take my authority over the devils trying to steal, kill, and destroy him and take his life?"

"Aha! I finally see now. The story isn't over. The ending isn't what I thought it was going to be at all! I did see him die, but I saw him die to himself. He is going to be saved if I rise and take my authority in the spirit over the devils attacking him and stand in the gap for him in intercession as his wife. That is why God is telling me to pray. That is why God said for us to pray for our enemies because we can change things through our prayers. We can change things if we bind the devils and proclaim the soul will be saved."

I will give you the keys of the kingdom of heaven; whatever you bind on earth will be bound in heaven, and whatever you loose on earth will be loosed in heaven (Matt. 16:19).

"How could I have been so foolish and blind? Why was I so immature in my understanding of the Scripture?" Amanda realized. "This whole time I thought that I was seeing correctly, but I was not seeing right at all. God had to show me all of this so I would care about my husband's soul. If I hadn't seen him dead and believed he was dead, I wouldn't have begun to intercede for him in prayer and in the spirit world. I would have just kept on allowing the enemy to attack him when I had the weapons to stop him. God, I am so sorry."

"Why was my heart so dark. Why was it so evil? Why didn't I care about him more? Why didn't I try harder to pray for him before? Why did it take me to see him as a dead man to begin to care about his eternal destination? I am a spiritual woman. I am constantly learning spiritual things, but I am no better than the Pharisees were. I knew the truth, but I didn't share it with the people that I loved. God, please forgive me for being so cold. Please forgive me for judging Nathanial so harshly when I myself was foolish," Amanda said. "This whole time You have been trying to teach me that I needed to care about my husband. You have been trying to show me what a hypocrite I am."

How can you say to your brother, "Let me take the speck out of your eye," when all the time there is a plank in your own eye? You hypocrite, first take the plank out of your own eye, and then you will see clearly to remove the speck from your brother's eye (Matt. 7:4–5).

"At one time I was glad that people were praying for me and believing for me to be saved, even when I didn't deserve it. I was just like him, in need of a Savior and in need of people who were spiritually mature and wise to intercede on my behalf. All this time God wanted me to care about my husband who was in front of me perishing. He wanted me to invest in his life and try to help him see the truth that I had."

"Now leave me alone so that my anger may burn against them and that I may destroy them. Then I will make you into a great nation." But Moses sought the favor of the LORD his God. *"LORD,"* he said, *"why should your anger burn against your people, whom you brought out of Egypt with great power and a mighty hand?"* (Exod. 32:10–11).

If Moses had not interceded for the people, then the Lord would have destroyed them, but God responded to Moses's prayers. He was merciful toward the people because of the prayers. Prayers do change things in Heaven! Prayers also change things on the earth. James 5:16 says, *"Therefore confess your sins to each other and pray for each other so that you may be healed. The prayer of a righteous person is powerful and effective."*

This whole time Amanda thought that this was about her husband. She thought that God wanted to discipline him and show him how bad he was, but really God was trying to show her that she wasn't as perfect as she thought she was. She still had growing and maturing to do. She still needed to learn about God's love and grace, so she could extend love and compassion toward others.

"If I couldn't even show my husband grace how in the world can I show grace to others?" Amanda wondered. "Now I see that I can change this. I can help my husband receive Christ, die to himself, and get the Devil away from him." She prayed, "God, you have given me power and authority over evil. You have given me a way to help my husband out of his problems and afflictions. Please help me be a better wife. Help me to love my husband as You love him. Help me to see that he can't be good outside of a relationship with You. Help me to intercede for him in the spirit. Help me to become a wife who can change his heart and mind about what a Christian really is."

"God, forgive me for being a religious person, a person who looks for the fault in others but doesn't do anything to intercede for them and help them. Help me to be a stronger Christian. I don't want to be this way, and I promise to write these things down for others to see my failures and my part of the story. I will obey You. I will confess my sins to others so I can be healed. I will trust You and Your word, where You tell us that the prayers of a righteous person are powerful and effective. I believe that if I pray and if I intercede You will help my husband. I believe You will open his eyes, draw back the curtain on the enemy's lies, and ensure that he comes to know You and dies to himself so he can be saved."

Amanda was shocked. Knowledge was what she needed the whole time. She needed more knowledge about who God was and what He wanted her to do. She needed to humble herself and not think she was better than others. God was gracious for giving her this knowledge. God had been kind when he forgave her for all the things she had once done. And now here she was, finding herself once again in need of forgiveness from Heaven. She, too, still made mistakes, even when she was trying to do the right thing.

This battle wasn't a battle between her and her husband. It was a battle between the Devil and God. God wanted her husband to be saved, but the Devil wanted him to go to Hell. She was standing right in the middle of the battlefield, and she had weapons to use against her enemy, Satan, but she wasn't using them at all. She was asking God to do something she was supposed to do. She was asking God for help when He told her to go and take what belonged to her.

Amanda noted that the Bible says, "As for me and my house, we will serve the Lord." She said, "My husband is in my house. He is one with me. If we are one, then I can stand in faith on his behalf. I can tell the Devil to get the heck away from my man. I can get him away from my husband's mind, and I can command him to stay out of our lives. I can also pray for the Holy Spirit to minister to him. I can be the helper to him that God has called me to be." She then prayed, "God, how didn't I see this before? How did I not understand?"

God said back to her, "Amanda, you are immature in your faith. There is more to learn. Stay humble and continue to receive corrections. Don't think more of yourself than you ought. If you stay on this path you will live. You will see that there is a lot you don't know and don't do perfectly yet, but if you're faithful I will teach you. You will help others come to Christ, including your husband."

Wives, in the same way submit yourselves to your own husbands so that, if any of them do not believe the word, they may be won over without words by the behavior of their wives (1 Pet. 3:1).

Did you know that men can be won by their Christian wives' witness? Did you know that there is more to the story than you sometimes see? Sometimes we think we know the ending of a story. We think we have all the information we need, but then God will show us that there is more information needed to make a verdict. Christians have power. We can do all things through Christ, who gives us strength, including ministering in our own homes. *Who would I be if I preached to others and let the man I love go to hell in my house?* Amanda thought. *I must intercede! I have to love him better and be a better helpmate.*

Mark 9:23 teaches, *"'If you can'?" said Jesus. "Everything is possible for one who believes."* All this time she thought her husband didn't believe in the Scriptures, but come to find out, maybe she didn't fully believe and trust God as she should have either. If she had believed all things were possible, she should have believed for her husband's salvation. "Oh, what a wretched person I am. Thank you, God, for having mercy on me," she prayed.

True humility requires us to acknowledge our shortcomings. It requires us to continue to press into the spirit world knowing we have never fully arrived. There is always more to learn about God. There is always more to understand. Let us never become arrogant and prideful in our religious traditions. Let us believe God is able and willing to save all people, even when they don't look like they deserve it.

None of us deserved our salvation. All of us still depend on God's grace and mercy every day. Today, Amanda was going to challenge herself with the same message she had challenged the people with during the church service. She was going to learn more about God and His word so she could minister to her husband. She was going to pray for him and intercede on his behalf. And she was going to command the devils to stay away from him because she had the authority to tell them they weren't welcome in their family or home.

Amanda was going to challenge herself to elevate her faith. She needed to strengthen herself so she could believe that Jesus could save someone who looked like they could never be saved. It would only be through dropping the religiosity and traditions understood by man that she could believe for her husband's salvation. He needed to be saved. He could be saved, and she could witness to him and win him to Christ. He was going to die, but not in the way she assumed. He was going to die to himself. His old man was going to die, so his spirit man could live.

This whole time God wanted her to care. He wanted her to care about the man who was perishing in front of her. She claimed to love him, but she didn't. She didn't know what God's love was until that day. God's love is patient. It is kind. It is long-suffering. It doesn't keep a record of wrongdoing. It forgives and doesn't delight in evil. Love wants what God wants for a person. Love wants to see a lost, wretched soul come to life. That is God's love. *"Love never fails. But where there are prophecies, they will cease; where there are tongues, they will be stilled; where there is knowledge, it will pass away"* (1 Cor. 13:8). So maybe if Nathanial did die it would be her fault. Maybe if he went to Hell it would be because she hadn't done enough to ensure he could come to the light and receive his salvation. Maybe after all the problem wasn't him. It was her and her inability to practice what she preached.

Sometimes it is easier to judge others and look at their weaknesses and failures, but are we ready to look at our own? Are we willing to go before God and humble ourselves and ask for mercy? Can we be honest with Him and with others and admit that we, too, need help? The prophecy she spoke of would come to pass but not like she thought it would. She didn't have all the knowledge yet. He was going to die, but not literally, just spiritually, so he could finally live.

"*No, I strike a blow to my body and make it my slave so that after I have preached to others, I myself will not be disqualified for the prize*" (1 Cor. 9:27). The racehorse would win. The horse they had bet on together was going to make it. They were going to go away into the future together, not apart. The future God had for them was bright. They were going to ride away into the sunset—and eventually up to Heaven, hand in hand in a horse-drawn carriage—because that was God's plan. His kingdom will come and His will be done on earth as it is in Heaven. God had given Nathanial a Christian wife for a reason, and indeed it was a good thing!

He was going to find Jesus sooner than he thought. He was going to be a changed man, a new creation, soon. Amanda didn't have to wait much longer. It doesn't take that long to see what God has promised come to pass. The hard part was over. The waiting wouldn't prevail much longer. Now that she knew her power and authority over her enemy she was going to use it, and she was going to get her husband back from the grips of Hell. She was going to make sure he was a part of her future. She was going to laugh without worry and fear because when the enemy thought he had won, he discovered he hadn't.

God isn't done writing this story. This is only the beginning, and there will be great laughter after. The family will laugh more than they've ever laughed before. God was going to use his humor and authenticity to lead others to Christ. He was going to use a man who once did awful things to do great ones. Let us not forget that Paul was once Saul. He once persecuted Christians, but one encounter with Christ changed everything and turned his life around. That will be Nathaniel's story too. He will be an on-fire Christian, not a religious one.

He will see the Lord move mightily in his midst. He will prove that God is loving, gracious, and kind, and he will get people back out of Satan's hand that Satan thought he surely had forever. "Haha!" Amanda said to Satan as she realized God's bigger plan. "You really thought that Nathanial was going to die and go to Hell. You really thought that his story was over. Well, you were wrong once again. This is just the beginning of his life." This whole time Satan heard Amanda prophecy that her husband would be dead, and he thought, "I got him." Then, just when Satan thought he had won, he discovered he hadn't won at all.

Like a good horse race it may look like one horse has the lead. It may look like things are hopeless and the horse you've bet on won't win. And then, out of nowhere, your horse catches up, takes the lead, crosses the finish line, and is crowned the winner. Nathaniel would conquer his enemies. He would prove himself to be a horse that could be disciplined and broken to win through listening to His master.

Meanwhile, Saul was still breathing out murderous threats against the Lord's disciples. He went to the high priest and asked him for letters to the synagogues in Damascus, so that if he found any there who belonged to the Way, whether men or women, he might take them as prisoners to Jerusalem. As he neared Damascus on his journey, suddenly a light from heaven flashed around him. He fell to the ground and heard a voice say to him, "Saul, Saul, why do you persecute me?" "Who are you, Lord?" Saul asked. "I am Jesus, whom you are persecuting," he replied. "Now get up and go into the city, and you will be told what you must do."

The men traveling with Saul stood there speechless; they heard the sound but did not see anyone. Saul got up from the ground, but when he opened his eyes he could see nothing. So they led him by the hand into Damascus. For three days he was blind, and did not eat or drink anything. In Damascus there was a disciple named Ananias. The Lord called to him in a vision, "Ananias!" "Yes, Lord," he answered.

The Lord told him, "Go to the house of Judas on Straight Street and ask for a man from Tarsus named Saul, for he is praying. In a vision he has seen a man named Ananias come and place his hands on him to restore his sight." "Lord," Ananias answered, "I have heard many reports about this man and all the harm he has done to your holy people in Jerusalem. And he has come here with authority from the chief priests to arrest all who call on your name." But the Lord said to Ananias, "Go! This man is my chosen instrument to proclaim my name to the Gentiles and their kings and to the people of Israel. I will show him how much he must suffer for my name."

Then Ananias went to the house and entered it. Placing his hands on Saul, he said, "Brother Saul, the Lord—Jesus, who appeared to you on the road as you were coming here—has sent me so that you may see again and be filled with the Holy Spirit." Immediately, something like scales fell from Saul's eyes, and he could see again. He got up and was baptized, and after taking some food, he regained his strength (Acts 9:1–19).

Sometimes we are shocked when a horse we didn't expect to win crosses the finish line. Sometimes, we are surprised when the underdog comes through, even when no one believes in him but his trainer. But one thing is for sure, people don't have to believe you are going to win the race. No one has the right to determine if you win or lose. God alone has the last word. He alone has the last laugh, and when He believes in a person He will help him to become who only He knows he can be. Nathaniel would be baptized. He would soon be free from the enemy's grip.

The name on his tombstone wouldn't say loser. It would say overcomer. His name would be remembered for winning great battles for the Lord. He would go down in history as an underdog who, despite all the odds and all the bets against his name, would win because Jesus Christ loved him and had a plan for his life. Luke 19:9–10 says, *"Jesus said to him, 'Today salvation has come to this house, because this man, too, is a son of Abraham. For the Son of Man came to seek and to save the lost.'"*

{ **19** }

Masks or Glass

In a good marriage people can be at ease and be themselves. The best marriages are marriages where two people come together and accept each other and help each other, even when the partner doesn't deserve it. Marriage is intimate. It is a place where people can rest in each other knowing they are genuinely loved for who they are, not who they pretend to be. If you have to put on a show or wear a mask when you are with your spouse, you'll never be happy in your marriage.

Actors and actresses will do their best when they are performing, when the thing they are acting out is genuine. When two performers must pretend to be in love, they may be able to convince others they are in love, but the truth is, most of these performers aren't in love with each other. They are just going through the motions for a good show.

God doesn't want us to have to put on a show in front of others. Life isn't supposed to be a drama where all the people are performing parts that are untrue to who they are. As we act out our lives on the earth before God, angels, devils, and people, we should aim to be genuine and show the world who we really are, not who we want them to think that we are. Some of the unhappiest people are those who pretend to be something they're not, and some of the happiest people are those who are themselves regardless of what other people think about them.

A spouse deserves to know who their partner is. It isn't loving, kind, or fair to be with someone and pretend that you are someone that you aren't. All people deserve to know the truth, but it is even more vital for a partner to know the truth because they are working together on an intimate level. Satan hurts people through deception. He hurts people when he can get someone to act like someone they aren't. God hates deception. He hates it when people wear masks.

One of the fundamental truths about Christianity is that God knows us for who we really are. There is nothing we can do to fool God or to make Him believe that we are a character we aren't. God knows when we are honest and He knows when we are not. God sees it when we go before other people pretending to be someone we aren't. He sees it when we pretend and perform. Going through the motions, pretending to act out a part, is of the enemy because it is the outward acting out of a demonstration of a lie.

God knew when Satan said in his heart that he was going to exalt himself above God. Satan may or may not have acted like he was against God, but God knew that he was, even when Satan continued to act out a role or a part toward God. *"You said in your heart, 'I will ascend to the heavens; I will raise my throne above the stars of God; I will sit enthroned on the mount of assembly, on the utmost heights of Mount Zaphon'"* (Isa. 14:13).

We can safely assume that Satan would have continued his job or duty toward God if God hadn't "cast" him out of Heaven. The word cast can describe acting or drama. It defines a group of people who portray characters driving a certain narrative. Satan was cast out. He was removed from the show and given a new role because his heart was no longer in the show of Heaven. His heart was removed from the love of God, even if he was still acting out his former part.

God doesn't want people to love Him, be religious, or perform religious things if their hearts are not right. God hates it when people pretend to be someone they aren't. He wants people to be honest and pure before Him. He wants their Christianity to be a relationship, where the characters are interacting out of passion, love, intimacy, and truth. The best scripts, the best performances, and the best shows are those that are genuine and come from the heart.

Coming up with a script and trying to play a part will never create the same level of impact. Impact on people's lives comes from being real. It comes from being honest. In all our relationships we will find the best success when we don't act like someone we aren't. Sometimes it is hard to see someone play a new part or change roles when we are accustomed to seeing them in a certain way, but the truth is, Jesus came to give us a new part. He came to get rid of the former character and identity and to replace it with something authentic—the us that we were always created to be.

James 1:25 says, *"But whoever looks intently into the perfect law that gives freedom, and continues in it—not forgetting what they have heard, but doing it—they will be blessed in what they do."* Understanding God and His word, then acting it out, is the only way we will ever be free. God's word tells us who we are. It tells us how we are supposed to look, act, and perform. It tells us who we really are, even when the world tries to mold us into another role. Many people live their lives thinking they are being authentic, but if people have not fully understood God and adopted His script for their lives then they are acting in the wrong role.

There are some performers who begin to believe they are the character that they are portraying. Lying is a very powerful force. If people act out lies for long enough then they begin to believe the lie. They begin to get confused about what is true and what is false. Satan, from the very beginning, has tried to get humankind to act out of character. He has tried to trick people into thinking they are something they aren't so they will act in ways that are contrary to their true identity. When people live the lie long enough, they assume, "This is me. This is who I am." But the truth is, they are living the life of a character that never was them.

Nathanial looked at his wife and was so sad. He felt like he had lost his best friend, his partner, his everything. The girl she was at the beginning of the relationship wasn't who she was anymore. *Why doesn't she act like the girl I once knew? Why does she act like someone else entirely? Who is this girl? I didn't realize I was marrying her. I thought I was marrying someone else,* he told himself. *I just want her to go back to who she used to be.*

The night Amanda had preached at his grandpa's church she came home and told Nathanial the good news. She was so excited and said, "Come here and talk to me! I have something so good to tell you!" He listened to Amanda as she talked about the things God had been sharing with her. She told him that he was going to be saved and that God had shown her that he was going to die because he was going to be baptized and born again. She told him that God loved him and had a good plan for him and that it was all going to be okay. But something about this sounded terrible to Nathanial. He teared up looking at the woman he had married and said, "I can't deal with this anymore. You are getting worse. You are so mentally ill. You are getting worse. I just hate this."

Nathanial thought that Amanda had been losing her genuine self in her new walk with Christ. All of these years he felt like she was slipping away from him and from her genuine identity. He was grieved because he believed she was living a lie. Nathanial had been raised in church. He had been around Christians who pretended. His mom was one of the worst, and his relationship with her was toxic and painful. She had acted like a Christian for years and put on the show, but at home she was something entirely different and everyone in their house knew it.

My wife is doing the same thing my mom did. She is going to end up in a mental institution. She is going to lose her mind just like my mom, he thought. *I want my wife to be okay. I just want my wife to go back to being normal.* Nathanial blamed religion for his mom's and wife's problems. He thought that the church was a place full of hypocrites, people who pretend to be perfect when they weren't. Some of the meanest people Nathanial had ever met were at church. That is why he said he wanted nothing to do with God or religion.

Nathanial perceived Amanda was going deeper into the part. He thought she was losing herself in the performance, and the truth was, he was right. Amanda was getting further and further away from the girl he had once met and knew. She was not the same person she had been when they met in high school. Amanda had received a new name, a new part, a new role, and a new identity, and as she walked with God she got deeper and deeper into the part. She became the character. But the difference between Amanda and his mom was that his mom was pretending to play the role, and his wife was authentically what she said she was.

The Devil does a great job of mimicking God. He has watched God and does his best to pretend to be God, but he isn't. The Devil is an actor. He is a deceiver, a character who pretends to be one thing, but he isn't. His true identity is not what people often see when he interacts with them. The Devil is a clown, a joker. He wears a mask to conceal his true identity because then he can trick people into thinking he is trustworthy, dependable, and sincere. This allows him to influence their behavior without them knowing what he is doing.

People who do magic tricks often present themselves as doing one thing while they do another. In the field of psychology this is called the art of misdirection. When people use the art of misdirection they create illusions so they can prevent recognition of the truth behind what they are doing or trying to accomplish. By focusing your attention on one thing, the person who has mastered this art can deceive your eyes and cause you to think you are watching something, so he can perform another deceptive act.

There are people who can steal from the purses and wallets of others without them ever knowing what they have done because they have mastered this art. The human brain is easily deceived. Satan knows it and he uses it to create entire narratives and shows. Unless people have the Holy Spirit to show them, they will never know the truth because there is a deceiver, a clown, a joker, who has mastered the art of misdirection roaming the earth. And human beings can't detect him until he has stolen everything from them without the supernatural insight and vision of God.

All of us need God to properly understand the stage we are on. People will not be happy acting out a part that isn't for them. Some people have acted out evil parts, like the man who played the Joker, and the devils behind this operation took his life by convincing him that he was that man. He played the part so much that his brain was rewired and reshaped to believe he was that. How dangerous is it to play around with Satan? How dangerous is it to pretend to be someone you're not, both with God and with mankind?

The truth is, Amanda agreed with Nathanial about some things, and one of them was that religious people and institutions are often big stages full of fake characters who believe that they are fooling others. Sometimes these actors even think they are the characters after a while because they have played the part for so long. Religious customs, traditions, and manmade parts outside of Christ will not lead to happiness any more than parts played by sinners and others who operate outside of the Church. When you are overly religious and you live a life without Christ you will find the same misery the world finds, and you'll never know why you aren't happy.

Colossians 2:8 explains, *"See to it that no one takes you captive by philosophy and empty deceit, according to human tradition, according to the elemental spirits of the world, and not according to Christ."* God warns us to be aware of empty roles and parts that are orchestrated by man outside of God. People can put on great religious performances. They can fool others and sometimes themselves with their performances, but if the show is done outside of God's direction, God's script, and God's ordained characters, then the show will be done in vain. It will be worth nothing in the end.

When Jesus used the word "hypocrites" to talk to the Pharisees and the religious scribes he was broadcasting that there are people who do all the right things for all the wrong reasons. He was warning us of people who wear masks, the people who do performances and skits, but these are not done from the heart. These performances are not authentic because the characters live their lives without believing in the part. When we don't believe in our hearts and aren't living out our genuine feelings and relationship with God, we will never make the impact another makes who means what they say, knows who they are, and knows what they are called to do.

The Greek word for hypocrite is hupokrités, meaning an actor under an assumed character stage-player. If we don't believe what we say we believe, we are hypocrites before God and before man. That is why we must be honest with God and with others in all things. We must not conceal our true identities by wearing masks. Our performances, good or bad, must be visible to all people, because when we pretend to be something we're not God doesn't like it.

Then some of the Pharisees and teachers of the law said to him, "Teacher, we want to see a sign from you." He answered, "A wicked and adulterous generation asks for a sign! But none will be given it except the sign of the prophet Jonah. For as Jonah was three days and three nights in the belly of a huge fish, so the Son of Man will be three days and three nights in the heart of the earth. The men of Nineveh will stand up at the judgment with this generation and condemn it; for they repented at the preaching of Jonah, and now something greater than Jonah is here" (Matt. 12:38–41).

Many people know the story of Jonah and the whale. We teach this story to our children, and we tell them about what God did in Jonah's life. But how many churchgoers would answer truthfully and say they believe that Jonah was indeed eaten by a whale and lived? Could you honestly answer before God and man that you believe this story? If the answer is no, then you are a hypocrite, and I mean that in love. But to understand who God wants us to be, we must understand when we are failing in our faith, and we must be honest about it, so we can ask God to help us mature and grow.

Hebrews 12:6–8 teaches, *"Because the Lord disciplines the one he loves, and he chastens everyone he accepts as his son. Endure hardship as discipline; God is treating you as his children. For what children are not disciplined by their father? If you are not disciplined—and everyone undergoes discipline—then you are not legitimate, not true sons and daughters at all."* God wants us to admit when we have missed the mark and failed. He doesn't want us to get so religious that we pretend and try to fool others into thinking we have arrived and are perfect when we aren't yet. God desires for us to be perfect, and there is nothing wrong with trying to reach and attain that goal, but sometimes we make mistakes, and when we do, we must be willing to turn, repent, and ask God to redirect us and help us do what He really wants us to do.

Jonah was a prophet. He did hear from God. Jonah loved God, and he thought he was doing the right thing by not preaching to the people who hated God and were doing evil things. He felt justified in turning his back on the people God wanted to save because he deemed them as unworthy. He deemed them as people who were too bad for God to save because he was comparing them to himself. God doesn't want us to look around at other characters and see if we are better or worse than them. He wants us to peer deeply into the law of liberty and compare ourselves to that standard.

In his religiosity, Jonah felt justified in ignoring those who were perishing. He felt like they didn't deserve to be told the truth, that they were less than him, and that they were not worthy of the salvation he had been given. That is why God took him into the whale, because Jonah needed to realize that he, too, sometimes displeased God. Until he was honest about his own imperfections and his failure to obey, he was unable to be set free. Jonah had to be honest with the sailors about his relationship with God. He had to say, "I am the reason this storm has arisen."

A failure to do what God said to do, which was to preach to the people the impending doom, was going to send those people to Hell. The truth was, God was very angry with those people and intended to destroy them for what they were doing. What they were doing was very wrong in God's eyes, but they needed a preacher, a prophet, a person to tell them what they were doing and to help them come into a place of repentance. And if Jonah refused to be that prophet, that preacher, and the one to bring the message, then they would never hear it.

How, then, can they call on the one they have not believed in? And how can they believe in the one of whom they have not heard? And how can they hear without someone preaching to them? And how can anyone preach unless they are sent? As it is written: "How beautiful are the feet of those who bring good news!" For Isaiah says, *"Lord, who has believed our message?" Consequently, faith comes from hearing the message, and the message is heard through the word about Christ* (Rom. 10:14–17).

God wanted Amanda to tell her husband the truth about his relationship with God. God wanted her to be honest with her husband about his impending doom without repentance, because if she was quiet and didn't tell him she wouldn't be doing her part. God gave her an important role. He told her to do the work of the ministry in her own home, and if she failed to do this part well, then her husband would be destroyed. But if she acted out the part in accordance with God's commands, did what God told her to do, and was faithful to the truth, then her husband could see his wicked ways and turn and change.

"But I have preached to him, God. I talk about you constantly. I always tell him," Amanda told God. He replied, "Yes, Amanda, you have talked about me to him, but you haven't addressed him directly because, like Jonah, you didn't believe he could really turn. As you have seen his ways and his behavior you have gotten colder and more distant. You have run away from him because you have felt like he was unworthy of the message."

The word of the LORD came to Jonah son of Amittai: "Go to the great city of Nineveh and preach against it, because its wickedness has come up before me." But Jonah ran away from the LORD and headed for Tarshish. He went down to Joppa, where he found a ship bound for that port. After paying the fare, he went aboard and sailed for Tarshish to flee from the LORD (Jon. 1:1–3).

The Pharisees and scribes were similar to Jonah in this regard because they said they believed God's word, but when the word was made flesh in front of them, they didn't believe. They didn't think that everyone could be saved. They didn't think that some people were worthy because of their outward performance. As Christians we must realize that people who are living outside of God are acting out of part. They need help with casting. They need help knowing who they are and what they are supposed to do, and if we don't help them to see what role they are supposed to be in, who will?

Then the word of the Lord came to Jonah a second time: "Go to the great city of Nineveh and proclaim to it the message I give you." Jonah obeyed the word of the Lord and went to Nineveh. Now Nineveh was a very large city; it took three days to go through it. Jonah began by going a day's journey into the city, proclaiming, "Forty more days and Nineveh will be overthrown." The Ninevites believed God. A fast was proclaimed, and all of them, from the greatest to the least, put on sackcloth.

When Jonah's warning reached the king of Nineveh, he rose from his throne, took off his royal robes, covered himself with sackcloth and sat down in the dust. This is the proclamation he issued in Nineveh: "By the decree of the king and his nobles: Do not let people or animals, herds or flocks, taste anything; do not let them eat or drink. But let people and animals be covered with sackcloth. Let everyone call urgently on God. Let them give up their evil ways and their violence. Who knows? God may yet relent and with compassion turn from his fierce anger so that we will not perish." When God saw what they did and how they turned from their evil ways, he relented and did not bring on them the destruction he had threatened (Jonah 3:1–10)

Jesus came to save the lost. He came to see the sinner returned. Jonah was a believer. He did know God, but when he wasn't extending the love of God to others whom God wanted the love extended to he failed in his role. God needed Jonah to play the part for His kingdom. He needed Jonah to proudly and boldly proclaim the truth to all people, regardless of what he thought about them or what they would think about him. The truth is, it doesn't matter what people think about us. If people don't like us because we are obeying God, that is their choice. But we must be willing to do what God says, not what people say, if we are going to demonstrate his power.

Amanda wanted her husband to accept her. She didn't want him to reject her, so she pretended to be something she wasn't for him. She wasn't bold and confident for Jesus. She thought she was, but she often failed to confront him and address him out of fear of rejection or confrontation. She often pulled back from being herself because she didn't want to rock the boat in their relationship. Yet sometimes the boat has to rock. Sometimes we need to be shaken up so we can get on the course God has for us.

Are you afraid of the storm? Are you afraid of what is going to happen? Do you sometimes pretend to be someone you aren't so others will like you? The Church is notorious for this. Church people can often get so caught up in playing a part that they forget to check if they are performing the script of Heaven or the script of man. It can also happen in marriages because we want people to love us. We want people to think we are special or worthy, so we put on a mask, we wear a part, and we pretend that we are something we aren't because we want to be accepted.

Then the sailors said to each other, "Come, let us cast lots to find out who is responsible for this calamity." They cast lots and the lot fell on Jonah. So they asked him, "Tell us, who is responsible for making all this trouble for us? What kind of work do you do? Where do you come from? What is your country? From what people are you?" He answered, "I am a Hebrew and I worship the Lord, the God of heaven, who made the sea and the dry land." This terrified them and they asked, "What have you done?" (They knew he was running away from the Lord, because he had already told them so) (Jon. 1:7–10).

Jonah had put on a mask. He told the sailors part of the truth. He told them he was running away from God, but they had gods, too, so they didn't realize who he was or which god he was running from. When they discovered who Jonah really was and which god he was running from, they were terrified, because they knew that Jonah's god was powerful and could destroy them and everything that they had. We must be careful not to shy away from the truth, pretending to be religious or pretending to be someone we aren't so others will accept us on their boat. We must ensure we are honest in our interactions with both God and man.

Amanda knew what she needed to do. From this day forward she needed to not shy away from Nathanial, even if it meant there was going to be conflict. If she loved him, and if she loved herself, she needed him to know who she was and what she believed. She needed not to worry about his reaction to her; she just needed to be herself, and he could either accept her or not accept her. And she needed to be honest with God, asking him to help her with her unbelief and re-ligiosity. It isn't enough to know God for ourselves. We must be dili-gent to ensure those around us have the opportunity to know too!

Things were amping up in their house. Nathanial knew she was getting deeper into the part. He saw that she was really believing what she said she believed. That is why he cried in their kitchen that night, because he saw that she was not putting on a show anymore. She really believed in God. But now she needed to convey that truth to him in a very personal way. She needed to bring it to him and tell him the truth of God's word for his life, because she believed it could heal him, deliver him, and save him, regardless of how wicked or bad he had been before.

Did she believe God's word that God was powerful enough to change anyone? Did she see her husband and all his sins and faults and still love him enough to help him become the person God knew he could be? Did she really believe in the God she said she did? Time would tell.

Then the eleven disciples went to Galilee, to the mountain where Jesus had told them to go. When they saw him, they worshiped him; but some doubted. Then Jesus came to them and said, "All authority in heaven and on earth has been given to me. Therefore go and make disciples of all nations, baptizing them in the name of the Father and of the Son and of the Holy Spirit, and teaching them to obey everything I have commanded you. And surely I am with you always, to the very end of the age" (Matt. 28:16–20).

You decide for yourself. Is this story fictional? Is it just an act? Did these people really exist? Is God and what He promises us real? What is the truth? Do you want to know? Or are you happy with your performances and shows? Are you happy living a lie, living behind a mask, and concealing your true identity? The choice is yours, but just remember, the best shows are the shows that are put on from the heart. The best stories are the ones that are true, even when they are dramatic. Make sure you don't tune in for just part of the show. The whole story matters. You have to know every part of God to see the truth.

{ 20 }

Play the Part

Jonah was asleep on the boat when the storm was raging all around him. He wasn't afraid to die because he knew that if he died, he was going to go to Heaven. The problem was, he didn't care about the people on the boat with him who wouldn't have made it to eternity. They worshiped false gods, and so did the people Jonah was called to preach to. Christians aren't supposed to keep God to themselves. They aren't supposed to sleep in peace while the world around them is perishing.

Jonah 1:5 tells us, *"All the sailors were afraid and each cried out to his own god. And they threw the cargo into the sea to lighten the ship. But Jonah had gone below deck, where he lay down and fell into a deep sleep."*

There are many Scriptures that God gives us commanding us to wake up and be alert. Part of being alert is paying attention not only to our own lives but also to the lives of others. Why didn't Jonah care that the sailors would drown with him but their eternal outcome wouldn't be the same as his? Why hadn't he tried to work with God to save the people that God called him to preach to? Religion can cause people to act like Jonah. It can cause people to fall asleep because they are secure and content in their eternity, but what about the eternities of others?

Every person we see has a soul. The people we pass in the grocery store, the people we work with, and the family members who annoy us and get on our nerves. No one deserves to go to Hell. Hell wasn't made for people. It was made for Satan and his angels. We shouldn't want anyone to go to Hell because God doesn't. Our hearts must be centered on salvation for all people. We must want what God wants to be in tune.

There is a flow, a rhythm that our heart needs to operate properly, just like there is a flow or rhythm to the waves. When people are out of the flow or rhythm in their hearts, things will rage around them, and they don't even care or notice. Everything may be going insane, and they remain peacefully asleep because they have become passive when they should be demonstrating a level of emotion. The world tells us to have emotional regulation, self-control, and numbness, but this isn't God's design for our lives. We must know that our enemy, not God, wants us to be numb.

Ephesians 5:12–14 explains, *"It is shameful even to mention what the disobedient do in secret. But everything exposed by the light becomes visible—and everything that is illuminated becomes a light. This is why it is said: 'Wake up, sleeper, rise from the dead, and Christ will shine on you.'"*

God wants to shine a light on the works of darkness. He wants the ugly things to be uncovered. His assignment for the Christian is to shine a light, pull back the curtain, and reveal what is hiding below the surface. When we pull back a curtain and expose the things that are behind it, there is often a big surprise, a big demonstration, a big show, because the things that are hiding that don't want to be revealed work very hard to remain hidden. Satan and his kingdom do not want to be discovered or identified. They want to wear a mask and pretend not to be there.

Performers often use their costumes to hide their identity. When you see a clown do you wonder who the person is in the clown suit? If you see a musician, do you wonder who the person is behind the act? Some people work harder than others to conceal their true colors. Some people spend a lifetime building up a false identity. There can be temporary comfort in a hidden and undisclosed identity, because when someone creates a false identity, they can run away from the truth and the light that is trying to help them remember who they really are.

When you hate yourself, you may not want to remember who you really are. If you are afraid of who God has made you to be or what God wants you to do you may try to create an identity somewhere else, hoping that you can remain concealed, incognito, and hidden from God and His plan for your life. Sometimes facing the truth is difficult. Jonah didn't want to face the truth. He wanted to create a new life, a new identity, and a new environment because he thought it would allow him to hide.

The word of the LORD came to Jonah son of Amittai: "Go to the great city of Ninevah and preach against it, because its wickedness has come up before me." But Jonah ran away from the LORD and headed for Tarshish. He went down to Joppa, where he found a ship bound for that port. After paying the fare, he went aboard and sailed for Tarshish to flee from the LORD (Jon. 1:1–3).

Notice that Jonah wasn't from Tarshish. He had no business there. Jonah wanted to depart from where he was really from and who he really was. He wanted to hide his problems and relationship with God, and he wanted everyone who knew who he really was to get far away from him. This position was his protective mechanism. It was his way of trying to get away from his responsibility and the truth God had for him. Jonah didn't want anyone, or anything, to recognize his problem. He didn't want to be responsible for his God-given assignment and role.

After Amanda received the news from God that her husband had the chance to be saved, she continued to talk to the Lord about what He would have her do. God told Amanda that her husband was hiding behind a mask. He showed her that she needed to confront him and be herself regardless of his response. God said, "Amanda, shine a light on the truth. Tell him what his sins are doing to him. Warn him of the impending storm if he doesn't change directions. Don't back down or go back to sleep. Stay awake and be involved. Care that he is perishing."

Amanda tried to wake her husband up from his sleep on a Monday morning. "Nathanial, wake up," she said, giving him a little shake. "I want to tell you what God has told me. You know those Mardi gras masks? Have you ever looked into the masks people would wear in Venice to hide their true identities? I have never looked into it much, but this morning God had me researching and I was learning about how masks have been used for generations to help people hide their identities! Even kings and royalty used to use them to be able to walk among the commoners."

Amanda kept trying to be playful with her husband. She wanted him to hear what she had heard from God. She wanted to share with him the things that she knew had been destroying their marriage. "Nathanial, God has been helping me to write this love story. It is our story and it is so cool." He responded by hollering at her in a thundering voice, "Amanda, get the f*** away from me. Stop talking to me about God. I don't give a s*** about your God. Why are you waking me up with this bulls*** again!"

Amanda ran into their son's bedroom crying. It was then that she noticed her son had a sign on his wall with a police officer on it. The sign said, "You have authority." Amanda knew she needed to go back into the room. She knew she needed to confront Nathanial, something she had not done in a long time. She couldn't run away anymore. She couldn't let him push her to another place, another room, a separate area, and pretend she wasn't hurt or in need of saying something. So, she turned around and marched right back into the bedroom.

"You are wrong for yelling at me," Amanda said. "You shouldn't be talking to your wife like that. You are called to be loving, kind, and respectful to me. You made a vow to treat me with compassion and care as the weaker vessel, and you aren't doing that." The two went back and forth for a long time, and before she knew it they were deep in a storm. The waves were high, the thunder was booming, the lightning was crashing, and the ship was no longer steady.

After a few minutes of fighting, screaming, and going back and forth like a vessel tossed around by a violent storm, Nathanial tried to escape. He opened their bedroom door and ran out. He walked into the living room where their children were and, in the calmest voice, said to them, "Good morning, babies." Amanda followed him with the same intensity and energy they had in the bedroom. She didn't want her children to hear the fight. She had tried to shut the door and keep it in their bedroom, but she wasn't going to be fake. She wasn't going to pretend to her children that there wasn't a storm going on because that would be a lie.

"You need to come back into the bedroom and talk," Amanda told him. "Don't keep running away. Don't keep on trying to hide. You have to face the problems. Let's talk about this. We have things we need to discuss." In front of their children, Nathanial said, "I don't want to talk to you. You are making me hate you. You are toxic. You are absolutely insane. Look at you. You are so out of control. You have no emotional regulation. You are yelling at me."

This was a part of Nathanial's act. His character loved to make her seem like the bad guy. He loved to make people think he was smooth, calm, and collected and Amanda was unraveled and insane. Even though Nathanial had a few minutes earlier threatened divorce, told Amanda he was going to do something to shut her up, and had been cussing, screaming, and telling her how much of a b**** she was, he was now pretending to be someone entirely different in front of their children. "Look at your mother," he said. "She is the one who is nuts."

Amanda knew what he was doing now. God had given her a playbook and a script, and He told her exactly who Nathanial was under the mask. For the first time in her life she knew that she was supposed to fight, speak up, and let the truth out at all costs. "Nathanial, you are expecting me to pretend you didn't just hurt me? You want me to pretend that everything is okay when my husband, the man I love, has been saying hurtful things to me? Why would I do that? Why would I come in here acting like someone I am not?" Amanda asked. "You came in here and put on a mask. You are trying to run away and hide. You came in here and pretended that you were okay in front of the kids. Why don't you show the truth? Why don't you want the truth revealed?"

Just then, Nathanial turned on some music. He chose "chill vibes" and blasted on the sound bar in the living room. He was trying with everything in him to tune out the sound of his wife. He was trying very hard to ignore the voice of God speaking through her, confronting him and his lies, his deception, and his hidden evils.

"See! Even this is a way to hide. You want to put on chill vibes music? You want to try to pretend as if you are chill right now!" Amanda exclaimed. "Amanda, you need to calm down. You need to calm down and then we can talk," her husband replied. "No, Nathanial, you are wrong," she shouted, "I don't need to calm down. When someone gets stabbed by another person they are going to have a reaction. If I saw someone getting shot in the street I wouldn't just say, oh well, let me go about my day then. This isn't a time to be calm. This is a time to demonstrate what is true and what has been done that is hurtful!"

For a few more minutes, they argued in front of the children. Nathanial was trying with everything in him to use his regular character and get Amanda off his case. He wanted her to go away, be quiet, and pretend that everything was okay. He wanted her to shut up and stop preaching to him and telling him what God wanted him to do. He wanted her not to hold him accountable. If he could just get her to focus on herself, and if he could just paint her out to be the villain, then maybe she'd believe it and back off.

But this time his character was unsuccessful. He couldn't get her to back off, as he had always been able to do before, because she knew that she had been anointed to confront. The storm wasn't bothering her because God had told her for weeks that a storm was coming.

Amanda knew there was an impending storm. She knew that something ferocious was headed their way, but she wasn't going to ignore the storm anymore. She wasn't going to let her husband die in the storm if she could do something about it.

When the two first started dating, they would have big storms and fights. Amanda used to stand up for herself and fight back, but there came a day when she stopped fighting because she wanted to keep the peace and stop the waves from crashing all around her. She thought that holding back the storm was good for her, for him, and for their children, but the truth was, the storm needed to rage, and Nathanial needed to know that God wasn't happy with him and if he didn't change, he was going to be destroyed.

After a little while of arguing in the living room, Nathanial agreed to go back into the bedroom away from the children. In the bedroom Nathanial continued to insist that Amanda stop talking to him about religion and God. "I don't want to hear it. This is a hard stop for me. If you don't stop talking to me about God I am not going to be with you anymore." Amanda looked at him calmly and said, "Okay, that is fine, because I am not going to stop talking to you about this. I am not going to let up or change. This is what I am called to do. I am going to continue talking to you about my relationship with God. So what actions are you going to take to do what you are saying you want to do?"

Amanda could tell that Nathanial was speechless and taken aback by her bold confrontation. He could tell that something was very different about her. Why was she so confident? Why was she not afraid of him and his yelling, cussing, threats, and confession to leave the marriage? *This is very strange and different,* he thought to himself. *She always let me get my way before. She has always let me back her down by doing these tactics.* Nathanial then began to bring up counseling, something he never wanted to do any other time when Amanda had tried bringing it up before. "When we were in counseling, we were told to respect each other's boundaries," he reminded her. "You are not respecting my boundaries by telling me about God constantly. That is the problem with you Christians. You just can't keep things to yourself."

"Blah blah blah. Counseling? You are just trying to use that against me!" Amanda herself was a counselor, and she said, "Nathanial, this isn't a boundary thing. You don't want me to talk about MY relationship with God, and I have a right to talk about God. You are the one who wants me to change and stop being honest. You want me to put on a mask, and I am not going to do that."

"And anyway, how many times have you respected my boundaries? You haven't ever," she continued. "How many years have I asked you to stop cussing at me, yelling at me, and calling me names? You can stop cussing when you go around clients or your grandparents. You respect them enough to control yourself, but you don't respect me. You don't care about my boundaries, do you? You just want someone to listen to us talk for one hour a week? Why aren't we talking all hours of the week? That is what a relationship is. It isn't about putting on a mask all week and for one hour being honest and talking. Let's talk now. Let's handle this now. What are you running for?"

Amanda knew what he was doing. He was hoping that by bringing up counseling he could go about his bad behavior for six days a week and then sit in a counseling office for one hour and pretend to be working on things, but Amanda knew that wasn't progress. Progress is facing the storm when the storm hits. It is working through the issues now, not later. There was no more time to delay. There was no more time to put things off. The issues needed to be addressed. They needed to be hashed out, regardless of how hard it may be.

Brothers and sisters, if someone is caught in a sin, you who live by the Spirit should restore that person gently. But watch yourselves, or you also may be tempted" (Gal. 6:1). A failure to confront someone for their sin is a trap for the person who omits their responsibility and it is also one for the person they refuse to confront. Satan can take sailors captive when no one is willing to say this is a problem and it must be fixed. Ironically, in the story of Jonah, the sailors who were unbelievers knew that they needed to do something to fix the problem when Jonah, who was the spiritual leader, should have taken the lead. But in the case of Amanda and Nathanial, she knew she had to take the lead or he wouldn't. She knew his life could be lost if she didn't speak up.

Amanda wasn't concerned about where she was going when she died. She knew she was going to Heaven as Jonah did, but she also knew her husband wasn't. She knew that if this ship went down, he was going to be lost in the sea forever. Storms are made when hot and cold come together. The clash between the heat and cold causes a storm to manifest. Was Amanda willing to be hot for God even if it meant the clash and the storm was here? The answer was finally yes! She loved Nathanial far too much to watch him drown without trying to offer him a lifeline.

Drugs, alcohol, and other substances can amplify what is already inside a person. When people use substances, they get "colder" in the spirit. They lose their fire. Even many mental health drugs work this way, by causing people to close up, stuff it down, and hide the heat that needs to come out. Not all emotions are bad. There is a time to let yourself be honest. There is a time to weep, wail, and cry out. If your husband going to Hell wasn't a time to show emotion when would be a better time? He may not like your character. He may want you to calm down and to go back into a shell, but it isn't the time to retreat and hide. "It is time to navigate the waters," Amanda decided.

She knew she was ready. She was a skilled sailor because Jesus had taught her how to survive in rough waters. Amanda wasn't intimidated by these waves or this storm anymore. She knew how to keep her boat afloat. She knew how to act with both precision and intention, even when everyone else was freaking out and fleeing for their lives. Nathanial was very scared, even though he acted like he wasn't.

But Amanda wasn't scared at all, even when she looked out of control in her crying, commanding, and confronting.

Nathanial was being carried by the sea. When people are afraid and don't know what to do they will often panic, and this panic can manifest itself in different ways. But skilled sailors don't panic when things are going crazy. They make a plan. They take action. They look at the storm and call out what God says because it is only through the power of Christ that we can calm a storm. When we use God's word and authority, and we speak boldly to the waves and to the things causing them, then we can take charge.

It is safe to assume that Jesus yelled at the wind and the waves. I doubt his voice was a squeak. As Jesus spoke to the sea around him, he commanded with authority. He spoke with a loud voice. Many Christians are told that it is wrong to yell, –that you need to calm down. You just need to be more dignified and controlled, but there is a time and a place to yell, shout, and proclaim what is true. There is a time to be undignified for God, and in these times, you can't worry about what the people around you think. You must be strong and care only for what the Lord thinks about your performance.

Jesus flipped tables. He confronted people and called them out for their sin. He shouted, as did many of his disciples. It isn't a sin to yell, cry, or be emotional. In fact, Amanda had preached at church the Sunday before and yelled almost the entire sermon under the anointing of the Holy Ghost. Don't let the Devil lie to you and tell you that it is wrong to be emotional, to yell, or to shout. Don't let him convince you that these characteristics aren't a good part of your godly character.

People need to see the emotion in your performance. They need to see what you really feel and how you are impacted by the circumstances around you. A good show doesn't come from concealing emotions, hiding the truth, and running away from the problems in your life. A good show is a show that is full of raw emotion, confrontation between the forces of good and evil, and a revelation of the truth behind the people who are before you.

Satan works hard to get people to put on masks. He works hard to stop people from being honest. He wants people to be quiet, keep to themselves, run away, or drown out the voice of truth. He wants Christians to refuse to speak, proclaim, go toward their battle, or address their problems. He knows that when a Christian comes for a fight, prepared and ready, he can't win, and the Devil knew Amanda had changed and she was not going back to the former intimidated woman he had for years kept in a shell to herself because she was afraid to swim.

Amanda wasn't at all afraid to swim. She knew how to swim. God had taught her. She knew that even if she was thrown overboard, she would continue to live. *Give it your best shot, but I am awake and I am not backing down this time. My God is with me, and He has given me a mission. I am not running from my mission. I am running to it,* Amanda thought. When a search and rescue team goes toward a life that needs saving, they can't be afraid. They can't let their fear and their emotions stop them from doing what must be done, and Amanda was on a search and rescue mission. She wanted to save the man she loved.

"*The engulfing waters threatened me, the deep surrounded me; seaweed was wrapped around my head. To the roots of the mountains I sank down; the earth beneath barred me in forever. But you, LORD my God, brought my life up from the pit. When my life was ebbing away, I remembered you, LORD, and my prayer rose to you, to your holy temple. Those who cling to worthless idols turn away from God's love for them. But I, with shouts of grateful praise, will sacrifice to you. What I have vowed I will make good. I will say, 'Salvation comes from the LORD.'" And the LORD commanded the fish, and it vomited Jonah onto dry land* (Jon. 2:5–10).

Amanda and Nathanial had both been acting out of character for quite some time. Amanda had adopted a passive character, a character who was not willing to show emotions for the man she loved because he punished her if she did. And Nathanial had always had the same character ever since she had met him. His character was mean, harsh, and cold. It was dangerous, aggressive, and willing to do anything to keep people away from his heart. Nathanial didn't want Amanda to love him. He wanted her to be a villain so he could remain one too.

Nathanial knew God's power working through Amanda had the power to unmask, reveal, and pull back the lies, revealing his authentic character, but he hated that because he didn't want to change. He didn't want to be different, as he had found comfort in this character, this identity, and he was terrified of returning and going the way God had commanded him to. "It is better if I go this way!" he told himself. "I know God told me to go another direction. I see the storm, but I don't want to go that way. I want to pretend this isn't happening. I want to pretend I am someone else."

This is when things got violent. Amanda confronted Nathanial about his lack of respect toward her boundaries in their early days, confronting him with what he did on New Year's, forcing her to go out, forcing her to cheat on her boyfriend, and pushing her to do things she didn't want to throughout the relationship. He became enraged and shouted, "I will f*** you up! I will f*** you up! Do you understand me? You are dead to me."

Amanda would have usually been afraid at this point. He had assaulted her many times before. His character wasn't above putting his hands on her and trying to harm her through violence. But for the first time in a long time, she didn't care. "If you do that you will be stopped by an angel of the Lord. Do you hear me? You would be stupid to put your hands on me again," Amanda warned him. "I know what I didn't know before, and that is that I have the protection of the heavenly hosts. An angel of the Lord would slay you on the spot if you tried to do anything to me. Do you understand?"

And Amanda meant what she was saying. She believed it. She wasn't blowing smoke. She was confident that God would send her help if this man tried to harm her again. She knew that God had enough of her abuse and that He was calling her to be strong and confront. "Explain. Define. Please tell me what exactly you mean when you say I will f*** you up? Do you think that is God's plan for you to threaten to kill your wife? Don't you know the Bible says a man is to lay down his life for his wife, not the other way around? Don't you see what spirit you are working under?"

We must remember that the actors on the stage aren't alone. It may look like they are, but there are those who are recording the show, controlling the lights and sounds, and there are those in the audience too. Many people are involved in a show, but you can't see all of them. Amanda knew that she had Jesus listening, watching, and observing this show. She knew that she had bystanders from Heaven willing and ready to intervene on her behalf if he was to take it to the next level.

Never forget that there is always a limo driver or carriage driver who hears and sees everything going on between the bride and the groom. There is always someone who is a quiet observer. Many times, the riders forget that someone else is observing, but Amanda hadn't forgotten. She knew who was driving this marriage carriage. She knew who was watching, listening, and recording the things going on, and she was going to please Him. She was going to make sure Jesus was proud of her for what she was doing and saying. Besides, God had sent her help before when Nathanial attacked her, so wouldn't He do it again?

The Devil tried to kill Paul many times. He sent vipers, he sent storms, he sent people to stone Paul, but Paul was not afraid of the storm, of the snakes, or of the people who hated him. He was willing to do anything to witness for Jesus Christ. He was willing to continue in strength, boldness, and courage, facing the enemy head-on.

Amanda was tired of the vipers. She was tired of the storm trying to tell her what she had to do and how she needed to act. "NO, thank you," Amanda said. "I have been given the authority to trample serpents. I have been given the authority to calm the sea, and I am going to continue to preach when he threatens to stone me."

Paul gathered a pile of brushwood and, as he put it on the fire, a viper, driven out by the heat, fastened itself on his hand. . . . But Paul shook the snake off into the fire and suffered no ill effects (Acts 28:3,5).

Being afraid to die will keep you from bringing the heat. It will keep you from going forward. Christians must not be afraid to die. We must be more concerned that others around us are going to die and not get to eternity. Only then can we make an impact. *"They triumphed over him by the blood of the Lamb and by the word of their testimony; they did not love their lives so much as to shrink from death"* (Rev. 12:11).

The Devil wants you to stay in the box he has for you. He wants you to play the part he has assigned for your life, and he hates it when someone acts out of character. He hates it when someone believes God's word and acts like a genuine, on-fire believer because Satan has no weapons he can use against God. He has nothing he can do to stop the light, the fire, and the exposure of him and his dark kingdom. Never forget that Satan wants you to act a certain way.

He wants us to forget that God is with us. He wants us to act like we are inferior to him. Satan wants us to stop showing others when they are wrong or when they hurt us. He wants us to pretend everything is okay, show no emotion, and mask our realities as Christians. As a director, Satan plans to control the villain and the good guy. He wants the villain to rage and have power, and he wants the good guy not to fight back and accept defeat.

God's script is entirely different. God's script says that the Christian holds the power and authority. His script tells us to confront, to address, and to be a character that is unafraid of the snakes and the threats to our lives. Christians aren't called to stand down and let the villains run the world. We aren't called to be quiet and pretend the world isn't overrun by evil. We are to shine the light on the evil and we are to call out the villains.

Of course they won't like it. A villain doesn't like a good guy. Villains want the good guys to stay in their homes and remain uninvolved in the story. Villains don't want to be exposed, stopped, or prevented from continuing to create chaos. But since when do we let the villains tell us what to do? Superheroes don't say, "Oh no, the storm has been created by the villain. We must remain silent. We must hide and pretend we don't see what is going on."

Villains create storms, but superheroes control the damage. When a villain tries to use threats, violence, and intimidation, a real superhero doesn't heed their threats and run in fear. True superheroes believe in their superpowers. They believe in their ability to overcome the enemy. Why would a good guy run and hide? It is the villain who needs to be afraid.

The best superheroes rip the mask off the villain. They reveal who is really behind the chaos and the dysfunction. Superheroes expose what villains don't want exposed. They reveal what the villains don't want revealed. "Who are you really?" They seek to know. "Take the mask off. Show us your true colors. Show us who you really are! Stop hiding behind a mask. Stop pretending to be something you aren't. You aren't all-powerful if you're a villain. And if you aren't careful, you will lose everything because you played the weaker part."

Do you think it's right to tell a superhero to calm down? Do you think it is right to pretend that the villain hasn't caused great damage and chaos? Or do you presume it is better to yell, to cry, and to make a scene if it means that people pay attention to what is going on around them? Isn't there a time to shout WATCH OUT!!! Oh, of course there is. Only a villain wouldn't want you to warn people. Only a villain would want you to stand down.

The word of the Lord came to me: "Son of man, speak to your people and say to them: 'When I bring the sword against a land, and the people of the land choose one of their men and make him their watchman, and he sees the sword coming against the land and blows the trumpet to warn the people, then if anyone hears the trumpet but does not heed the warning and the sword comes and takes their life, their blood will be on their own head. Since they heard the sound of the trumpet but did not heed the warning, their blood will be on their own head. If they had heeded the warning, they would have saved themselves. But if the watchman sees the sword coming and does not blow the trumpet to warn the people and the sword comes and takes someone's life, that person's life will be taken because of their sin, but I will hold the watchman accountable for their blood.

Son of man, I have made you a watchman for the people of Israel; so hear the word I speak and give them warning from me. When I say to the wicked, 'You wicked person, you will surely die,' and you do not speak out to dissuade them from their ways, that wicked person will die for their sin, and I will hold you accountable for their blood. But if you do warn the wicked person to turn from their ways and they do not do so, they will die for their sin, though you yourself will be saved" (Ezek. 33:1–9).

{ 21 }

Drop the Act

If a director has written a script and the characters aren't adhering to it the director has reason to change the character's assignment. He can say you aren't allowed on the set anymore. A part of being a director is overseeing the implementation of the script. If you have characters who refuse to play their given part, they are rebellious and working in opposition to the show. These people don't deserve sympathy or remorse for the outcomes of their lives. But sometimes good directors give second chances.

God is a God of second chances. He gave both Paul and Jonah a second chance. Paul was headed to Hell for his persecution of Christians, and Jonah was running from God for not performing his part of the script either. God rescued both Paul and Jonah. He gave these men another chance to turn their lives and their futures around. People must realize when God is giving them another chance and be thankful for what they are being given. It took Jonah a little while to see that God had given him another chance because he was still mad at God for saving the people he didn't believe should be saved.

Christians must be careful that we don't wish death on other people. Do we consider the severity of Hell? Do we really understand that Hell is a terrible place of eternal judgment? It is one thing to say we understand Hell and eternity and another thing to put into practice in our relationships with others. Jonah didn't think it was fair for the people of Ninevah to be given another chance, but he had been given one, so why didn't he want God to extend the same grace? Even after

Jonah agreed to preach to the people, his heart was still cold toward them. He still felt anger that God might deliver them.

Jonah had gone out and sat down at a place east of the city. There he made himself a shelter, sat in its shade and waited to see what would happen to the city. Then the Lord God provided a leafy plant and made it grow up over Jonah to give shade for his head to ease his discomfort, and Jonah was very happy about the plant. But at dawn the next day God provided a worm, which chewed the plant so that it withered. When the sun rose, God provided a scorching east wind, and the sun blazed on Jonah's head so that he grew faint. He wanted to die, and said, "It would be better for me to die than to live."

But God said to Jonah, "Is it right for you to be angry about the plant?" "It is," he said. "And I'm so angry I wish I were dead." But the Lord said, "You have been concerned about this plant, though you did not tend it or make it grow. It sprang up overnight and died overnight. And should I not have concern for the great city of Nineveh, in which there are more than a hundred and twenty thousand people who cannot tell their right hand from their left—and also many animals?" (Jon. 4:5–11).

If we have been hurt by others, or if we see that they have done some really terrible things, it can be hard for our human minds to extend forgiveness. Forgiveness isn't always easy. God wants us to have compassion for others because it helps us to be appreciative of the grace and compassion extended to us. God values life. He doesn't want to destroy even the animals, so how much more does He not want to destroy human life, even when it deserves to die?

God was working with Jonah to unveil the truth about his heart's condition. He was working with Jonah to show him how to love others and not judge them. Christians must be careful to never forget that we have been lost and found. While there are various sins and degrees of sin, the truth is that all sin leads to death. Despite the sin a person is caught and entangled with, sin is sin, and it will lead to death if it isn't drawn out of a heart.

Hating someone is likened to killing them. True love confronts. It shines the light into the dark places because it realizes that even though there is evil there the person can still have a chance for redemption. God looked at all of us while we were sinners and chose to deliver us from our affliction. God offered us a lifeline when we didn't deserve it. Are we willing to do the same for those around us? Are we able to put aside our own hurts and care about the well-being of another more than we care about our emotional wounds and opinions of right and wrong?

"Blessed are you when people insult you, persecute you and falsely say all kinds of evil against you because of me. Rejoice and be glad, because great is your reward in heaven, for in the same way they persecuted the prophets who were before you. You are the salt of the earth. But if the salt loses its saltiness, how can it be made salty again? It is no longer good for anything, except to be thrown out and trampled underfoot.

You are the light of the world. A town built on a hill cannot be hidden. Neither do people light a lamp and put it under a bowl. Instead they put it on its stand, and it gives light to everyone in the house. In the same way, let your light shine before others, that they may see your good deeds and glorify your Father in heaven" (Matt. 5:11–16).

People who have not accepted Jesus are lost at sea. They are engulfed by the waves, drowned, and killed. They are hungry, thirsty, and surrounded by darkness, and they are in desperate need of light, food, water, and hope. The Church is called to be the lighthouse. We are to call out into the sea and say, "Come this way because over here there is hope, light, food, and water. Over here there is rest from the storms and the engulfing waves. Do you want help?"

Sailors have been known to be some of the crudest people. The phrase "cuss like a sailor" has its roots in the reality that sailors were crass, rough people. Amanda's husband was this kind of sailor. He was harsh, crude, and nasty toward her. It was hard for her to be gentle, loving, and warm toward him, but she knew that God was telling her to. A part of her vows to him was that she would be a committed, loving wife. She had vowed to be his helper, and right now he needed help. Would she offer help? Would she put her hurt and emotions aside and continue to press in toward a drawing vessel that looked like a pirate ship?

Pirates are mean though. Don't they deserve to die? Amanda thought. God responded, "Yes, they do, but so did you and aren't you glad you didn't? Don't hate him, Amanda. Love him because that is what you promised to do. Do the right thing even when you don't feel like it. Don't let your emotions deter you from doing what is right. Overcome emotions. Obey my voice and attempt to rescue him, even if he looks like he is committed to die."

Jonah was sitting outside of Ninevah watching to see if God was going to destroy it. Amanda was watching to see if God was going to destroy Nathaniel. "God, are you really going to save him? Are you going to help him?" she asked. "I want to know what is going to happen. You said you were going to destroy him, and now you're saying you aren't. I want to know what is true. I want to know what is going on."

Fishing is hard work. Casting out a net isn't always easy. There are times when you don't want to fish. You don't want to throw the net out, especially if you have fished all night and caught no fish. When you feel like you've tried, toiled, and worked to fish and haven't caught anything, you sometimes think, well, what is the point of fishing anymore? What is the point of continuing to work in this spot? There isn't anything here, Jesus! But when you trust God and you want to please Him you will try even when you are tired of trying. Luke 5:5 reflects this, saying, *"Simon answered, 'Master, we've worked hard all night and haven't caught anything. But because you say so, I will let down the net.'"*

To cast a net or a line in fishing means to throw out, to extend one's line, but the only way you can extend a line is if you feel there is something in the water that is worth bringing in. If you don't believe that there is something in the water to catch and you don't want to catch anything, are you going to extend the line? Are you going to trust Jesus when He says there is something there? If you don't give up, you will see that there is something there!

When they had done so, they caught such a large number of fish that their nets began to break. So they signaled their partners in the other boat to come and help them, and they came and filled both boats so full that they began to sink. When Simon Peter saw this, he fell at Jesus' knees and said, "Go away from me, Lord; I am a sinful man!" For he and all his companions were astonished at the catch of fish they had taken (Luke 5:6–9).

Have you ever wondered why Simon Peter said, "Go away from me, Lord; I am a sinful man," after Jesus helped him to catch fish and achieve his goal? Is it because he didn't believe in the catch? Is it because he assumed that there was nothing of value in the place he was fishing? Did he perceive in his heart that he hadn't believed that his fishing would produce anything at all? These are hard truths, and Amanda felt just like Peter one day. She realized she had thought that her husband couldn't be caught. She thought there wasn't anything there when she looked at the man she had vowed to love.

Jesus didn't call us to a life of ignorance or a life of comfort. He wants us to do the hard thing sometimes. He wants us to face the truth in our lives because it is only the truth that can heal, deliver, and set us free. Sometimes Christian's think being comfortable is the goal of Christianity, but what if it isn't? What if our comfort isn't what we are supposed to be pursuing? What if the uncomfortable parts of our lives, the hard parts of our lives, are the parts that God wants to take and reshape so we can walk in our proper position with Jesus?

The word of God is a sword. It is supposed to sharpen us as the Church. It is supposed to convict us to our heart and our core because when we are convicted and repent, we become sharper Christians. When Peter and Amanda were confronted with the truth of their hearts, and they were convicted of their sins, they realized Jesus was there to sharpen them, not leave them as they were. Sometimes, in the sharpening process, there will be uncomfortable moments and realizations. Things that hurt but need to be drawn out of the water because there is a heart in there that is worthy and special to the Creator of it.

God sees the evil things in a man's or woman's heart and wants to draw them out of their lives. He wants to remove it so they can be healthy. Christians aren't perfect. They are on a mission to become perfect, but if you live your life thinking that God will never need to discipline you, correct you, or show you the ugly things in you then you are deceived. To be sharpened by God's word we must be confronted with the truths that we may want to avoid dealing with.

For the unbeliever, the word of God should pierce the heart too. But the unbelieving heart and the Christian heart are not the same. The Christian heart is being circumcised. It is being cut and molded to a certain form because it has already been made new. The unbelieving heart is different because the unbelieving heart needs to be completely pulled out and replaced if it even has a chance to change or become anything of value.

When a baby is circumcised there is a process of cutting and molding. Romans 2:29 says, "*No, a person is a Jew who is one inwardly; and circumcision is circumcision of the heart, by the Spirit, not by the written code. Such a person's praise is not from other people, but from God.*" To be eligible for circumcision, the person must first repent and turn to Christ. Then and only then will the Great Physician begin his procedure.

Jeremiah 17:9 teaches, "*The heart is deceitful above all things and beyond cure. Who can understand it?*" There is only one cure for the human condition and the human heart. The only cure is salvation, or rebirth, through the death and resurrection of Christ. When a heart is unchanged it will always lead to evil, but when a heart has been changed Jesus can begin to circumcise that heart. He can begin to show the world that the person has indeed been set apart as a vessel fit for service. Not all vessels have the same capacity. Not all vessels are equal in their value.

2 Timothy 2:20–21 says, *"In a large house there are articles not only of gold and silver, but also of wood and clay; some are for special purposes and some for common use. Those who cleanse themselves from the latter will be instruments for special purposes, made holy, useful to the Master and prepared to do any good work."*

People are vessels. We are ships and God wants to use us, but if a vessel is to be what it can be, there is a process that must take place. Becoming a Christian is just the beginning of our walk with God. After we are saved there is a refining process. Some people will make it to Heaven, but they won't be gold. They will be silver. Some are going to make it to Heaven and be commoners, and some will make it to Heaven and be special and set apart.

"Flee the evil desires of youth and pursue righteousness, faith, love and peace, along with those who call on the Lord out of a pure heart" (2 Timothy 2:22). Jesus wants to purify us. He wants to shape our hearts, but we must be willing to lie down on the operating table. If we aren't willing to work with God, doing the work of fleeing evil and pursuing righteousness, it isn't possible for us to become all that God wants us to become.

Amanda wanted to be a vessel of honor. She wanted to be one who was set apart for special purposes. She was always competitive, and she said to God, "Please, God, let me be one of the special-purpose vessels. Let me be molded into a better version of myself. I don't want to remain where I am. Even though this hurts and it is hard, I want to go forward. I want to be circumcised in my heart."

A pure heart must be cultivated. To be pure, you must stay alert and diligent. You must be willing to do the hard work that cultivation requires. If you want to be a good performer you must practice, and if you want to be a good Christian, you must allow Jesus to tell you when you need to be course-corrected and accept this criticism as a blessing. Our prayer should be, "Thank you, God, that you love me enough to not leave me as I am."

Amanda was thankful that the Lord had revealed her part in the struggling marriage. She was thankful that God cared enough about her to confront the hatred she had allowed to enter her heart. 2 Timothy 2:24 says, *"And the Lord's servant must not be quarrelsome but must be kind to everyone, able to teach, not resentful."* When we resent someone or something, we feel bitter. We feel cold and distant because we have often been hurt by our former efforts.

God doesn't call us to be bitter. He calls us to be kind and to teach without our pain leading the way. We must lead with our pain. We cannot let our pain lead us. We must let the truth of God lead, and the truth of God wants to deliver and set the oppressed people free. *"Opponents must be gently instructed, in the hope that God will grant them repentance leading them to a knowledge of the truth, and that they will come to their senses and escape from the trap of the devil, who has taken them captive to do his will"* (2 Tim. 2:25–26).

Notice that this doesn't give us an excuse not to confront. Christians are indeed called to confront, but not in hate or in resentment. Christians are called to care about others more than they care about themselves. *"Not looking to your own interests but each of you to the interests of the others"* (Phil. 2:4). We must know the evil one has captured that person's soul and that God has positioned us to pull them back onto the ship from their drowning in the storm. We are positioned to help free them from the captor that is trying to sink them and steal their life.

Who, being in very nature God, did not consider equality with God something to be used to his own advantage; rather, he made himself nothing by taking the very nature of a servant, being made in human likeness. And being found in appearance as a man, he humbled himself by becoming obedient to death—even death on a cross! Therefore God exalted him to the highest place and gave him the name that is above every name that at the name of Jesus every knee should bow, in heaven and on earth and under the earth, and every tongue acknowledge that Jesus Christ is Lord, to the glory of God the Father" (Phil. 2:6–11).

God gives us a position with Him in Heaven so we can humble ourselves and help others escape the snares of Satan. We are given our position, not to be comfortable, but to be uncomfortable, because we care about the lives of others more than we care about our own lives. It was through Jesus's willingness to humble Himself and love others who didn't deserve to be loved that He could achieve the name above every name. He was exalted in Heaven because he was humble on earth.

Do we want to be like Jesus? Do we want to be exalted and given an important, special purpose in Heaven? Or are we content with being saved and watching the world around us go to Hell? Are we content with seeing those we love drown without offering a lifeline to them because they have hurt us before? One of the hardest things Amanda would ever probably do was offer a lifeline to the man who didn't deserve it after what he had done to her, but she was going to do it anyway, not because he deserved it, but because he didn't and neither had she.

Doing what is right is far more important than doing what we think is right. Marriage, love, and commitment aren't about your feelings. It isn't about cards, chocolate strawberries, and fuzzy feelings. True love is about rescue. It is about willingness. It is about caring for another person more than yourself. That is what love is about. Many in the world miss love because they are chasing their own comfort. They are looking for what they can get and have to be comfortable.

Some people want the title of "wifey" or "hubby." They want the romantic, cute pictures, the honeymoon, and the shallow appearance of love. But real love isn't shallow. Real love is deep. It is persevering and willing to go to hard places, faraway places, to restore and bring back those who have been lost at sea. Are you willing to risk your life to save the one you have vowed to love until death do you part? Are you willing to jump into the storm, the water, and the roaring waves so you can save a soul that God wants saved?

It isn't comfortable to jump off a boat into the water to save someone who is drowning. People go through serious training regimens to become lifeguards, marines, navy sailors, firemen, or those in other rescue positions. If you are going to save others it doesn't just happen. People who rescue know the dangers associated with what they are doing, but more than that they know that the person needs their help. They don't wait around for someone else to do the job they could do. They see the need and they do the job, because if they don't, who will? Maybe someone will and maybe they won't. Are you prepared to face the repercussions of your immobility when you could have done something?

In theater a cast is a group of characters influencing the script and the show. The cast is largely responsible for the show's success or failure. Did you know you are a part of the cast? What happens if you don't act? What happens if you stop performing? Will the show go on? Will someone else do the role you have been called to do? Or will they not, and will everyone know about your failure to act when you should have given it all you had?

In theater casting is very different than in fishing. To be cast out of a place, show, or role means that you are removed from the cast. You are no longer a part of the cast or the show. People are cast out when they fail to act, when they are called to do a role, but they don't. God has called us to act out our role. He has called us to cast out evil and to remove it from the show. We are called to act against the characters that aren't supposed to be leading or directing the show.

Demons have various personalities. There are demons who are characters of lust, anger, and fear. These personalities, or characters, seek to influence the people who are performing. They want to be given the chance to speak, act, and perform too. But because they are background characters, they need the lead characters' permission to do what they are trying to do. They need to be given a place to do what they want to do, but Christians can cast them out. Remove them from our show. We can tell them they aren't welcome in the performance because we are giving the Holy Spirit full lead.

We have a reason to act out. We have a reason to tell people to drop acts that aren't benefiting them. We have a reason to command unholy personalities to stay back and stay down. Why would we permit evil to remain if we could do something about it? Why would we tell demons they can speak and have a voice if Jesus told them to shut up and be muzzled? Do we want to be like Jesus? Do we want to silence the enemies and rescue those who have been captured by them? Then we must learn how to act. We must learn and train to do the job we have been called to do. Don't run away. Don't shy back. You are being called for this part!

The director thinks you can do the part well. He sees the potential in you for the job. Do you want the part? Are you willing to study and learn the script, the characters, and the set? Are you willing to join this show? Or would you rather sit back and watch? Would you rather be an observer only? Maybe you'll make it to Heaven, but you won't be set apart. You won't be mainstage if you don't do something to distinguish yourself from the rest.

Do not conform to the pattern of this world, but be transformed by the renewing of your mind. Then you will be able to test and approve what God's will is—his good, pleasing and perfect will (Rom. 12:2).

{ **22** }

Curtain Call

After the completion of a show the characters all come together before the audience in a curtain call. The audience will either applaud or they will boo, depending on the perception of the show. Generally, people applaud the show if the performance was enjoyable to watch and the characters did a good job. Yet there are times when the audience shows their displeasure with the show. Not everyone who watches the show will like it.

People generally find characters that they identify with. They find parts of the story that speak to them or resonate with them in their hearts. A person's perception of the characters, the performance, and the storyline is not always indicative of the show. They usually have far more to do with the heart and the perceptions of the audience. Performers who want to be successful must always remember that they aren't doing what they are doing for applause.

A good performer does what they feel they should do and they are themselves regardless of the response of the crowd. The crowd's applause or their contempt is irrelevant to a performer. Performers perform because they love their part. They do what they do because they love their job. A good performer is passionate, and their heart is in what they are doing. Our hearts' position matters greatly in all aspects of life, and performing and demonstrating our hearts to others is only an outward expression of who we genuinely are inside.

Some people in the crowd and in the casting stage of a show want to be the villain. They like the role of the bad guy, and they find joy in rooting for the person who is set on doing evil. Amanda always wondered why some people wanted to have this part in a story. She didn't get why someone would willingly choose to audition and play a villain. She wanted the part that was true to her heart. She wanted to do the right thing. She wanted to be a character of integrity, honesty, and value.

In life and on the stage there are villains and good guys. Some people want to live criminal lifestyles and some people want to be police officers. Some people choose to walk in disobedience to authority, society, and all the people who have tried to help them, and some people try to find peace with others who are trying to benefit them and help them to become a better version of themselves. When Jesus was dying on the cross, He demonstrated to us that there would always be two groups, two people, two types of characters.

One of the thieves on the cross wanted to stop the character of the villain. He wanted to change. He wanted Jesus to remember him and forgive him for his poor performance. The other guy, however, didn't want to change, even until death. This criminal, although guilty of the same types of crimes, refused to repent, refused to change, and refused to accept the free gift that could have been given to him. In life people have discretion. They have free will to choose their outcomes and their fate.

People have no excuse for continuing to do evil. Everyone has been given a choice to control themselves and to change their futures if they are tired of living a life of misery, turmoil, and violence. God doesn't want people to live their lives as part of the Devil's kingdom. He doesn't want the Devil to own a soul in this life or the next. Jesus died for the sins of the whole world because He wanted to give people a lifeline—a way out of the struggle and the role of playing the villain character.

God gave this earth to man. He allowed man to take ownership and possession of it. A part of God's word that He refuses to violate is the authority He has given man, both for good and for evil, to use their own discretion and individual choice. When a police officer has been given discretion, they are permitted to decide what is and isn't appropriate for them to do. They are permitted within legal bounds to do what they think is right, but if a police officer abuses their position and does evil with their discretion, they will be faced with the repercussions of the law, just like the criminal is punished for their wrongdoing.

God holds all people accountable. Whether you are a criminal or a police officer you are still held by the law to follow it and adhere to it, whether you want to or not. But one thing we know is that people who refuse to submit to the authority of the system they are a part of will face consequences for their choices. But wise people don't want to be punished. They don't want to break the law because their hearts are good and they love doing the right thing. Wise people don't need someone to make them accountable to the law.

Wise people follow the law with or without monitoring by others. Good performers would perform the same way with ten people or with ten thousand people watching them because what they are doing is from their heart. A superhero isn't a superhero because people applaud him. They would be doing the same thing with or without public recognition because in their heart they hate evil and want to stop it from happening.

Criminals or villains often don't understand the role of the good guy, just like the good guy doesn't understand the role of the criminal. An ugly heart that hates cannot get why anyone would go out of their way to help others, be kind to others, or forgive others who have done wrong to them. It is common to see villains reminiscing about the pains and wrongs that others have done to them. They hold onto these things and never let go, then they hurt others because they have never healed from their pain.

Healing and forgiving others, acknowledging that no one is perfect, is a sign of maturity and personal responsibility. God commands us to forgive others, even those who don't deserve it, because

He has forgiven us. People who live their lives holding onto wrongs, refusing to forgive, and hating everyone and everything around them will never prosper because they refuse to follow the laws of God.

Proverbs 28:13 explains, *"Whoever conceals their sins does not prosper, but the one who confesses and renounces them finds mercy."* Villains want to conceal their identity. They want to conceal their hurt, their pain, and the truth behind their mask and their mistreatment of others. Villains never face the truth. They keep running and hiding, pretending to be someone they aren't, because they don't want to forgive and move forward, acknowledging that even villains can sometimes become good guys if they are humble and repent publicly before God and man. Being humble and owning our wrongs is hard sometimes, but it is far better than living a life apart from truth and love.

1 Peter 4:8 tells us, *"Above all, love each other deeply, because love covers over a multitude of sins."* Covering is very different from concealing. When something is covered, it is protected, even when there is something there. When a person covers their grill they are acknowledging first that there is a grill that needs to be covered. There isn't an ignoring of the grill, a hiding of the grill. There is a covering over it.

God sent Jesus to cover our sins. He didn't promise us that we wouldn't have sins to cover. He told us that we would need to confess our sins and continue walking with Him, accepting the covering we don't deserve, but He freely gives because He loves us. True love doesn't conceal or hide the sins in the lives of others. It doesn't pretend, mask, or act like the sin and the wrong aren't there. Love covers. It acknowledges the sin, hates the sin, and confronts the sin, but it forgives and works to protect anyway.

Jesus asks us to be real, honest, and to evaluate our performance so we can improve. Many of the people in the Bible weren't perfect, but it was their commitment to repentance because of a respect for God's authority that kept them receiving the promises. Rebels don't want to repent. They don't want to respect the system that is above them. They want to continue what they are doing because they are rebellious, just as Satan was.

Have you ever felt bad for the villain in the story? Have you ever wanted them to just do something different and to change because you believed that they could if they would only apologize and act differently? Amanda did. She always felt pity and sorrow for villains. She always thought that she could change them if she could only love them more, talk to them, and teach them the truth about their behavior, but do you know what the truth is? No one can save a villain who is determined to continue in that part. When someone has committed in their heart to be something, even something they shouldn't be, we can't make them change. The director can't convince them to apply for another role, and the characters can't either. In this life we all come in alone and we will all leave alone. The choices of others do impact us, but ultimately, we are given the right to choose by God.

Amanda knew what she needed to do. She needed to play the part God had given her and she needed to play it with all of her heart, not holding a thing back. She needed to demonstrate to Nathanial that God was real and that she believed what she was preaching to him. She needed to continue on in her role, even when he tried to make her stop. That was her role. That was her responsibility, and she could only play one role at a time. She couldn't take over his part and do his role for him. His role was his responsibility alone.

Some went out on the sea in ships; they were merchants on the mighty waters. They saw the works of the Lord, his wonderful deeds in the deep. For he spoke and stirred up a tempest that lifted high the waves. They mounted up to the heavens and went down to the depths; in their peril their courage melted away. They reeled and staggered like drunkards; they were at their wits' end (Ps. 107:23–27).

Some people get to their wits' end in the storm. They realize their ship is going to go down and they are in need of salvation, and when they do the Lord will save them regardless of the former things. *"Then they cried out to the Lord in their trouble, and he brought them out of their distress. He stilled the storm to a whisper; the waves of the sea were hushed. They were glad when it grew calm, and he guided them to their desired haven"* (Ps. 107:28–30).

But notice that this says the word "some." Some people realize and call out for help. Some people choose to continue heading in a tubulous direction, not fearing the wind, the waves, or anything else around them. They hear the other sailors saying, "Stop!" They hear the roar of death surrounding them, but they are too proud to say I NEED HELP! They are too proud to change and go in another direction.

The Church's job is to preach and teach the unfiltered word of God. We are to make sure people are close enough to Jesus to look at Him and tell Him they aren't interested in what He is offering. People aren't telling us they hate Jesus. They aren't telling us that they hate the Church. When people say, "I don't want what you have. I don't want to play that part! I am not interested," they aren't telling the other characters as much as they are making a statement to the one who is running the show. The other characters may observe it, but they aren't the ones who make the final say or ruling about the future of that character.

"Some sat in darkness, in utter darkness, prisoners suffering in iron chains, because they rebelled against God's commands and despised the plans of the Most High" (Psalm 107:10–11). People who are confined in darkness, suffering in the chains of evil today, have chosen to rebel. They have chosen to sit in that place. Jesus is willing to forgive them, but are they willing to admit that they need Him as their Savior? In all stories there are many characters. Some are good and some aren't, and the Bible makes this very, very clear.

As they were going out, they met a man from Cyrene, named Simon, and they forced him to carry the cross. They came to a place called Golgotha (which means "the place of the skull"). There they offered Jesus wine to drink, mixed with gall; but after tasting it, he refused to drink it. When they had crucified him, they divided up his clothes by casting lots. And sitting down, they kept watch over him there. Above his head they placed the written charge against him: THIS IS JESUS, THE KING OF THE JEWS.

Two rebels were crucified with him, one on his right and one on his left. Those who passed by hurled insults at him, shaking their heads and saying, "You who are going to destroy the temple and build it in three days, save yourself! Come down from the cross, if you are the Son of God!" In the same way the chief priests, the teachers of the law and the elders mocked him. "He saved others," they said, "but he can't save himself! He's the king of Israel! Let him come down now from the cross, and we will believe in him. He trusts in God. Let God rescue him now if he wants him, for he said, 'I am the Son of God.'" In the same way the rebels who were crucified with him also heaped insults on him.

From noon until three in the afternoon darkness came over all the land. About three in the afternoon Jesus cried out in a loud voice, "Eli, Eli, lema sabachthani?" (which means "My God, my God, why have you forsaken me?"). When some of those standing there heard this, they said, "He's calling Elijah." Immediately one of them ran and got a sponge. He filled it with wine vinegar, put it on a staff, and offered it to Jesus to drink. The rest said, "Now leave him alone. Let's see if Elijah comes to save him."

And when Jesus had cried out again in a loud voice, he gave up his spirit. At that moment the curtain of the temple was torn in two from top to bottom. The earth shook, the rocks split and the tombs broke open. The bodies of many holy people who had died were raised to life. They came out of the tombs after Jesus' resurrection and went into the holy city and appeared to many people. When the centurion and those with him who were guarding Jesus saw the earthquake and all that had happened, they were terrified, and exclaimed, "Surely he was the Son of God!" Many women were there, watching from a distance. They had followed Jesus from Galilee to care for his needs. Among them were Mary Magdalene, Mary the mother of James and Joseph, and the mother of Zebedee's sons (Matthew 27:22–56).

Some people continued to insult Jesus and His message. These characters wanted Him to be dead. They hated Him and they refused to acknowledge anything that He taught them. Even though He was dying for their sins, they refused to offer back the same love to Jesus that He was offering to them. Jesus believed in them. He did everything to help them change, but they didn't care. They didn't want to change.

Other characters were once on the side of evil, like the Centurian soldier who knew that He was the Son of God after He witnessed what happened on the cross. These people were once totally opposed to the truth, but they decided to change after they got close to Jesus. Some people, like Paul, do change when they are confronted. They do realize what they have done and want to be different.

And other characters love Jesus with everything in them like Mary. These charaters are constant and unwaviering in their belief in the truth. They follow Jesus closely. They stay by His side through everything, even when it means they may be in danger personally. These characters walk closely with Christ. They follow Him and have a close relationship with Him because they have taken the time to fellowship with Him.

Christians can be at peace when they have tried to witness the truth and live boldly as the friends of Jesus Christ. When we have not denied Him and we have done everything in our power to share the gospel message, regardless of the outcome of the other characters around us, we must choose to continue on with Jesus, knowing that He understands our pain and suffering when we lose someone that we thought was going to perform with us forever.

Loss is difficult. It is hard to process. Some losses are eternal and some aren't. We will see and celebrate with the people we love again one day when those people have accepted the gift of salvation. Christians do have the hope of tomorrow, but our hearts still pain for those whom we once loved and tried to minister to but who chose to curse us and ignore us, even when we wanted them to be safe in the arms of their Savior.

Amanda had gotten comfortable permitting the evil in her husband to remain in her house. She had stopped fighting against the evil because she was afraid of the evil in her husband. She let the evil remain near her and her children for far too long. She let the "robbers" come into the home that was meant to be sanctified, safe, and holy, and she didn't resist them anymore because she was trying to keep the peace. But Jesus was angry about this. He didn't want the evil to be permitted to rule and reign in a holy sanctuary.

Jesus entered the temple courts and drove out all who were buying and selling there. He overturned the tables of the money changers and the benches of those selling doves. "It is written," he said to them, "'My house will be called a house of prayer, but you are making it 'a den of robbers'" (Matt. 21:12–13).

Jesus didn't come to bring peace among men. He didn't come to live in union with evil. Jesus came to drive out devils. He came to destroy the works of the enemy. Jesus came to make holy places holy again. He came to remove the evil from the world and the lives of those who wish to be free. Are you a character who wants to see this mission fulfilled? Are you a character that adheres to a friend of God in His script? Or do you want to play a different part? What are you auditioning for? What are you willing to act out with all of your heart?

What is said here may not be religiously acceptable. The Pharisees and the scribes may boo the show. All those who love evil will also root for the bad guy to win. It may be hard to accept that Jesus does sometimes flip tables. It may be hard to perceive that He isn't always quiet and permitting of sin and evil. Jesus has been misrepresented by many today, just as He was misunderstood by many in the days that He walked the earth as a man.

People see what they want to see. They watch the show through the lens of their own hearts. There is a time to be mad and to do something about it. There is a time to say enough is enough. Jesus is long-suffering. He does permit imperfect people into His kingdom, but He is not tolerant of evil. He is not a man who is going to endorse evil and injustice.

"Do not suppose that I have come to bring peace to the earth. I did not come to bring peace, but a sword. For I have come to turn 'a man against his father, a daughter against her mother, a daughter-in-law against her mother-in-law—a man's enemies will be the members of his own household'" (Matt. 10:34–36). There are households that are divided. There are households that will face violence because there are two opposing forces in the hearts of those who live in the house.

"Persecution Will Come"

"I am sending you out like sheep among wolves. Therefore be as shrewd as snakes and as innocent as doves. Be on your guard; you will be handed over to the local councils and be flogged in the synagogues. On my account you will be brought before governors and kings as witnesses to them and to the Gentiles. But when they arrest you, do not worry about what to say or how to say it. At that time you will be given what to say, for it will not be you speaking, but the Spirit of your Father speaking through you.

Brother will betray brother to death, and a father his child; children will rebel against their parents and have them put to death. You will be hated by everyone because of me, but the one who stands firm to the end will be saved. When you are persecuted in one place, flee to another. Truly I tell you, you will not finish going through the towns of Israel before the Son of Man comes. The student is not above the teacher, nor a servant above his master. It is enough for students to be like their teachers, and servants like their masters. If the head of the house has been called Beelzebul, how much more the members of his household!" (Matt. 10:16–25).

People thought that Jesus, the master, was Satan. They accused him of being full of demonic power. Jesus promised us that as the members of His household we would face the same thing. People would look at us and talk about us as if we were evil because we are full of the power of God and we are performing God's plans and purposes on this earth as we were commanded to do by our Father. Amanda's story wasn't over. It was just beginning. She would go and preach and teach and there would be many who didn't like her performance.

But regardless, she would tell this message to all people everywhere. What she had been told in secret she would shout in the streets. And when she did, the persecution would come. She would be accused of being evil, of being full of the Devil, and of being part of something unjust. But Amanda knew the truth. She knew she was pleasing to her Father in Heaven. She knew she was doing God's work, and she had the anointing of the Holy Spirit. And you know who doesn't like that? Satan.

So, if you don't like this story, and you are rooting for the enemy, maybe it is because you are him. Maybe the master of your house isn't Jesus, but it is the Devil himself. Only a devil would want you to side against the message of Jesus. God wouldn't want that for anyone, but He lets you choose today what you are going to do. Do you know what happened to Nathaniel? Do you wonder what his outcome was? Well, if you are reading this story, you likely already know.

"So do not be afraid of them, for there is nothing concealed that will not be disclosed, or hidden that will not be made known. What I tell you in the dark, speak in the daylight; what is whispered in your ear, proclaim from the roofs. Do not be afraid of those who kill the body but cannot kill the soul. Rather, be afraid of the One who can destroy both soul and body in hell. Are not two sparrows sold for a penny? Yet not one of them will fall to the ground outside your Father's care. And even the very hairs of your head are all numbered. So don't be afraid; you are worth more than many sparrows. "Whoever acknowledges me before others, I will also acknowledge before my Father in heaven. But whoever disowns me before others, I will disown before my Father in heaven" (Matt. 10:26–33).

Don't ever deny Jesus. Don't ever deny the message of the cross. Don't ever say that God isn't able to deliver His people. God is and will deliver those who ask Him for help. He will ensure that the promises in the word of God are manifest in the lives of all who believe. It doesn't matter who likes the message. It doesn't matter who tries to stop it. God is not a man that He should lie. When He says someone is dead, they are. If Jesus curses you, it is only a matter of time before the roots wither and you are no more.

"A man's enemies will be the members of his own household. Anyone who loves their father or mother more than me is not worthy of me; anyone who loves their son or daughter more than me is not worthy of me. Whoever does not take up their cross and follow me is not worthy of me. Whoever finds their life will lose it, and whoever loses their life for my sake will find it" (Matt. 10:36–39).

Amanda didn't need anyone else to believe her when she said her husband was going to die. She didn't change her prophecy just because it seemed hard to believe. She kept on writing. She kept on documenting what the Spirit of God was saying. She kept on recording the truth. Then, she published it. Why? So the whole world could see that truly there is a God who lives and loves His people. God is a good God. He is a protector, a defender, and a deliverer.

What happened to Nathanial was his own fault. It was his own doing. He chose his fate because he didn't believe the prophecy. He didn't believe that God was powerful, supreme, and able to do what He said He would do. Nathanial thought he was better than God.

The fool says in his heart, "There is no God." They are corrupt, their deeds are vile; there is no one who does good. The LORD looks down from heaven on all mankind to see if there are any who understand, any who seek God. All have turned away, all have become corrupt; there is no one who does good, not even one. Do all these evildoers know nothing? They devour my people as though eating bread; they never call on the LORD. But there they are, overwhelmed with dread, for God is present in the company of the righteous. You evildoers frustrate the plans of the poor, but the LORD is their refuge.

Oh, that salvation for Israel would come out of Zion! When the LORD restores his people, let Jacob rejoice and Israel be glad! LORD, who may dwell in your sacred tent? Who may live on your holy mountain? The one whose walk is blameless, who does what is righteous, who speaks the truth from their heart; whose tongue utters no slander, who does no wrong to a neighbor, and casts no slur on others; who despises a vile person but honors those who *fear the LORD; who keeps an oath even when it hurts, and does not change their mind* (Ps. 14:1–15:4).

Amanda kept her vow. She loved her husband until death. She stayed by his side because she had promised that she would. She did everything in her power to be his helpmate. She tried to drive the devils out of his life, but he wanted the devils. He wanted to be the villain. That was the character he had chosen, and he didn't care what the director thought he should be. He didn't care what the other characters wanted. He only cared about himself.

Those who run after other gods will suffer more and more. I will not pour out libations of blood to such gods or take up their names on my lips. LORD, you alone are my portion and my cup; you make my lot secure. The boundary lines have fallen for me in pleasant places; surely I have a delightful inheritance. I will praise the LORD, who counsels me; even at night my heart instructs me. I keep my eyes always on the LORD. With him at my right hand, I will not be shaken (Ps. 16:4–8).

God gave Amanda a play-by-play of everything ahead of time. He told her what was coming. She saw the storm approaching. She saw the plot of the enemy against her husband's life. She watched the sharks circle his dead heart. She watched them thirst for his blood. She screamed and shouted at the top of her lungs, "Watch out! Wake up! Come here! Please don't stay where you are!" But he didn't want her help. He didn't want God's help. He hated her and her God and that was his choice.

Therefore my heart is glad and my tongue rejoices; my body also will rest secure, because you will not abandon me to the realm of the dead, nor will you let your faithful one see decay. You make known to me the path of life; you will fill me with joy in your presence, with eternal pleasures at your right hand. Hear me, LORD, my plea is just; listen to my cry. Hear my prayer—it does not rise from deceitful lips. Let my vindication come from you; may your eyes see what is right. Though you probe my heart, though you examine me at night and test me, you will find that I have planned no evil; my mouth has not transgressed.

Though people tried to bribe me, I have kept myself from the ways of the violent through what your lips have commanded. My steps have held to your paths; my feet have not stumbled. I call on you, my God, for you will answer me; turn your ear to me and hear my prayer. Show me the wonders of your great love, you who save by your right hand those who take refuge in you from their foes. Keep me as the apple of your eye; hide me in the shadow of your wings from the wicked who are out to destroy me, from my mortal enemies who surround me (Psalm 16:9–17:9).

This part of Amanda's performance was over, and thank God, because it was a difficult set to go through. It isn't easy watching a sea monster come up onto the dock and steal your best friend. It isn't easy watching the man you love and know could be more fail to reach his destiny and his future. It hurts to imagine the demons of Hell feasting on the flesh of a person who could have ruled over them. But in the future sets there will be laughter for Amanda and her children. Sometimes it hurts to look back, but God tells us to never forget Egypt.

God doesn't want us to pretend we weren't once slaves. He doesn't want us to forget what He did for us. God wants us to be thankful that we were spared. He wants us to appreciate that we weren't taken out by the Red Sea and that we have been given fresh manna and quail. Amanda was on the way to the promised land. She was going to make it, but it would require her to live by faith throughout the sets in between here and there. What do you think? Who are you in the story or in the audience? Your heart matters. Your perception matters, but it doesn't matter as much as God's.

Then from his mouth the serpent spewed water like a river, to overtake the woman and sweep her away with the torrent. But the earth helped the woman by opening its mouth and swallowing the river that the dragon had spewed out of his mouth. Then the dragon was enraged at the woman and went off to wage war against the rest of her offspring—those who keep God's commands and hold fast their testimony about Jesus. The dragon stood on the shore of the sea. And I saw a beast coming out of the sea. It had ten horns and seven heads, with ten crowns on its horns, and on each head a blasphemous name (Rev. 12:15–13:1).

Amanda and Nathanial should have walked together hand in hand into eternity. The carriage should have taken them both away together. That was God's plan. That was the script God had written, but there is another cunning, lying creature who joined himself in the story. Amanda had no idea that when they got engaged, said their vows, and walked hand in hand down by the water at *The Boathouse* that their story would both start and end there– on the shore of the water. The water that would take her husband's life but would permit her to live and be spit out on the dry ground, urging her to go forward with the message of salvation and repentance for all people through Christ Jesus.

"Flowers, flowers, here we go again with the flowers," Amanda said as she watched people around her throwing bouquets and shouting for her success and rooting her on. Amanda remembers picking out the flowers for her wedding bouquet. She chose purple, her favorite color. *Does the beginning of a thing and the end of one really end with flowers*, she wondered as she looked at the flowers on her counter after the funeral. *Flowers*, she thought, *for celebration and for mourning*. But Amanda didn't want flowers. She wanted revenge against her enemy for what he had done.

Her enemy wasn't her husband. It never was. Her enemy was the Devil and all who worked for him. She knew her true enemy and she was going to make him pay. In this next set more people will be saved. More people are going to come to find Christ under her ministry than ever before. Amanda was going to war. She was going to take out as many demons as she could before Jesus took her to her forever home. She was going to make the kingdom of darkness pay for what it had done to her family.

Amanda didn't want the demons to have any rights or any say-so in the show as long as she was in it. She wanted them cast out entirely. She wanted them away from her and everyone she encountered. In this next set, she was going to take her authority over the Devil. She was going to do what Jesus commands: *"Heal the sick, raise the dead, cleanse those who have leprosy, drive out demons. Freely you have received; freely give"* (Matt. 10:8).